WARRIOR'S MARK
BOOK ONE

S.E. LOWER

Marked by a Vow

Warrior's Mark: Dragons
SE Lower

Marked by a Vow

Copyright © 2025 by Susan Lower writing as SE Lower

Editing: Fenley Grant

Proofreading: Lara Abramson

Cover design: Book Covers by Melody

Language note: This book uses different Native American words to stand in for the shifters' ancient language, a tribute to the folklore and culture of the fictional people who gain animal spirit guides at their coming-of-age. The end of the book contains a pronunciation guide.

S.E. Lower

www.selower.com

ISBN: 978-1-945274-15-2

Foreword

Legends are woven from the whispers of the past, echoes of battles fought, love lost, and spirits bound by fate. This story is no different.

Gwen's journey begins on a mountain steeped in ancient magic, where dragon shifters guard secrets older than time itself. Their power is sacred, their existence fragile, and in the shadows of prophecy, their survival is anything but certain. Gwen never expected to become entangled in their world. She came for family, for duty, for a life that was never meant to be hers. But destiny rarely asks permission.

Inspired by folklore and the deep spiritual bonds of tribal origins, this series is a tale of sacrifice, resilience, and the undeniable pull of fate. It is about the choices we make when everything is on the line—the ones that define us, reshape us, and test the limits of what we are willing to lose.

As you embark on this journey, prepare to step beyond the boundaries of the known and into the heart of a legend waiting to unfold.

Welcome to the mountain.

One

Behind her, the mountains rumbled as Gwen raced down the mountain passage on her skis. Bent low, her pack on her back, she was gaining speed. She kept between the evergreens. The pine needles covered her as she descended. Again, the mountain rumbled and sounds of cracking and crumbling made her heart race. The storm above hit sooner than expected, tossing the helicopter off course. She'd had to jump several feet from the aircraft to land on the snowcapped peak, the thin air almost suffocating at the higher elevation. Had her sudden landing caused the snow to shift? Or did the helicopter's propellers break the peak's serene stillness and silence? No matter, she needed to reach Sentinel Peak before dark. If not, she would die trying. Three days was not nearly enough time.

The mountain agreed with her and promised to grant her wish with the sudden release of snow. Afraid to look back, she skied faster, bent lower, and dodged the trees to get through the pass. Her heart raced along with her. The sound of the avalanche swallowing up her trail chased her.

She'd either outrun this, or the mountain would bury her body in its cold, unyielding clutches. Gwen raced for the first option, leaning to avoid a tree. Her skis lifted her off the ground from the sudden slope. Flying in the air, she tilted her face in the wind, savoring the short flight before her skis slammed back into the snow-padded mountainside.

Almost there, she could see the clear path of snow beyond the trees. Here, the passage became narrow, and sprays of snow and ice flew out from behind her, a wave of white death collecting momentum in her wake. She dug her poles in deeper, moving faster, propelling herself ahead of the avalanche.

Either the mountain had decided it, too, wanted to claim her, or it had decided to aid in her mission with a clean slate for anyone trying to track her.

Darkness blotted out the sun for a minute, a shadow stretching ahead of her. Gwen tilted her head, her hood blocking her view, and she looked ahead again.

Suddenly, a tree came into her line of sight. She leaned, and the pole in her left hand snapped in half from the impact of her misjudgment. Off balance, she tossed the other pole and used her legs to keep her skis in motion, gliding them out to the side, left, then right, left, then right. The systematic motion of constant movement distracted her from thinking about the tide of colossal death behind her.

As soon as she burst through the tree line, the snow spewed out like a child spitting milk from its nose. She bent down and kept her gaze focused ahead. She'd made it, but a boulder sticking out of the snow tried to snag her and toss her away. The avalanche suddenly twisted and knocked her skis out from under her. She slid, riding the cold waves of snow and ice. One layer after another pushed her forward. Her pack and rifle pulled against her back as if the mountain attempted to rip them from her. She held onto the straps, screaming until she slowed. Above her, a roar muted all other sounds.

Gwen tried to release her booted feet, her skis stuck in the mass of snow. She glanced behind her as another gush of snow rose. Head turned, body curled into a ball, she protected her head with her hands. Around her, the ground trembled and quaked as something large blanketed her.

It surrounded her and protected her as the avalanche rolled over them. She covered her ears to block out the roar of the mountain, the hiss of the ice, and its deafening roar.

Then silence.

Gwen counted her heartbeats to a hundred. Whatever fell over her kept the snow from packing around her body. She waited, held still, and heard heavy breathing. Her heart skipped a beat. Then two.

Breathing. Deep. Labored. Breathing.

Slowly, she pulled her arms away, her vision adjusting to the shrouded darkness. Crushing pressure forced the last of the air into her lungs, feeling the brush of heat inches from her face. An outline of scales rose and fell above her. "What the—"

Warmth pressed against her, a furnace against the biting wind, blocking out the mountain's attempt to bury her. The heated ceiling lifted, letting light flood in through the reflection on the snow at her side. A scream curled in her throat. She pushed it down, watching as hues of red, blue, and orange glimmered across the opal scales, like the southern skies of Antarctica. So beautiful, delirious. Was this real? Had the avalanche taken her sanity?

A snort of warm steam fogged her goggles and jolted her. *This can't be real.*

Unable to resist, she reached up and ran her gloved hand across the waves of color. Above her, the scales rippled, and the beast chuffed, bringing her out of her stupor.

Gwen pulled her goggles and her scarf down. Wiggling in her confined area, she reached for her rifle. What kind of beast could land on a person and shield them? If it thought of her as prey, it had another thing coming.

The enormous beast lifted its head, giving her more light, then air. She swung the weapon around as the beast rose on its front feet. Gwen rolled from underneath it and tripped over her skis. Sprawled out, face-first in the deep snow, her rifle in her hand with the barrel pointed above her head, the beast stepped on both the weapon and her hand. She couldn't move either of them.

Growling, the beast lowered its head and glared at her. Gwen rolled slightly to her side to get a better view. She cringed, her breath escaping her for the longest moment of her life. One large reptilian eye watched her, dared her, and a row of sharp teeth warned her of their bite.

Dragon.

On the mountain?

She'd landed in the beast's territory.

All the stories . . . they're true?

"Please . . ." Her heart beat in a frenzy of frantic. "Don't hurt me."

It stepped back, and Gwen scrabbled against the layers of crusted and broken snow. Tree limbs and rocks jabbed into her backside. She stretched her neck to look up at a large silver and black dragon standing before her—blue-tipped wings folded on its back.

The beast lowered its head, a sign to show her it meant no harm. It didn't slow the pace of her rapid-firing heart or ease the pain in her lungs, sucking for deep breaths to find her calm. Falling back into the snow, she muttered, "A dragon, seriously?"

She expected to find a wolf, maybe a bear. She tried to catch her breath. *A dragon.* She panted, fighting back a panic attack. This wasn't what she signed up for.

Beneath her, the tremors of another avalanche higher on the mountain brought her back to reality. "I get it," she whispered to the mountain, gulping in another deep breath of crisp, cold air. "I'm going."

A firework of snow erupted from the clouds above, falling like thick confetti. What other way could the mountain celebrate such victory? She didn't like others invading her space, either. She closed her eyes briefly to ensure she hadn't imagined things.

The dragon keened. A set of talons clasped around her. Gwen jolted. Her eyelids snapped open.

"No. Stop! Wait!" But even as she screamed, the dragon opened its wings and took off with her in its clutches.

Two

She shivered in his arms, more from the terror of seeing his dragon form than the cold, he feared.

Taran dropped the woman in the snow near his cabin and soared away. Once he flew far enough over the trees to ensure the darkening clouds shielded him from view, he shifted into a man. Jogging back, he found where he had kicked off his boots before his dragon took over. Taran had shredded his clothes in the shift, thanks to his dragon spirit's impatience. Thank the Great Hunter. He kept an emergency pack on his snowmobile behind the cabin and an extra set of clothes in the bag. Getting dressed took longer than he liked. What if she tried to ski farther down the mountain?

Part of him wanted to let her go, observe her struggle, and see if she possessed the true grit written on her face when she tried to point a rifle at him. Her fear made him bow to her, the moment of weakness like a thorn between his claws. Her fragile form against his chest, the tremor of fear in those eyes, caused a burning deep inside him. Protectiveness. Yes. Because, as a human, she was frail.

The northern wind howled. This female courted danger.

His dragon senses tingled with the mountain's raw energy, the sharp thread of her fear weaving through him.

Circling the side of the cabin, he slowed, grabbed a few logs from the woodpile, and went to greet his uninvited guest.

She lay sprawled in the snow, wiggling to sit up. A rifle case and pack slipped from her shoulders. Taran tensed. *Hunter.* His upper lip curled. He dumped the wood.

The sharp *thunk* startled her. Propped up on her elbows, she sucked in a breath, wide eyes locking on him.

Satisfaction curled through him. A fresh snowfall loomed. He ought to have left the rifle on the mountain.

"How did you get here?" Taran crossed his arms, towering over her.

Farther up the mountain, the avalanche rumbled on. When she didn't answer, he tried again. "Lost?"

Best to act like he hadn't just been a dragon, carrying her down off the mountain to safety.

"I landed wrong." She reached for her ski, wincing.

Taran exhaled slowly. Only a fool skied down this part of the mountain. "What hurts?"

"My knee." She rubbed her leg, chewing her lower lip. His gaze lingered longer than it should have.

"You're a bit far from the resort, aren't you?"

"I need to get to Sentinel Peak. Is it far from here?"

"You came down the passage?" The mountain rumbled above them. Taran lifted his chin, scanning the peaks in the distance. Snow could travel far—too far. The sound of falling trees made him uneasy. Thankfully, his cabin was low enough beneath Crag's Cliff to stay clear of the worst.

"Yes." She met his gaze, her look one of mild disbelief.

"You're lucky you made it this far. This side of the mountain can be deadly."

"I had help." Her head tilted, goggles shifting, revealing only the barest hint of her eyes. "A dragon . . . It . . ."

Taran's pulse quickened. *So that's why she carries the rifle.* Was she a soldier or a spirit hunter? Both types hunted his kind, seeking to steal spirit animals for their power.

"I've heard of snow angels, but I haven't heard of a snow dragon around here," Taran said.

She seemed to sense she'd reached a dead end on the dragon subject and changed tactics. "Do they happen often? The avalanches?"

Taran leaned close to her left ski. "Only when someone disturbs the sensitive parts of the mountain."

She shuddered, her snowsuit muffling her tremors. "I'm not sure where I am. Can you direct me? I need to get going."

"You won't be going anywhere with that leg." Taran pushed her rifle further from her. "How did you get on this side of the mountain?"

"The storm threw me off course." She pulled down her ski mask, looking at him directly. "Do you know where Sentinel Peak is located?"

"I do."

"Can you tell me how to get there?"

"I might. Are you going to tell me what you're doing here?"

Her cheeks flushed dark pink. "I told you: I need to get to Sentinel Peak. If you'll direct me, I'll be on my way."

Taran pressed his hand against her injured knee. She sucked in a sharp breath, glaring at him, fists digging into the snow to hold herself up.

"I don't think you're going anywhere."

She opened her mouth, then snapped it shut. Taran unclipped her boots from her skis. She flinched as they released. He offered his hand, his shoulder bearing her rifle. "Can you stand? Or do you need me to carry you?"

Her lips turned blue, shivers rippling through her body. The cold didn't bother him—his dragon blood ran hot—but a human would find the bitter winds chilling to the bone. She pushed herself up, wobbling, nearly falling back. Taran caught her, jerking her upright. She reached for her pack, but he was quicker, striding toward the cabin.

"Hey! Those are mine!"

He ignored her, stepping inside and leaving the door ajar. She took a step to follow, then cried out in pain, clutching her knee.

Taran dumped the pack and rifle on a table, then quickly returned for her. Outside, he hoisted her over his shoulder before she could protest.

"Hey! Put me down!"

Her voice, thick with pain, made him flinch, and for a moment, he almost let her go. She grabbed his belt, fingers digging into the leather. Taran adjusted his grip, one hand sliding across her backside, the other supporting the back of her knees. She stiffened, sucking in a breath.

An odd sensation tickled at the back of his mind, causing the hairs on his neck to rise. He set her gently on the rug in front of the fireplace, where he could assess her injuries. Her goggles shielded her eyes behind their tint. Her snowsuit was torn—one rip along her pant leg, another at her left elbow.

He grabbed a blanket from the couch and tossed it at her. She wasn't going to freeze to death on his watch. His dragon's protective instincts surged, and he realized keeping her close was his only option.

"You'll want to get out of your snowsuit. There's a shower by the kitchen. I can help if you need it. The hot water will warm you until the fire does."

"I'm good. Thanks." She crossed her arms, looking up at him with dark strands of hair spilling from her hood. Slowly, she lowered it.

Taran crouched beside her. He reached for her goggles, pulling them down. She flinched, her stunning green eyes locking onto his. They were a mesmerizing mix of watery hues, but the dark circles beneath them and the gash across her cheek broke the spell.

"Anything else hurt?" He grabbed another blanket and some pillows from the couch, stepping back to give her space. "Need help getting out of that suit?"

She pulled back. Her eyes narrowed at him.

Taran stood. "Do you have any spare clothes? These will get damp soon, and you'll catch cold."

"No." She attempted to rise. "I'm good. I can take care of myself."

Taran grabbed her pack and dropped it beside her with a soft thud. His body heat had already dried the dampness inside his boots, but she needed to shed the layers before she chilled. Maybe then, some color would return to her pale cheeks.

"Have it your way. I'll be outside." Without waiting for her reply, Taran grabbed the rifle.

"What are you doing with my rifle?" Her voice was sharp with alarm.

"You never answered why you had it."

"Hunting."

"Why does a woman need a highly sophisticated rifle to hunt in state game lands? You know it's illegal, right?"

"Is it illegal to defend oneself?"

"I thought you said you were hunting?" He tilted his head, lifting a brow.

"I was . . . I intended to."

"With a rifle in a restricted area? I'm the game warden here. Taran Vasumen."

"Gwen Riley. May I have my rifle back?"

Taran tested her name, liking the sound of it. "No. You'd best get out of those clothes before I get back."

"Is that a threat?"

"I don't waste my time with threats." He turned toward the door. "The storm is moving down the mountain. It's starting to snow. I'd best grab more wood."

The cold air behind the cabin brought a welcomed relief. He stashed the rifle in his truck, trying to calm his dragon. He didn't trust her. Without the military-grade rifle, he might have believed she was just another thrill-seeker bragging about skiing the mountain or hunting for a legendary buck. But too many hunters came through these parts, tracking shifters to steal their animal spirits.

Taran grabbed an axe and set to work, snowflakes drifting heavily around him. High in the mountains, Mother Nature threatened another wave of bitter cold. *She shouldn't be here.*

A growl reverberated through his chest in response.

The mountain isn't meant for humans. How had she made it this far? The elevation should have stolen her breath, the thin air too thin for most humans. Was she something more than she seemed?

His dragon spirit was at odds with his human thoughts. Something about her . . .

Maybe the lack of oxygen was affecting him, too.

He should have taken her straight to Crag's Cliff, to Aluk. As the eldest, Aluk held the alpha position over all the other packs and clans on the mountain. *But you already sense what she is, don't you?* His dragon's voice rumbled in his mind. *You can't leave her to someone else.*

But with her leg injured, taking Gwen to the resort in Avalanche Ridge seemed like a better option. For now.

Hopefully, the shock of the incident would wear off, and she wouldn't mention seeing a dragon. But if she was a hunter . . .

She smells like one of us, his dragon rumbled.

She smells like trouble. Taran's grip tightened around the axe.

Aluk would decide her fate.

Taran loaded a stack of wood into his arms and headed back inside. Her scent filled the cabin—fresh snow, pine, and something dark and earthy, almost familiar.

His dragon spirit stirred, his protective instinct sharpening.

Mine.

Three

As soon as Taran was out of sight, Gwen patted her pockets in a frantic search. Her phone. She needed her phone. Panic gnawed at her, but she fought it down. Without her phone, Peter couldn't track or contact her, and if he couldn't find her, she might not make it to him in time.

"No. No," she muttered.

Her fingers found the shards of crystal hidden in her hip pocket. The sharp edges bit into her palm, and she pulled them out, eyes stinging. Broken pieces. She tossed them into the fire. They sparked, flashing as they caught the flame. To a shifter blood, they'd appear as clear as glass, but to Gwen, they were useless now.

With a grim sigh, Gwen unzipped her snowsuit. She pulled her arms free and pushed the suit down, mindful of her aching knee. Kicking off her boots, she saw the slashes in the cloth. Her phone must have fallen in the snow when the dragon had grabbed her.

The dragon . . . Her mind reeled. Taran. His aura made her skin hum with heat. Unlike other shifters, his spirit tried to draw from her, feeding off her energy. She clenched her jaw, glancing over at the fire. Did he sense it? Her blood magic?

She couldn't tell if his powers extended beyond strength and the other usual shifter traits: sharper sight, hearing, reflexes, longer life span. The kinds of traits that could keep her brother alive for decades.

Grabbing the couch, Gwen pulled herself to her feet and tossed her snowsuit aside. Hopping over to the table, she grabbed her pack and sank into a chair. Digging through the pockets, her relief was short-lived. She found the other soul crystals, but none were whole, and the small aetherium crystal wasn't enough to hold a dragon spirit.

Her heart sank. The avalanche had probably shattered them, or perhaps Taran's strength had crushed them when he'd tossed her pack aside. The crystals had to grow in strength with a captured spirit, but none were useful now.

Except one. Gwen's fingers brushed the last surviving crystal. It was enough—just barely. It had to be. Her brother's life depended on it. Unlike shifter males, who could survive the loss of their spirit, her brother's faint shifter blood meant he would die without one.

She couldn't stay here. Not with a dragon watching her every move. She had to get to Sentinel Peak and capture a wolf shifter's spirit before Cedric learned about Peter's ailment.

Cedric, who had taken her in and claimed her as his daughter, wouldn't hesitate to make Peter an example. She had to act fast.

Her fingers curled around the lone surviving crystal. *One left.*

"Think, Gwen," she muttered, pushing back the panic threatening to choke her. *Dragon.* Taran Vasumen may have saved her from the avalanche, but he was still a dragon. She needed one crystal for one spirit, but could this small crystal hold a spirit as powerful as his?

She swallowed hard, thinking this was all her fault. Peter wouldn't be in this trouble if not for her. His father's faint line of shifter blood was nothing like the blood magic flowing in her veins. For years, he protected her. The more powerful spirits he scouted for the hunters, the bigger the reward Cedric gave him. But then the spirits became an addiction, a way to enhance his strength and agility. He burned through too many, too fast.

Dragons, according to myth, had stronger spirits and lived longer than the other shifter bloods. Still, any shifter spirit would keep Peter alive. She had to focus on that. Her brother's life depended on it.

The rest could wait. She'd deal with Cedric later. He might punish her for sneaking off, but if Peter's addiction was discovered, Cedric would make an example of him. She couldn't let that happen. Not again.

The hunters in the compound had told stories of shifters, but never of dragons. Gwen felt the prickles of magic race down her skin, the dampness of her clothing cooling her flesh. She pulled the map from her pack, the weight of time pressing down on her. *Three days.*

After tucking the crystal into her bra, she dug deeper into her pack. She needed to keep moving.

Then the door creaked open.

"Find what you need?"

"No phone," Gwen muttered, pulling out her socks. "But I've got warm socks." She held up the pink hiking socks, offering them as if they were some kind of victory.

"You wouldn't be able to contact anyone, anyway. No signal reaches this mountainside. Is there someone you wanted to call?"

Gwen shrugged off the question, keeping her focus on the map. *Someone who might die if I don't reach him in time.* But she couldn't tell Taran that. "Can you show me where I am?"

"I can show you the way to the bathroom and lend you some clothes. Your lips are still blue."

Inside the one-room cabin, the fireplace crackled, throwing shadows over the open kitchen. With no bed in sight, she assumed the closed door opposite the bathroom held one. The heavy log beams overhead gleamed in the firelight. Outside, the sky churned, a deepening gray swallowing what was left of the day. Gwen limped toward the window, but his voice stopped her.

"You need help to find the bathroom? Because that's the wrong way."

She stared outside, her shoulders slumped. The mountain stretched out before her, wild and untamed. A prison of now. *Too much time is slipping away.* "It's not late enough for it to get dark."

"The mountain's not done with her tantrum. Storm's covering us fast. When I went for wood, the snow had already filled my tracks." He held out a flannel shirt. Thick. Warm. Big enough to swallow her whole. Gwen hesitated. *Taking help from him is dangerous.*

Though tall, she remained shorter than Taran. At five foot seven, with curves that had made running from hunters a challenge, she wasn't used to feeling small. But next to him—towering, solid, unreadable—she did.

"Shirt. Hot shower. Change," he said.

Gwen wavered, gripping her pack tighter. "I've got warm socks. I'll be fine. A little chill won't kill me."

A lock of dark hair fell over his forehead, but his arm never lowered. The firelight caught in his eyes, dark depths swirling with something unreadable. A challenge. A warning.

She hesitated too long.

Taran lunged. He swept her up again in his arms.

"Okay. Okay. I'll do it. You don't have to carry me. Please don't touch me."

He dropped her. Not roughly, but with controlled ease inside the bathroom.

The space was small, walled in pine planks, holding only a toilet, tub, shower, and sink. No windows. No escape.

"Toss your damp clothes out in the hall so I can hang them up." His voice carried a quiet command. "I better hear the water in five, or I'll be back to help you."

"Over my dead body." She snatched the shirt from his hand, glaring.

"Given the mountain's previous attempts, I don't think today's your day." His expression darkened. "You're going to warm up. I'm going to make you something to eat. Then we'll address your presence here and the next steps of what to do with you."

Gwen pressed her lips tightly together, barely holding back a retort.

For Peter's sake, she couldn't afford to screw this up. She needed to get to Sentinel Peak.

She *needed* Taran Vasumen's dragon spirit.

Her fingers clenched around the damp fabric of her bra, pressing the crystal tighter against her skin. She couldn't take the risk of him finding it.

The hot water chased away the deep-seated chill, but it couldn't rid her of the tension coiled in her muscles. Tomorrow, she'd be sore. Bruised from the avalanche, from the dragon's claws, from everything. But she had no time for pain.

She had to move.

If anyone asked, she came to Sentinel Peak searching for answers about her past.

The truth, however, was far more dangerous.

When the water cooled, Gwen grabbed a towel left by the sink, dried off, and reached for Taran's shirt. The fabric smelled like him—wood smoke and the crisp bite of mountain air. She ignored that thought, tugging it on. The oversized garment draped over her curves, the shirttails hanging low enough to cover her. Good. Bracing herself, she pulled on her socks, gritting her teeth against the sharp pulse in her knee. It was red, swollen, and angry.

She needed her pack.

Hobbling into the main room, her stomach lurched at the sight of Taran at the table rifling through her things.

"Hey! That's mine!"

She stumbled, catching herself on the kitchen island before propelling forward. He flung her supplies onto the floor.

"I need to make sure you don't have any more guns." He ignored her attempt to stop him.

Her breath hitched. The soul crystal was safe, pressed against her skin beneath the lace of her bra.

"I don't have any guns in my pack." She sank to the floor, retrieving her things, her pulse throbbing in her throat. Any wrong move sent sharp pain radiating up her leg, but she didn't care. She had to secure her supplies before he destroyed them.

Taran turned the bag upside down. The rest of her belongings spilled out.

"You've got ammo." His voice held an edge. Almost a growl.

Gwen's fingers curled into a fist. "Of course, I do. You don't think I'd carry a rifle for protection and not have any ammunition, do you?"

His dark eyes flickered, assessing. "What do you think you need protecting from here?"

You.

"Bears. Lions. Wolves." *Dragons.*

A muscle in his jaw ticked. "A rifle won't protect you."

She met his gaze, refusing to back down. "It's better than nothing."

His eyes narrowed. "What makes you think you need protection?"

"My business is *not* your business."

"It became my business the moment you landed on my doorstep."

He placed her in a chair. She shoved her scattered belongings back into her pack, heart pounding as he slowly unfolded the map Peter had given her.

Stupid. *Stupid.*

His gaze traced the route she'd marked. And there it was—the weight of his judgment, pressing down on her like a dark cloud. Then, something changed. His pupils contracted to slits, flickering back before she could blink. The rich red hue deepened, and for a breath, an unfamiliar current prickled under her skin, like a whisper of electricity.

A dragon's power brushing against hers.

"You should have headed further east," he said, more somber than sarcastic.

Gwen snatched the map from him, stuffing it into her pack. "I lost my compass. If you'd be kind enough to point me in the right direction, I'll leave first thing after the storm clears."

His response was instantaneous. "You're not going anywhere."

The words slammed into her like a blow.

He sounded like Cedric.

You're not going anywhere. Not now or ever. Your place is here. You'll learn to accept it.

Her pulse spiked. Not again. *Not this time.*

"You can't keep me here."

Gwen surveyed the cabin for her rifle, wanting to escape.

"I can and I will." Hot, lazy licks of warmth against her cheeks caused her skin to prickle.

"I'm going to Sentinel Peak, and neither you nor an entire army will stop me."

"We'll see. First, we'll go to the resort tomorrow and have your knee looked at. I'm sure there will be more questions since you're trespassing on private property."

"This is state game lands, and you're the game warden."

"I am the game warden, but the state game lands are below us, not above us. Above us is privately owned by my family. I'm guessing your map doesn't include everywhere on the mountain."

She shook her head.

"We'll visit my brother Conleth in the morning and then see what my eldest brother, Aluk, has to say on the matter."

She couldn't afford to lose another day chatting with his family. Did his brothers have a dragon spirit too? "Then we'll head to Sentinel Peak?"

"Why do you want to go there?"

"I—I have family there."

Taran tilted his head, studying her too closely. "In Sentinel Peak?"

Careful. Think. She couldn't tell him the truth. Not yet.

She nodded. "Frostwood originally, but they migrated to Sentinel Peak. I-I have a brother, and I'm trying to find him."

Taran's brows pulled together. "Your brother lives in Sentinel Peak?"

Not exactly. Not in the way you're thinking.

She forced herself to hold his gaze. "He's in trouble. I need to get to him."

Taran was silent for a long moment. Then, quietly, he asked. "And you came alone?"

Stay in control. Stay ahead of the questions. She lifted her chin. "I had no choice."

His expression didn't soften. If anything, the muscle in his jaw ticked again, and a flicker of something dark passed through his eyes.

"You expect me to believe you hiked up this mountain in the middle of a snowstorm to track down a lost brother?"

She exhaled sharply. "I don't care what you believe. I just need to get to Sentinel Peak."

Taran crossed his arms, unmoved. "And why didn't you just go to Frostwood first?"

Her stomach turned. *He's testing me. Looking for cracks.*

She forced herself to hesitate, as if the answer hurt. Like the truth was painful. Then she whispered. "Because they don't want me."

That made him pause.

She pressed her advantage. "I didn't come up this mountain for fun. I didn't plan to get caught in an avalanche. I just need to get to my brother before it's too late."

The words were truer than he knew.

Taran ran a hand over his jaw, exhaling. "You're not going anywhere tonight. The storm's getting worse."

A fresh bolt of panic shot through her. No. No more delays.

She clenched her fists under the table, nails biting into her palms. "And tomorrow?"

His dark gaze pinned her to the chair. "Tomorrow, we'll see what my brothers think."

Another wall. Another delay. Peter didn't have another day to wait.

Taran leaned in slightly, his voice quieter, but no less firm. "If you're lying to me, Gwen, I'll find out."

Her pulse pounded, but she met his gaze head-on. "I know."

If she didn't get out of here soon and reach Peter in time, the truth wouldn't matter.

"It's likely that the storm will continue into the evening and throughout most of the night. Rest. I'll take you to the resort after the storm passes."

"But not Sentinel Peak?"

"It'll be spring before the pass opens from all this snow to travel there. I hate to disappoint you, but this time of year it's closed to tourists. It's practically a ghost town, anyway."

"Ghost town?" Gwen's fingers curled into fists beneath the table. *He's lying.*

Abandoned?

Gwen forced her breathing to steady, but inside, panic pressed harder. *Peter wouldn't have sent me here for nothing.*

She gripped the edge of the table. *Think.*

"You're telling me no one lives there?" she asked, trying to keep the doubt from her voice.

"Like I said, a few people stayed, but it's not a place you just pass through." Taran studied her, his expression unreadable. "Especially not in the dead of winter."

Then why did Peter send me here?

The weight of the soul crystal pressed against her skin. It had to be Sentinel Peak. The hunters captured spirits from these mountains. She needed proof. A sign that she wasn't chasing ghosts.

She met Taran's gaze. "There has to be someone."

"You don't give up easily."

She lifted her chin. "Isn't that much obvious?"

He moved toward the kitchen. "You should eat."

She almost laughed. Eat? Like she could stomach food when every second slipping away could mean Peter's death.

Still, she couldn't afford to push Taran too hard. Not yet.

Play along. Stay patient.

She inhaled deeply and reached for the mug of hot tea he set near her.

"The storm should be done by morning?"

Taran leaned against the counter and crossed his arms over his chest. "Should be. But you won't get far in this weather. Even if I let you go."

The words sent ice through her veins. *If he let her go.*

Gwen schooled her expression. "I don't need permission."

His lips pressed into a firm line. "No, but you need your knee, and you need to not get yourself killed."

A sharp retort burned on the tip of her tongue. *Stay smart.*

She pushed away from the table. The moment she put weight on her leg, a sharp pain bolted through her knee, nearly buckling it.

Taran was there in an instant, catching her arm before she could fall. His grip was firm, but careful, his heat soaking into her skin. Burning.

She jerked away with a hiss. "I've got it."

Taran backed away. "Sure, you do."

She hated the way his voice wrapped around her, steady and unshaken. Too perceptive. *Too much like he can see right through me.*

She rubbed her arm where he'd touched her to relieve the pain. "Look, I appreciate your help, but I'll be fine on my own."

Taran pulled back his shoulders, standing at his full height. "Don't leave this cabin."

A chill that had nothing to do with the storm raced down her spine. "You can't keep me here."

His gaze darkened, flickering with something deep and knowing. "You're right. I can't. But I can take you to the resort once the storm has cleared, and it's safe to travel."

"How long before that happens?"

He didn't answer. The infuriating man just turned and strode into the kitchen, leaving her with nothing but the silence and the pounding of her own pulse.

Three days.

Patch, the compound medic, was uncertain. He said Peter wouldn't last longer than that. And she—she promised him a favor to buy his silence.

After three days, he'll be dead *anyway.*

The words echoed in her head, a sick twist in her gut.

But Cedric would know. And he wouldn't just kill Peter for violating one of the sacred rules. He'd make sure the others watched while her brother suffered.

Three days.

Was it enough time to reach Peter?

Four

No one entered the dense forest to the west of Sentinel Peak unless they had a death wish. The woods whispered secrets of those who ventured through its gates. Shadows moved where none should exist, and the air carried an unnatural stillness, as if something long buried still listened.

Deep in the mountain, a molten heart lay dormant, but Taran felt its pulse as if it thrummed through his own veins. The fire called to those marked by it. When the mountain stirred, the heart curled beneath the surface, pushing toward the peak.

A catastrophe far worse than an avalanche loomed.

Even now, the mountain quivered and quaked like a woman in the aftermath of making love.

In his gut, he knew she wouldn't listen. Stubbornness rolled off her in waves. He'd seen that look in her eyes. She'd try to leave. He couldn't let her.

She lay curled in front of the fire, wrapped in blankets, face half-buried in a pillow. Even asleep, she wasn't at peace. The way her fingers clutched the fabric, the slight crease between her brows—she was wound tight, even in rest.

The dragon growled low in his mind, displeased by her rejection. *She's afraid.*

She's dangerous.

So are we. The dragon's presence coiled in his chest, heat pressing behind his ribs. *You can feel it, can't you? The mountain waking. She is connected to it as she is to us.*

Taran lowered himself to the floor, careful to keep his distance.

Her body tensed, and those dark, sooty lashes fluttered open.

"Don't. Touch. Me."

"I'm not touching you."

She narrowed her eyes. "Then what are you doing?"

"Making sure you don't do anything reckless."

Her gaze darted to the door, then back. "You think I'm going to run into a blizzard with a busted knee?"

"I think you haven't stopped looking for an escape since you got here."

She scooted back, putting more space between them. "You could've just locked the door."

His lips twitched. "Locks mean little on this mountain."

A flicker of something crossed her face. Doubt? Fear?

"You have a problem with this?" He motioned between them, moving a few more inches away from her.

"I have a problem with you touching me."

"Me or men in general?" His nostrils flared. The beast inside him stirred. *If anyone laid a hand on her . . .*

Shadows swept across her face. "I don't know you."

Fair. But his dragon knew *her.*

"Then you'll understand why I choose to stay near you."

Her lips pressed together, but she didn't argue. Instead, she shifted carefully, adjusting the blankets around her injured knee. The slight whine she tried to hide didn't escape him. His dragon rumbled low in his chest, a sound she wouldn't hear with human ears. *She's hurt. She should not be in pain.*

Taran clenched his jaw. *She doesn't trust us yet.*

But she will.

He exhaled slowly, focusing on the fire instead of the woman before him. Flames danced in the hearth, licking over the wood in a slow, mesmerizing rhythm. But it wasn't the only fire stirring.

Deep in the mountain, something pulsed.

His dragon spirit lifted its head inside him, alert.

The mountain shifts.

Taran sensed it, too. A tremor, subtle but certain. The fae's curse still lived in the veins of this land, entwined with the veins of their ancestors and the spirits they inherited through their shifter blood. A far worse entity than time dwelt within.

Now, this woman—*their mate*—had landed at its peak and disrupted its slumber.

She burrowed deeper into the blankets. Her movements were cautious, careful not to jostle her knee. In the firelight, he caught the glint of gold in her gaze before she closed her eyes again. Faint, but unmistakable. He stiffened.

Not human. Not fully.

The fire crackled, casting dancing light and shadows over them.

"Sleep. You're safe."

She blinked, startled by his words. Then, slowly, she found a comfortable position and settled.

But Taran knew the truth.

She wasn't safe. Not as long as the mountain still remembered.

And it always remembered.

For a long time, Gwen remained stiff and unyielding. She took long, slow, breaths. Taran matched her rhythm, the controlled inhales and exhales calming his dragon spirit. Even so, unease coiled inside him. Leaving her, even for a moment, went against every instinct.

She's ours. We stay. His dragon's growl rumbled in the back of his mind, a possessive thread wrapping tight around his senses.

She doesn't trust us yet.

She will.

Gwen carried secrets that could endanger his people. He needed answers, but those wouldn't come until she trusted him enough to offer them. Until then, taking her to Sentinel Peak was out of the question. Not without knowing her motives.

Yet, despite every warning in his mind, his dragon rumbled with satisfaction at her nearness. Where she went, the beast within him would follow. Fate had made them inseparable, whether or not she accepted it.

In the early hours of the morning, she sighed, her body finally surrendering to exhaustion. The tension holding her rigid eased, and her breathing evened out. Taran barely moved, unwilling to disturb the moment. Sometime before dawn, she shifted in sleep, her body curling instinctively toward his warmth. The scent of her, crisp like mountain air and wild like untouched forests, filled his lungs.

His dragon preened. *Ours.*

You don't know that for certain. Taran countered, although until now, his dragon had never taken such drastic measures where a female was concerned.

She came to us. To our part of the mountain. Ours.

He brushed a stray lock of hair from her face, memorizing the feel of silk against his fingers. He had no right to touch her. No right to want her. But the beast inside him didn't care about right or wrong—it only cared that she was his.

She winced in her sleep, and he pulled away.

As the first light of morning crept through the window, he carefully put more distance between them. He replaced himself with a pillow, creating the space she'd insisted on while ignoring the hollow ache it left behind.

Still, the questions gnawed at him.

Why had she come over the mountain?

Her reckless descent ahead of the avalanche, the map she carried charting a path straight to Sentinel Peak didn't add up. She must have flown to reach such an altitude before the storm.

Which meant someone had dropped her there.

His dragon growled, unsettled. *Trapped? Hunted?*

Taran's jaw tightened. *Or she's hunting something of her own. A brother?*

The idea sat like a stone in his gut. Why not come from below if she knew about his people? Why risk the deadliest part of the mountain?

The map troubled him the most. The borders were inaccurate, sketched from recollection, or outdated information no stranger should have possessed.

She's not an outsider. His dragon insisted. *The mountain would not have let her pass if she were.*

Which is why it sent an avalanche rushing after her.

The mountain was alive, ancient, aware. And it did not grant passage lightly.

The snow erased any chance of tracking where she'd come from, but that mattered less than where she intended to go.

Sentinel Peak was no longer inhabited.

Years ago, its people scattered, fleeing after the first tremors threatened to bury them alive. Some took the warnings seriously and abandoned their ancestral land. Others too disconnected from the mountain's spirits refused to believe in the danger. Many dismissed the volcano, the curse, the whispers of the fae's lingering presence as myths.

But those who stayed had learned otherwise.

The curse still lived beneath their feet, woven into the land.

Over time, their people faded. Bloodlines thinned. Fewer children were born with the ability to bond with a spirit, and without that connection, finding a mate became nearly impossible.

His people were dying.

His dragon snarled. *We will not let them fade. We will not lose her.*

Taran exhaled slowly, steadying the storm within.

And Gwen, an outsider with her half-truths and misplaced map, had arrived just as the mountain stirred again.

Coincidence?

He didn't believe in coincidences.

She is meant for us.

Or she's a threat.

Then we protect her. Or we stop her. His dragon spirit was unwavering.

Taran's jaw tightened.

Whatever she'd come to find, whatever she hunted, he would make sure it wasn't at the cost of his people.

Five

AFTER THE SUN CLEARED away the storm clouds, Taran waited while Gwen dressed. She pulled a ribbed turtleneck down over her head, the fabric catching on her tangled hair, before falling into place. Yellow edged the bruise on her cheek.

She carried that bruise before she hit the mountain. Someone hurt her.

His fingers curled into a fist. So many questions, and she'd offered no further answers. He wanted to demand them from her, shake the truth free.

But Gwen looked like the kind of woman who'd bite her tongue bloody before giving into pressure. He needed her trust. *And forcing her would only push her further away.*

Taran grabbed the rifle and led her outside. While she'd slept, he'd dug out the snowmobile. Another storm could come, and he wouldn't risk being stranded. Gwen eyed the machine warily, then shifted her weight onto her good leg.

"How far?" she asked.

He handed her the pack she'd brought with her. "A distance."

She slid the straps over her shoulders, keeping her hands tucked into the sleeves of her coat. Instead of climbing on behind him, she settled onto the seat stiffly, balancing without using him for support.

His dragon bristled. *She won't even hold on to us?*

She wouldn't. He'd seen the way she flinched when he got too close. He didn't know why, but whatever had been done to her ran deep.

Taran started the machine. The engine's purr filled the silence as they cut through the crisp morning air, the snowmobile carving a steady path toward the resort. The wind carried her scent along with pine from the surrounding trees. His dragon stretched toward her, and Taran fought against it.

She came here to search for her brother. He intended to discover why.

Avalanche Ridge Resort came into view, its cedar beams standing strong against the morning light. Taran slowed as they neared the entrance, parking alongside the other vehicles.

A small village of cabins scattered about in clusters, with road signs and trails leading to shops, the ice pond, or the designated ski slopes. Snow covered the ancient stones of the mountain to make a base. The resort gave him one more reason he couldn't let himself grow attached to this woman.

Before he could offer to help, Gwen dismounted, careful not to put too much weight on her injured knee.

She didn't sway. Didn't stumble. Didn't ask for assistance.

Taran had seen pride before, but hers had sharp edges honed in armor.

Still, when she took a step and her knee nearly buckled, instinct overrode reason. He caught her arm, steadying her before she could protest. Heat jolted through him, brief but potent. Her body tensed as if he'd burned her.

She jerked free, retreating a step.

"I said don't touch me," she muttered under her breath.

Taran narrowed his eyes but didn't press. *Why does she react like that? Fear? Pain? Something else?*

The scent of firewood and fresh bread drifted from the dining hall as they entered. Gwen's expression gave nothing away, but her gaze flicked over the room, taking in exits, cataloging people. Looking for an escape? Or someone?

His dragon stirred. *She's hunting.*

His cousin Ben stepped into view, leaning lazily against the doorway. His gaze swept over Gwen's stiff posture; his easygoing smirk faded.

What do we have here? Ben's voice slipped into Taran's mind.

Taran scowled, ignoring him.

"I'd ask you where you've been," Ben said aloud, "but I can see you've had your hands full." Ben winked at Gwen.

Gwen crossed her arms over her snowsuit. The color drained from her face.

"Ben, this is Gwen. I found her trying to outrun an avalanche above Crag's Cliff."

Ben's brows lifted. His gaze darted between them, unreadable, before landing back on Gwen. They exchanged a silent glance, before Taran declared, "I'm taking her to see Conleth."

A quiet growl rumbled from Gwen's stomach. The scent of fresh eggs and sizzling bacon thickened the air, a stark contrast to the canned soup and bitter coffee she'd endured back at the cabin. She had refused to take anything else. The protein bar she grabbed from her pack was hardly enough after what she'd been through.

She clutched that pack now, her fingers tightening over the straps, her gaze evasive.

Ben tilted his head. "Why don't you let her grab some breakfast first? You can arrange the meeting with Aluk, then take her to see Conleth."

"I'd rather get this over with and be on my way." Gwen murmured. She cast her gaze downward.

The change in her body language made Taran's dragon stir uneasily. She was holding something back. Her avoidance of Ben's gaze confirmed his suspicions.

Another growl from her stomach. His dragon bristled. *We should feed her.*

Taran clenched his jaw. *She's not ours to take care of.*

She is.

His dragon's certainty made something tighten in his chest. He shook it off.

Ben extended his arm toward Gwen. "Why don't I escort you to breakfast, and Taran here can check in with the boss man?"

Taran tensed. His fists curled at his sides before he realized it. Ben's gaze flicked down, his lips curving in the same direction.

Taran forced his hands to unclench, wiggling his fingers to shake off the tension.

"Shouldn't I be going with you?" Gwen asked, something in her posture giving her away. "I want this over with so I can leave."

Then she batted those dark lashes. Maybe intentional. Maybe not. But Taran noticed.

His dragon noticed.

Ben, however, remained unfazed. At six-foot-four and already mated, he was impervious to flirtation.

Jealousy struck deep, laced with a possessiveness Taran didn't care to examine.

She's not ours.

His dragon only rumbled, dissatisfied.

Ben smirked knowingly. "Come on, Gwen. You'll think clearer on a full stomach."

Taran exhaled through his nose. He didn't like it, but he let her go. For now.

"Tell Kaya she is my guest," Taran said.

"No. Really. I couldn't." With her hands raised, she tried to back away.

"You're hungry. We can hear your stomach grumbling," Taran said.

She bit her lip, her face turned red as a beet. It wasn't his intention to embarrass her. His dragon nudged him. *Feed her.*

"Don't let her out of your sight," he said to Ben.

"Your name is Gwen?" Ben asked, and Gwen nodded.

"Well then, Gwen, let's get ourselves some breakfast. Kaya makes the best omelets this side of the mountain."

"Kaya." Gwen looked back at Taran, wary.

"My mate . . . er . . . wife." Ben glanced back over his shoulder at Taran. "Aluk's down in his chambers."

Taran watched as Ben led Gwen toward the dining hall. *Don't touch her*, he projected into Ben's mind.

Gwen walked stiffly, shoulders tight, fingers curled around the straps of her pack like it was a lifeline. The sight unsettled him. She looked more like someone heading into prison than sitting down for breakfast.

He shouldn't care.

But he did.

Ours.

With a frustrated huff, he turned on his heel and made his way toward the lower chambers beneath the resort. Enforcers nodded in acknowledgement as he passed, but Taran barely registered them. His dragon still bristled at the sight of Gwen walking away with someone else, and it took effort to shove the feeling aside.

She's not ours, he reminded his dragon again. But it wasn't sinking in the way it should.

He found Aluk in his lair, still in his dragon form, the massive creature's dark navy scales gleaming under the lantern light. The air crackled with energy as Aluk shifted, the dragon spirit receding, leaving behind a man who was every bit as formidable as his beast.

"I heard the avalanche. Glad I didn't have to come find you," Aluk rumbled, pulling on a pair of sweatpants. His soot-colored beard matched the color of his long, wild hair. Twice the shoulders' width of Taran and a foot taller, the alpha of the Vasumen clan bore no resemblance to his younger sibling.

Taran rolled his shoulders back. "I rescued a woman skiing down the backside of the mountain." He unhooked the rifle from his back and laid it on a nearby rock. "She carried this on her back."

Aluk's gaze narrowed. "Then she saw your dragon form."

"I couldn't stop the shift. My dragon spirit took over at the sight of her skiing ahead of the avalanche. I dropped her in front of my cabin and shifted out of sight. With the shock, I don't think she has pieced it together yet."

Aluk scratched his chin. "How did she get past the slopes?"

Taran crossed his arms. "I don't know."

"She had to have been airdropped."

"My thought too." He hesitated, then added, "She claims she has family in Sentinel Peak. She has an old map with markings of town and surrounding areas."

Aluk's gaze darkened. "Is it possible?"

"Maybe."

Taran watched as Aluk took the rifle, sliding the bolt and cocking the gun with practiced ease. The weapon let out a sharp *click* as Aluk inspected it, his expression unreadable.

"Yet her weapon is military-issued," Aluk said, finally. "It is more likely she is a government scout or working with the hunters. You should have left her buried in the mountain."

Taran stiffened. "The avalanche would have killed her."

Aluk nodded, keeping the rifle.

Taran's dragon growled in his head. His fists clenched at his sides. "Saving someone's life isn't a choice."

Aluk's sharp gaze pinned him in place. "Except this time, your dragon decided for you."

"I have never lost control of my dragon like this," Taran paced. "Under other circumstances, I would call for a rescue team to pull her from the snow. I couldn't risk not getting to her in time."

Aluk studied him for a long moment. "You think she's your mate?"

Taran cupped the back of his neck. Heat spread through his body, tightening around his ribs. *Mate.* The curse had stripped them of their fated mates centuries ago. *Mate.* It wasn't possible.

And yet—

His dragon insisted. *Mate.*

Taran forced himself to breathe. "I don't know what to think," he admitted. "But I get the impression she's on the run. Whoever or whatever she's running from has her afraid enough to carry a high-powered rifle for protection." He motioned to the weapon, still in Aluk's grip.

"She entered my territory and avoided coming from the south," Aluk said.

Taran frowned. "Where else could she descend, avoiding our defenses? The old compound is an icebox on a hill. No one goes there anymore, not even our kind. Humans can't survive beyond Crag's Cliff, not with the pressure in the air."

Aluk's eyes turned a dark shade of gold. "Or could they? The mountain has been dormant for decades. Until yesterday. You can sense the change. The air smells warmer, and the pine's scent is stronger."

Taran growled low in his throat. "They are not allowed to hunt us anymore. They don't belong here."

Aluk lifted his chin and stretched his neck. "Perhaps they want what lies in the forbidden valley." Aluk waved his hand. "We are called to this mountain to protect its secrets. With a hunter on the mountain, we must protect our people."

Taran's stomach clenched. "Gwen?"

His dragon had decided no matter what Aluk said, or what she was hiding, his spirit would not let go.

Aluk's brows lifted slightly. "The female's name is Gwen?"

Taran nodded, swallowing the lump climbing in his throat.

"We can't afford any risk. Return her to where you found her and let the mountain cover your tracks."

Ice crept down Taran's spine. "I can't take someone to their death."

She wouldn't survive to see another sunrise. A protective surge shot through him. In the short time he'd had her under his watch, something inside him had shifted. Handing her over to the mountain, letting it swallow her whole, went against everything in him.

Aluk's eyes darkened, losing some of their gold hue.

"We don't know if she is one of the spirit hunters," Taran argued. "She could've been their prisoner. She is looking for her brother in Sentinel Peak. There is something about her I can't explain."

Aluk rubbed the back of his neck. "I will ask you one more time, brother. Is she your mate?"

"All I'm saying is I think we shouldn't eliminate her until we know what brought her here." He needed more time—time to understand the connection between them, to figure out why his dragon reacted to her like this.

Aluk crossed his arms. "Are you questioning my authority?"

"She could be connected to the mountain."

Or to him.

The thought sent a fiery spark through him, awakening something primal and familiar to his dragon.

Aluk dug a finger into his beard as he considered. "Those with dark blood magic haven't been seen in centuries. Hunters. The fae. It makes no difference. She will return to her pack, update their maps, and hand us over to them. They'll come for us. For our land. For our gifts from the Great Hunter."

"Then I'll keep watch over her. If she is a hunter, we can use her as bait to track the others. To protect our people." And maybe, just maybe, he could figure out what she meant to him.

Aluk's expression didn't soften. He grabbed the rifle and shoved it into Taran's chest. "This is a government-issued rifle, brother. Your duty is to your people first. Eliminate the threat."

Taran's fingers curled around the barrel, his dragon coiling tight, ready to spring. "No."

The growl in his throat was met with an equally deep one from Aluk. His alpha's dominance crashed down like a tidal wave, suffocating and unrelenting. Taran held firm for as long as he could until his knees hit the cold stone.

"If you can't protect your part of the mountain, I will send Ben on your behalf," Aluk warned.

Taran's chest burned, fury clawing through him. His fingers gripped the rifle against his chest tightly, but he refused to bow his head.

"Do you challenge me, brother?"

"No." Taran gritted his teeth, forcing himself back to his feet. "You are my eldest brother and my alpha. But I *must* know if she is my mate. Give me time. A couple of weeks."

Aluk snorted. "You have a couple of days. If you do not know by then, she is not your mate."

Taran didn't answer. He didn't need to.

Because deep down, he already knew.

She belonged to him.

And he belonged to her.

As a human, was Gwen subject to the same workings of fate?

Heat filled his veins, unbidden and insistent. His thoughts tangled with Gwen—her scent, her eyes, the way his dragon had reached for her without hesitation. He tried to separate desire from the undeniable pull of something deeper. Something bonding. Her soul called to his, and resisting it was like trying to hold back the avalanche.

"Good." Aluk's voice deepened with the spirit of his beast. "Realizing she's not your mate will make your task easier."

Taran didn't respond.

He watched his brother shed his sweatpants and shift back into the gigantic beast he found earlier in the lair. *You know what you need to do.* Aluk murmured into Taran's mind.

He did know.

But that didn't mean he could do it.

Six

Avalanche Ridge Resort sat northwest of Sentinel Peak, its rustic lodges nestled high in the mountains like a secret carved into the wilderness. According to the map posted outside the resort lobby, Sentinel Peak wrapped halfway around the mountainside, bordering the state forest. It was marked like any other tourist town, but remote and secluded.

Except no one lived in Sentinel Peak.

Unless Taran lied.

The more time she spent here, the more her suspicions grew.

Why would he lie?

Because they all lie.

The resort's isolation made it the perfect hideaway. Hidden from the world, it was an ideal refuge. And yet, the map she carried was more valuable than she realized. If updated, it could become a bargaining chip.

Cedric would pay a fortune for this discovery.

The black market for animal spirits was too lucrative for Cedric to ignore. An entire community of shifter-bloods, thriving in secrecy? He wouldn't just send hunters. He would send an army.

She understood why Taran lied.

Shifter-bloods are selfish.

Cedric's words echoed in her head. *It wouldn't kill them to share their gifts with the rest of the world. They let the spirits die and wander when others may benefit.*

She'd heard that speech a thousand times. Hunters combed these mountains because of it. Cedric sent them, searching for spirits to bind, to sell. The price of a captured spirit—alive, contained—lined his pockets in gold.

She knew how the system worked. She had listened to the scouts at the compound, absorbing every whispered report. Her brother, Peter, shared what they discovered: the hidden places, the traps they set, the creatures that roamed beyond human sight.

And the shadows that whispered.

Men who heard them claimed it was a curse.

Cedric called it an opportunity.

His price for freedom was simple: give him what he wanted, or stay trapped on the mountain forever.

Peter deserved a different choice.

If all else failed, Gwen knew where to find a wolf spirit near Crag's Cliff—the shifter's prison.

A place few even knew existed.

The shifter-run prison sat higher in the elevations, buried in snow and hidden in the rocky slope. The government pretended it didn't exist, but Cedric had a way of obtaining information from the right people.

Peter had assured her, *Stay north, near the forests of Sentinel Peak. The wolf spirits will come to you.*

Easy pickings.

But the avalanche had thrown her plans into chaos. It had pushed her far past the prison, deep into uncharted territory.

And all around her, the auras of shifter spirits pressed against her senses.

It was like being brushed by a thousand unseen hands, an intimacy she neither wanted nor could escape. Her gift—her curse—made her hyperaware of them. Their presence thrummed beneath her skin, a constant, aching pulse.

Did Cedric know about this place?

Avalanche Ridge wasn't marked on any map she took from the compound. This region was supposed to be restricted territory, protected by the government, disguised as nothing more than state lands.

She knew better.

Across the mountain, other towns were bustling with tourists. Why hadn't anyone ever spoken of this one?

Why had no one discovered the dragons until her?

Gwen decided to keep the knowledge of more dragons to herself. It might prove useful later should Cedric decide to punish her for leaving the compound without his permission.

The mere thought of his displeasure sent a prickling sensation across her skin.

When Taran didn't return after breakfast, Ben led her to the resort lobby, settling her near the grand stone fireplace. The warmth of the flames flickered over her skin as she watched families bundle up for the slopes or sling their ice skates over their shoulders. Laughter and clinking silverware drifted from the dining hall, mixing with the scent of fresh coffee and maple syrup.

Kaya's western omelet—Ben hadn't been lying when he said his wife made a mean omelet—paired with orange juice had had hit the spot. Real orange juice, not the powdered kind Cedric's scouts drank. The coffee was strong enough to make her rethink her loyalty to caffeine substitutes.

Maybe she'd send Taran a bag of dark roast after she and Peter were safe.

Anonymous, of course.

If she succeeded in taking his dragon spirit and leaving him human again, she'd be the hunted.

Gwen rubbed her knee absentmindedly, pushing the thought aside. The plan hadn't changed: find a spirit for Peter. Get out.

But there was one problem.

Ben.

To her dismay, he carried the spirit of a dragon, too.

Taran had mentioned a brother or two. One of them was the alpha. Did he have a dragon spirit too?

A ripple in the still water. Her awareness washed over the resort, touching other spirits. Besides the dragons, she sensed wolves, bears, and mountain lions. One spirit, feathered and distant, hovered on the edge of her perception. An eagle? A falcon? It was too faint to identify.

She tore her focus away, instead drinking in the space around her. The resort was beautiful, all polished wood and stone, flooded with natural light from the towering windows and skylights. She shouldn't feel at ease here, but the open space, the sturdy beams above her, made her feel . . . free.

A dangerous feeling.

"Do you need anything?"

Ben's voice pulled her from her thoughts. He stood close, not hovering but always within sight. She had noticed he never strayed far. Whether it was curiosity or suspicion, she wasn't sure.

She ignored the fleeting desire to return. "Where did all these people come from?"

Ben glanced around as if seeing the lobby through her eyes.

They looked human. They acted human. But were they all shifter-bloods?

His dark eyes glistened with something unreadable. They reminded her so much of Taran's. "About everywhere, I'd guess."

"So, they're not all . . . you know . . ." She was careful not to tip her hand. "Local?"

Ben tilted his head, his brow furrowing at her question. His frown deepened as if she were considering whether to answer, but then his gaze shifted past her, and a flicker of relief crossed his face.

"I've got it from here."

Taran's voice sent a ripple through her, steady and sure. He stepped close, his hand lifting toward her back before dropping away at the last second.

Good.

She didn't need him touching her. Simply imagining the contact sent a jolt through her, quickening her pulse. With so many shifters surrounding her, her skin had become hypersensitive, teetering on the edge of pain.

Too many spirits. Too many shifters.

If Peter had known about this place, why had he sent her to Crag's Cliff instead? Why not here? The spirits were so abundant around them.

Ben cleared his throat, altering the mood. "Well then, I'll get back to my duties. They'll be wanting the roads cleared." He shot Taran a pointed look. "I'm surprised last night's storm didn't delay you."

"We took the snowmobile."

Ben grimaced as he glanced at Gwen. "Must have been a fun ride."

She forced a small smile. "I'm looking forward to the ride to Sentinel Peak." She stood, putting the weight off her bad leg.

Taran ignored her remark. "Did you enjoy breakfast?"

"Very much. Thank you."

"Good," he said. "Because you'll be staying here as my guest for a while."

Here? She couldn't stay here. She had *two days* at most to get what she came for.

"You see that?" Taran nodded toward the window. She followed his gaze.

A world of white stretched before her, blanketing the mountains in an endless, suffocating expanse. The sky had darkened, thick gray clouds curling low, promising more snow.

"You won't get off this mountain alive."

Her pulse thrummed as Taran and Ben exchanged a look. Their gazes locked, and a silent exchange passed between them.

She had heard of this ability. True shifters had the ability to communicate without words. They didn't need spirit crystals like Cedric and his hunters. The spirits captured and bound to those without a natural claim lost this gift. Watching them now, witnessing it firsthand, sent a strange thrill through her.

Ben shook his head, his lips pressing into a thin line. "I hope you know what you're doing."

Gwen's tongue stuck to the roof of her mouth.

She should argue. Object. Demand he take her to Sentinel Peak.

Instead, the weight of Taran's decision settled over her like the storm looming outside.

She wasn't leaving.

Not yet.

If she stayed, she wouldn't have to take Taran's dragon spirit. She could find another.

She owed him that much.

He had saved her from the avalanche, given her shelter, respected her boundaries in a way no one else ever had.

Last night, his presence near her had kept her on edge. Not because she feared him, but because no one ever obeyed when she said no. The only person who had respected her refusal to be touched was Peter.

Her mother had acknowledged her sensitivity a few times.

Her father never had.

And Cedric? He taught her the consequence of refusing.

"I know you don't trust me," Taran said. "But I need you to give me your hand. No questions unless you will answer some yourself."

"No."

She clasped her hands behind her back.

Taran's eyes softened. "Have I not been respectful this entire time?"

Her fingers curled into her palms, the heat of her blood singing just beneath her skin. The tips of her fingers prickled, going numb.

His voice's sincerity made her pause. How long could she keep refusing?

She *hated* that something so simple caused her discomfort.

Because *he* asked without demanding, she slowly extended her hand.

Her fingers trembled.

Taran slid his palm beneath hers, warm and solid, a contrast to the cold press of fear coiling in her gut. The moment their skin met; tingles swept up her arm like the delicate stroke of a flame.

"Are you going to read my palm?"

"Are you going to tell me what you're really looking for in Sentinel Peak?" Taran's thumb brushed over her wrist, and her pulse jumped.

Gwen sucked in her breath as the energy of his dragon spirit seeped into her, coiling through her veins, warming her from the inside. She forced herself to blink, to focus, to keep from triggering her own gift.

"My brother is waiting for me there." *Or he will be in two more days if Patch keeps his end of the deal.* Taran didn't need to know that. "You claimed no one is in Sentinel Peak, yet the map indicates otherwise. Where are the people if not there?"

His thumb moved in slow circles over her wrist. She clenched her jaw, resisting the way her body reacted.

His touch grew warmer.

"Is this why you don't—?"

"I have sensitive skin," she cut in. *Among other things.*

Taran's amber eyes deepened, his pupils becoming narrow slits. The change sent a thrill through her, an unsettling awareness of just how close she stood to a predator.

His jaw sported a five o'clock shadow.

For the first time in her life, she *wanted* to touch someone.

To trace her fingers along the rough edge of his jaw, to see if it felt as coarse as it looked.

The thought sent a jolt of panic through her.

She tried to step back.

Taran tightened his grip.

"Then accept my apology in advance," Taran murmured.

He lifted her hand, bending toward her wrist.

Her breath caught in her lungs.

His tongue traced a deliberate pattern across her skin, searing heat marking its path.

The touch was too much.

Too hot. Too intimate.

A sharp jolt of sensation bolted through her. Gwen tried to jerk her hand back, but his grip held firm. A sound escaped through her teeth, something rough, something feral.

Not a scream.

A growl.

Slowly, Gwen exhaled. Her breath trembled as it left her lips.

Taran's gaze locked onto hers, swirling with anguish. The raw emotion in his eyes made her heart lurch.

Then softly, he blew against the burning mark on her wrist.

A shiver rolled down her spine. The contrast of heat and cool air sent her senses into disarray.

She stared at the reddened skin, stunned.

What just happened?

Flinching, she jerked her arm closer to her chest.

Taran let go, and the moment his touch disappeared, reality came crashing back.

Her pulse pounded in her ears. The sting on her wrist faded from the surface and sank deeper, etching into her blood.

A lump formed in her throat. Blinking hard, she forced back the prick of tears threatening to spill.

Then, with a jolt, she stepped back.

A *giant* step.

"What have you done?"

Seven

"I see Aluk sent me too late."

Taran's gaze narrowed on the person behind her. The earthy scent of pine needles and mint filled Gwen's lungs as she whirled around, her injured knee buckling beneath her. A sharp protest of pain shot through her, and she would have collapsed if Taran hadn't caught her by the arm. She groaned, biting back the agony, the coppery tang of blood lingering on her tongue.

An older, more mature version of Taran stood behind her. His essence screamed dragon. The scent of charred embers clung to his spirit's aura, blending with the earthy musk. His long, dark shaggy hair and neatly trimmed goatee set him apart from his younger brother, who had little facial hair and a darker bronze complexion. The resemblance was undeniable, yet he carried a heavier weight in his eyes, the kind forged from responsibility and experience.

Gwen clutched her wrist. The mark throbbed in time with her heartbeat. A faint burn of ozone tainted the air. Her breath came in short, panicked gasps. The searing pain spread like wildfire under her skin. *He. Marked. Her.* Gripping her wrist tighter, her fingers turned white at the ends. No amount of pressure dulled the brand's angry burn.

If Cedric saw this . . . if he found out . . .

No, no-no-no.

Her ribs ached from how hard she fought to breathe. She imagined Cedric's cold, assessing stare, the way he picked apart every detail, knew every secret thought concealed. He'd call her a traitor. A liar. And Peter—

Waves of nausea rolled through her, twisting her stomach in knots. She squeezed her wrist to her chest as though it could somehow shield her from the weight of what had just happened. He branded her, jeopardising everything with a mark.

"Why would you do this?" She glared at Taran.

This is what she got for trusting a stranger.

Gritting her teeth, she braced against the heat crawling through her veins, fighting the unnatural sensation of something foreign threading itself into her very essence

"I did what I had to do." His gaze held hers, intense, pleading for understanding but offering no apologies.

No apologies. She wanted to lash out, but hesitated at his expression. As quickly as it came, it vanished behind the hardened mask he wore, but it had been there. A crack in his confidence.

Taran's older version crossed his arms, his gaze flicking between them. "She has no clue what you've done."

"Is this a brand? Did you *brand* me?" she demanded.

Taran's older version said, "Aluk will kill you."

The surrounding air warmed slightly.

"Aluk will understand. I either marked her to show my intentions or . . ." Taran's eyes glazed over, unreadable.

Taran's older version snorted. "You should lick her mark and then carry her to my office."

She blinked. "Lick?"

"My saliva will stop the burning," Taran said, reaching for her wrist.

Before she could recoil, he pressed the flat of his tongue to her seared flesh, dragging it slowly over the darkened brand. The scent of his warm breath, tinged with spice and smoke, enveloped her. Relief, not pain, followed a tremor. The fire beneath her skin cooled, the violent tingling subsiding to a dull throb.

"How . . ."

"Can I carry you, or would you prefer to limp to Conleth's office?" Taran asked. "Either way, one or both of my arms will be around you."

Knowing she wouldn't make it far, she said, "Carry me if you must, but no skin-on-skin contact."

Taran's brows lifted slightly, but he said nothing.

She stared at the mark. The dragon's head was now a permanent part of her skin, its mane forming an ancient symbol she didn't recognize. Panic coiled around her chest. This mark. This claim. Was it reversible? Would it keep her from stealing Taran's dragon spirit? What if this ruined everything?

"I gave you my mark to protect you," Taran said, carrying her through the resort's grand halls. The plush surroundings clashed with the war raging inside her. He kept his hands carefully placed on the fabric of her clothing, mindful of her request, yet his grip was strong, possessive.

"To protect me from what?" she asked.

He carried her past a room where men and women waited on leather couches near a reception desk for spa services. "How many other humans have you seen since you arrived?"

Was this a trick question? Was he testing her?

"None, but I haven't exactly been mingling."

She needed to focus on why she had come here. Cedric promised her protection, but it cost her brother's freedom. Peter deserved a life away from Cedric's grasp. Taran might claim this mark was for her safety, but she wasn't naïve. She saw through his deception.

Trust no one.

"*Not even me,*" Peter had once told her.

She had to stay focused. She needed to find a shifter spirit and escape.

"When will the storm clear?" she asked. "How much longer until I can leave?"

"We can discuss it later."

Tempted, she nearly rested her head against his shoulder, but the throbbing in her wrist reminded her why such an action would be a bad idea.

"Forever," Conleth said.

She stiffened. "Forever?"

"When a dragon brands his mate, it's forever." Taran's older brother, Conleth, said, waiting in the medical suite of the resort. The antiseptic sting of alcohol mingled with citrus in the air.

Taran set her down on the examination table and took a step back. "We hadn't discussed that part yet."

Gwen's stomach dropped.

Dragon.

His mate?

"You admit it?" she asked, focusing on Taran. "You're the dragon who rescued me."

Conleth smirked. "She's not shocked. You went past that when you claimed her."

Gwen braced herself against the medical table, glaring at them both. "You're both dragons?"

Conleth ignored the question. "Push up your leggings or take them off."

Her fingers hesitated at the fabric.

"May I?" Conleth asked.

"Don't touch her." A growly undertone rumbled through Taran's words.

"You want me to examine her knee or not?" Conleth looked between the two of them. "That's what I thought."

She hesitated before nodding. Taran hovered close, his fingers clenching at his sides. She inhaled slowly, steadying herself as Conleth unwrapped the bandage.

The magic inherited from her mother in her blood stirred, hungry. Her senses brushed against Conleth's dragon spirit, testing, seeking. Unlike Taran's, it didn't retreat. Instead, it flared to life, standing its ground.

Conleth's gaze flicked up sharply. Had he sensed her probing? She clenched her jaw, pulling back her magic.

"You'll need to ice it," Conleth said, reapplying the bandage. "And stay off it."

"Days or weeks?" Gwen asked, dreading the answer.

"A few days at least."

The room closed in on her. That was too long. She needed to move. To plan. To get out of here. Three days, and she had two left.

"Gwen?"

Taran's fingers barely brushed her sleeve, but she flinched anyway. His touch was careful, almost hesitant, and yet it sent a ripple through her blood.

She forced her gaze to meet his. His eyes swirled with dark amber and golden shades of brown, hypnotising her in their stare.

"Are you okay? You look like you're in more pain."

She blinked, suddenly hyperaware of how much he was watching her. *Reading* her.

"Oh. Um." She flexed her fingers, wincing. "My wrist hurts. The mark stings."

Conleth straightened from looking at her knee. "May I see?"

"Look. Don't touch," Taran warned.

Gwen extended her arm, wrist up. The darkening brand remained the same, but under her skin, the pain continued to spread. Her blood boiled and sizzled in protest, magic twisting violently against what Taran had done. Against what he'd made her. *His mate.*

Taran and Conleth exchanged a glance. A silent conversation passed between them again. Then, without another word, Conleth turned away.

"I'll get you some cream to soothe the burn." He pulled open a cabinet, the metallic clang of the latch clicking in the silence. "You'll need to ice your knee often and avoid putting any weight on it until the sprain heals."

"I'm a fast healer."

Conleth studied her for a beat too long, something flickering in his expression. "I'm sure you are. But at least rest it for a few days before you attempt putting weight on it."

Too long. Peter didn't have a few days.

"So, I can't ski?" she asked. Casual. Like she wasn't already calculating how fast she could move on a bad knee.

"I wouldn't recommend it." Conleth handed Taran a small tube of ointment.

Taran uncapped it and squeezed a thin line onto her wrist. Gwen rubbed the cream in, the scents of herbs and something faint like eucalyptus filling her nose. It eased the burn slightly, but the mark itched beneath her skin, as if it knew it didn't belong to her.

Conleth's voice broke the silence. "Guess you'll be hanging around for a while."

He directed his comment at Taran, but it settled over Gwen like a noose.

Staying was never part of the plan. But now?

"Do I have another choice?" Her throat tightened.

There went getting Taran alone. The brand seared against her skin; a relentless reminder she couldn't touch him. She had no time to waste. Her gaze flicked to Conleth, her magic stretching toward him, testing the space between them.

His dragon sensed the intrusion instantly

A crease furrowed Conleth's brow. Gwen yanked her magic back. She hadn't meant to let it escape, but with the itch of the mark, she feared she couldn't control it.

"Aluk will be thrilled to return to Crag's Cliff." Conleth handed Gwen her bandage back. "I assume you want to do this yourself."

She wrapped her knee, the weight of his scrutiny making her fingers falter. He didn't correct her, didn't tell her if she'd wrapped it too tight or too loose. Just watched. Then, just as silently, he stepped away.

She pulled her leggings back down, and Taran extended his hand in an offer of assistance.

The world seemed to narrow to that one simple act. His fingers were rough from use, his palm steady, waiting. She hesitated.

Then she ignored it, pushed off the table, and landed on her good leg instead.

Taran sighed. "I can get you some crutches."

"Don't bother." She rolled her shoulders back. "My knee already feels better today compared to yesterday."

Most people needed weeks to recover. Gwen wasn't most people. Her body always had a way of recovering at a faster rate.

"If you don't take the crutches, then I am going to carry you."

Her stomach dipped. "I'll take them."

She needed an excuse to return anyway, to see Conleth again.

Conleth disappeared into another room and returned moments later. She slipped each crutch under her arms, grateful for the excuse to focus on something other than Taran's nearness. The burn on her wrist throbbed worse than the pain in her knee. Worse than the ache building inside her whenever Taran came too close.

"Should I have you check anything later?" she asked, lowering her lashes as she glanced at Conleth.

Taran rumbled low in his chest.

"I believe your mate can keep an eye on your mark. Since you're a fast healer, I don't foresee any future visits." Conleth pulled out an iPad and tapped on the screen.

Mate.

The sight of the sleek, modern device caught her off guard. Technology wasn't foreign to her, but seeing it here reminded her she had lost her cellphone.

She needed to find another phone. Contact Patch and get Peter.

Time was slipping through her fingers. Cedric would return soon and discover her gone.

Taran guided her down the hall, not complaining when she lagged behind.

"Where are you taking me?"

"You need to rest."

She opened her mouth to protest, but the glass elevator doors slid open, revealing a breathtaking view of the snow-covered peaks. For a moment, her pulse slowed, her mind going quiet. This place held a distracting, dangerous beauty.

They reached the top floor. The doors opened, and he stepped aside, waiting for her to enter an enormous suite.

"You'll stay here from now on."

Here? In the heart of their territory? Surrounded by shifters and their spirits? How would she get to Peter?

Her fingers curled tighter around the crutches. "What about the cabin?"

Taran's gaze became smoldering. "You would prefer to go back there? With me? Alone?"

Smug bastard.

Without this mark tying her to him, she might have found the cabin the perfect place to retreat. No one would have realized she had left the mountain or that Taran's dragon spirit was missing until it was too late. This complicated everything.

"I'm not big on being around people," she said.

His lips twitched. "I noticed."

Gwen pressed more weight into the crutches, grounding herself. "Perhaps one day, when the mountain is safe, we'll return."

She frowned. "Because of the avalanches?"

He held her gaze. "The avalanches are the least of our problems."

His words, not the cold, sent a tremor through her.

Eight

"Thirsty?"

Taran moved around the island counter inside his suite, motioning for Gwen to sit at the bar. She leaned her elbow against the surface, fingers tracing absent patterns while her gaze stayed locked on the raw, irritated mark on her wrist.

"Shall we discuss your dragon?"

His hand hovered over the icebox handle. Tension knotted between his shoulders. Folks around these parts knew about his dragon. Most averted their gaze, feigning ignorance. It's what kept them all protected this long.

"You rescued me."

His fingers tightened on the handle. "Are you a hunter?"

With a slow exhale, he opened the icebox, the cool air wash over his too-warm skin.

"Do I look like a hunter?"

No, she looked . . . *bewildered*. She had expected him to be a monster? And now she wasn't sure what to do, seeing he wasn't.

"Well, you tried to kill me."

He grabbed a towel, wrapping the cubes inside, giving his hands something to do.

Her brows pulled together. "Kill you?" A flush crept up her neck. "I . . . What would *you* have done if a giant dragon landed on top of you?"

He pressed the ice down on her wrist, watching the way she stiffened at the contact.

"You have an odd way of thanking a man for saving your life."

She exhaled, near laughter. "You'll have to forgive me. It's not every day a giant dragon steps between me and an avalanche."

Something about the way she said it stirred unease in him. It seemed superficial. He studied her as she stared at the mark, her expression unreadable.

"How do you know about my kind? You're not surprised at what I am."

She shrugged. "My brother has shifter blood. Shifters are no secret to my family."

His dragon stirred at that.

"This is the brother you're trying to find?"

She lifted her eyes to his, and he felt that familiar pull again. The one he hadn't been able to shake since he first saw her. *Mate.*

Taran leaned back against the counter, crossing his arms. "Is he the one who gave you the old map?"

"No." Her shoulders slumped. "I found it."

He pushed off the counter, unfolding his arms and leaning on his elbows before her. "You *found* it?"

She licked her lips before answering, a quick, nervous gesture, but his dragon noticed. Focused on it. His stomach tightened, heat curling low in his gut.

He grabbed a glass and filled it with water before he forgot what they were actually talking about.

"Your brother," he said after a beat. "Is one of us? What family do you come from? I don't recognize any Rileys from the mountain."

He caught the slight shrug of her shoulders from the corner of his eye. "You can ask him." Her fingers curled tighter around the crutch. "I don't know, which is why I can't stay here."

Taran slid the glass of water to her, careful to maintain the space between them. His eyes caught on the mark at her wrist. A flicker of heat stirred low in his chest, familiar and wrong. His dragon rumbled in quiet approval.

Gwen followed his gaze. "Is this why you lied to me? Because you intended to brand me and keep me here?"

Taran cupped the back of his neck, digging his fingers into the tense muscles. "I would never lie to you. The clans and packs protect Sentinel Peak. The town and the land stretching between it and Mist Haven are all within sacred territory. Now that you know what I am, you can't pass our protective boundaries to leave."

Her hand clenched into a fist. "So, I'm a prisoner."

"That *brand* is my *mating* mark." He waited a moment, allowing the words to sink in. "You're safe here only because of me." He omitted the escalating tension with his eldest brother, and the brewing conflict over their bond.

Gwen's eyes darkened. "Sentinel Peak is on the other side?"

"Correct."

This mountain belonged to the dragon, but Sentinel Peak belonged to the wolf bloods, who refused to surrender their claim even centuries after the curse. If she had wolf blood, he would have sensed it by now. But she wasn't one of them. And the curse ensured no female had bonded with a spirit in generations.

His jaw tightened as the weight of their past pressed down on him. When their ancestors had imprisoned the fae queen in the mountain, denying her and the wolf alpha their bond, the queen's wrath had torn through them, severing the shifter women's ability to connect with spirits.

And yet, Gwen bore a mark.

A sign that she belonged to him. That she was meant to be *his*.

"You are a danger to those living on this side of the mountain. If you had attempted to come up the mountain, you wouldn't have made it this far north."

"You can't stop me from going to Sentinel Peak and seeing my brother."

She pushed to her feet too quickly, nearly toppling. Her face twisted with pain as she caught herself on the crutch.

Gwen hopped to her feet. Flinching, she reached for a crutch.

Taran moved before he could stop himself from stepping around the counter. "I can and I will."

His dragon rumbled in his chest at the thought of her trying to leave.

Long ago, Sentinel Peak saw its fair share of visitors, but none of them knew the truth about the shifters. None of them threatened to expose what lay hidden in the mountains.

"When it's safe, I'll take you there. I promise."

Gwen's lips parted, then closed again. He could sense the defiance in her.

"You can fly me there. You're a dragon." She leaned in slightly, the eager look in her eyes making something primal tighten in his chest.

The Great Hunter help him.

His mouth parted, ready to say yes just to see her smile, but his people needed protecting. Their safety pulsed like a vow in his blood, and beneath it all, his dragon stirred, already hers, already restless with want. Not for duty. For her.

"One day." Her eyes widened. A deep flush spread up her cheeks to the tips of her ears.

He didn't think. He just acted. "If you wish to ride me, mate, I assure you there are other ways more enjoyable than being on a dragon."

Taran held still, every muscle strung tight as her eyes searched his. She parted her lips, then hesitated, gaze lingering on him. A slow smirk tugged at the corner of his lips.

"Hungry?" Taran moved closer. His gaze dropped to her lips, not minding at all the way she drank him in.

Gwen's breath caught and hitched. "I should finish my drink," she murmured.

"Then rest. You shouldn't be standing and putting pressure on your bad leg."

He kept his distance, but every step away dragged at him. Leaving her behind? Impossible. He marked her, and his dragon decided she belonged to them the moment he swooped her off the mountain.

"I'm not staying here. I'm going to see my brother, and neither you nor an entire army of dragons will stop me," she said.

"Not an army, Gwen. Just me. And I don't lose."

A few hours later, after Gwen rested, Taran left her near the fire in the lodge's lobby. The warmth of the flames painted golden light across her features. He didn't like leaving her.

Ben ordered the check-in staff to keep watch over her while Taran assisted with snow removal. As he approached, Ben tossed him a set of keys.

"I'm surprised Aluk wants us to clear the pass," Taran said.

"Aluk left for Crag's Cliff. Conleth is in charge." Ben yanked out a pair of gloves from his jacket. "There are too many guests. We'll use the traditional method."

Taran scoffed. "Even in summer, they'd have to fly in for an emergency."

"Which is why I'm clearing the landing pad." Ben didn't wait for agreement. "You're handling the roads."

Ben's voice dipped, just enough to make Taran's shoulders tense. "Aluk told me to remind you," Ben said, "Bring your woman to the prison. She's a risk."

Heat flared low in Taran's gut, sudden and electric, like the first crack of lightning. "She's under my protection."

Ben didn't blink. "You claimed her?"

"I did."

An unreadable shadow skimmed across Ben's face. "But is she your mate?"

Taran's jaw tensed. "I said yes."

"That's not what I asked." Ben crossed his arms.

"Did Aluk put you up to this? He's forgotten what it is like to find his mate."

"Our spirits don't forget." Ben glanced toward the mountain beyond the ridge, eyes turning gold reflecting his dragon. "He'll carry the loss of his first for a lifetime, and then his dragon's spirit will store it away for the next."

Taran knew that truth too well. "His dragon spirit won't let him move on."

"Fate did not bring him Naomi, and fate didn't take her away. I think his struggle isn't the curse or losing her. The disconnect between him and his dragon... wasn't it the dragon who took control of your father before the end?"

Taran swallowed hard, but the image rose from memory anyway. Naomi's body lit in firelight, then consumed by it. Their father lost the battle between soul and spirit and pulled further away until he perished before Taran reached of age to merge with his dragon. Neither his brother's mate, or his parents left a trace, but ash in their wake. He'd been too young to remember much about them. Yet, Naomi's name still cut his brother deep when spoken.

"Conleth and I always wondered if he chose Naomi out of obligation."

Ben stretched his fingers. "I never questioned it. When I met Kaya, my dragon whispered her name to me. Claiming her was like breathing. I didn't think. I just knew. She's my everything."

"Then you understand the torture of having a mate you can't touch or one in danger until proven trustworthy." He itched to return to Gwen.

Ben's shoulders hunched. "Aluk may seem harsh, but think about it. She is the first female to land on this side of the mountain."

"I have thought about it," Taran admitted. "She's different."

Ben's voice deepened, his dragon rising beneath the surface. "A woman with a military rifle is definitely not here for skiing. She could be a hunter."

They walked through the snow toward the garage, where vehicles and equipment were stored.

She could be our downfall.

His dragon didn't care. She was his.

"Aluk warned me, and I'm not saying he's wrong," Taran admitted, turning the keys over his hand. More than once, he glanced back toward the resort. Would she try to run while he was gone?

"You are sure Arden will alert us if anything happens to Gwen?" he asked. "With Aluk gone to Crag's Cliff, what about Conleth?"

"You should talk to Conleth." Ben's voice returned to normal. "Did you take her blood?"

Taran froze. "Why?"

"If it's dark, if her family is buried in the mountain's core, the curse could explain her showing up here."

"The fae are gone," Taran countered. "No one has seen them since the war."

"Disappearance doesn't mean extinction," Ben said. "Their bloodlines wouldn't have faded away. Why else would the mountain react to her that violently?"

"Fae and shifters do not mate."

"Then why hasn't your mark healed?" Ben pressed. "Shouldn't it have sealed when you sealed the mark with your saliva?"

Taran balled his hands into fists. "You've been talking to Conleth."

His brothers always dug into the past, especially Conleth. Over the years, he'd unearthed fragments of knowledge. Whispers of the curse. How their ancestors' choices condemned their people.

"She's not a shifter," Taran said.

"But she could have other blood. Not just human."

Her eyes held a glint of darkness, and when he stood close, his dragon quieted, settled, but already knew the answer he kept avoiding to explain why her mark hadn't healed.

Taran slid into the truck, the door shutting with a hollow thud that echoed too loudly in the air. Snow still clung to the edges of the road. Clearing them would take time, and it might not be a bad idea to discuss the possibility with Conleth.

He needed to bring it up. Not just Gwen's injuries, but the bond forming too fast, the way his dragon stirred every time she entered a room. And he still hadn't touched her. Not really. Not the way a mate should.

"Fat chance," Taran muttered.

The hunger to return to her pressed hard against his ribs, more instinct than thought. His dragon didn't like the distance. It paced behind his heartbeat, restless, ears pricked for any sign of danger.

Arden and the other staff would keep her safe. Arden ran a youth program at the resort, mostly for teens. He guided them and prepared them for the time when they would go into the darkest part of the forest to seek their animal spirits. He could handle watching one stubborn, injured woman.

She wouldn't get far. Not with her knee.

Taran's hands gripped the wheel. He didn't head toward the lodge. He took the turn for the landing pad. The unease didn't lift. Every mile between them scraped at his soul.

The curse began centuries below with a fae-blooded female. Beautiful. Dangerous. Royal. She'd enchanted a male shifter into loving her, or so the old stories claimed. In the end, the elders sealed her beneath the mountain to stop her from unraveling them all. But her punishment had cost more than a single life. The curse burned through every female born to their bloodline, stripping them of their spirit inheritance.

War followed. The fae vanished into the mist and shadow. But their vengeance never left the mountain.

And now Gwen was here.

If her blood held vestiges of that magic, she could be bound to the curse afflicting his people.

And he'd brought her into the heart of it.

Nine

GWEN GLOWERED AT THE mark on her wrist, the skin hot and stinging beneath Taran's mark. She leaned back against the pillowed bench near the grand fireplace, keeping her distance from the trickle of people passing through the lobby.

The mark fought for permanency. Would it give up and fade if she kept resisting him?

The sizzle in her blood said no.

She watched the window fog beneath her breath. Outside, the slopes stretched toward the horizon, empty save for a few skiers carving through the fresh powder. Twice, she caught sight of a runaway snowboard carving a lonely path down the mountain. Off to the side, untouched snow blanketed the rockier terrain—secluded, unmarked.

If the helicopter pilot knew the area better, he would've dropped me there instead.

But even with the setback, she'd bought herself time. She depleted her meager savings on the helicopter, paying for the flight time to help her escape the compound.

And she wasn't going back.

A sharp prickle ran down her spine.

The surrounding shifters hummed with spirits, a pressure she could feel beneath her skin like an impending storm. The man who kept checking on her—Arden—was the worst. His presence screeched in her bones, his scent like feathers. An eagle spirit.

Her fingers twitched against her lap.

Cedric would have loved someone like Arden. A shifter with the ability to fly? The type of spirit to turn an ordinary man into something more? He would've made Gwen steal it.

Her stomach twisted. *Not anymore. You're not that person anymore.*

Except she was.

She might have escaped Cedric and his hunters, but she wasn't free—not as long as Peter was dying.

The compound had taken everything from her. Her childhood. Her choices. Her body, warping it into a tool, a weapon. She had learned young what your ability could do when, in a moment of pain and fear, she'd accidentally absorbed a man's spirit. His shifter-blood spirit had rushed into her, latching on like wildfire, burning her from the inside out.

Cedric had witnessed it.

And instead of horror, he'd seen possibility.

Her father, a human, hadn't been able to handle the truth.

To her, Cedric was protection. To Cedric, she was an investment.

Every mission, every hunt, Cedric kept her at his side. The more spirits she absorbed, the more it hurt, until she learned to suppress the agony, to separate herself from the calling of her blood.

But Peter had been different. Unlike her father, Peter didn't fear her. He protected her.

She needed a new spirit for Peter. One strong enough to sustain him.

Taran's dragon called to her, but she couldn't take his spirit. Not just because he'd marked her — the risk was too great. Ben was off-limits too.

That left Conleth.

Taran's brother.

His dragon pulsed with vitality, a powerful, burning presence. She could sense it even from here. He was exactly what Peter needed.

"Can I get you anything?" Arden's voice dragged her from her thoughts. He was watching her again, his sharp eyes unwavering. His long dark hair was pulled into a bun, his bronze skin and angular features setting him apart from the other shifters.

"A phone?" she asked.

"We have few of those here. Perhaps Taran may assist you when he returns."

Her lips pressed into a thin line. "Did he tell you not to give me a phone?"

Arden didn't flinch. "The phones are out."

Not a yes or a no.

Gwen tilted her head. "You don't have a cell phone?"

"A cell phone wouldn't work here. There are no towers in this part of the mountain."

She narrowed her eyes. "And landlines?"

"The storm took them out."

Gwen pushed back her hair. "What about email? Can I at least send an email? You can watch me type it."

Arden's lips thinned. She put him in an uncomfortable corner.

Gwen lifted a hand before he could answer. "Understood. No service. No internet. Mountain and snowstorm. Gotcha."

Silence settled between them.

Arden's gaze flicked past her, out the window. He was careful not to hover, keeping a respectable distance like Taran, Ben, and Conleth. She had no doubt Taran made sure *everyone* knew not to touch her, that he had given orders for them to keep their hands to themselves.

The consideration, the restraint—it only reinforced her choice.

Conleth's dragon was a better option.

She let her head rest against the cold glass, staring out at the snow-covered world. The resort's main slope stretched into the distance, the occasional figure gliding over fresh powder. But beyond the groomed trails lay something wilder. Jagged outcroppings. Heavy drifts. Dense trees.

If she had landed there, then maybe she wouldn't be trapped inside a shifter stronghold with no way to reach Peter.

Arden cleared his throat. "Perhaps I can get you some paper, and you could send a note? The mail carrier should arrive tomorrow."

A thoughtful gesture.

But by tomorrow, Peter might already be dead.

Gwen hugged her arms around her waist, shoving back the rising panic. "I have to get to Sentinel Peak. I don't suppose you would help me?"

Arden's expression didn't change. "No. The mountain is unsettled. You're safer here."

Her mouth opened, ready with a retort—but nothing came out.

It wasn't his fault. He wasn't the one holding her here, wasn't the one keeping her from Peter. Arden was just another cog in the machine, another shifter following orders. Focusing her frustration on him wouldn't help.

She *could* take his spirit.

Arden was strong, no doubt about that. His eagle spirit would sell for a fortune in the black market. But his strength wasn't what Peter needed.

Instead, Gwen forced a slow smile. "How about skis?" She pressed her palm to the glass, feigning casual interest. "Do you know where I can get a new set?"

Arden didn't take the bait. "Yes, but skis won't do you any good with an injured leg."

Gwen's hand slipped from the glass.

How many people knew about her injury?

The bandage helped. Resting for a few hours had taken the edge off the swelling. But Taran had taken her crutches. He told Arden to release them solely when necessary, accompanied by a female.

Even now, she could feel the invisible leash tightening.

"How else am I to get to Sentinel Peak?"

Arden tilted his head, his dark eyes catching flecks of gold in the firelight. "Between here and Sentinel Peak lies danger. Is risking your life worth a few days' wait?"

"Yes." A tear slipped down her cheek, warm against the cold air, sliding over her lips. The salt stung her tongue, bitter with desperation. More spilled down her face. "You don't understand."

"No," Arden admitted. "I do not. It is not my place to try."

He lifted his chin, looking down his nose at her. "Taran protects you here. To forgo that protection would be unwise."

Gwen turned away, rubbing her cheek against her shoulder to dry her face.

Outside, the world stretched wide and white, a frozen landscape swallowing the horizon. Sentinel Peak rose in the distance, its jagged outline disappearing into the thick, churning clouds. More snow was coming. Soon, the mountain would bury itself in silence.

Her throat ached with the weight of words she couldn't say. If they found out what she was, or what she could do—

She had to leave.

The crystal tucked into her bra pressed into her skin—a sharp, constant reminder of why. *For Peter.*

She swallowed hard. "Even when the snow stops, I'm still trapped here. Do you know what that's like?"

Arden blinked. The gold in his gaze softened, silver swirls breaking through.

"What you call a prison is freedom to another. You are a guest here. The mate of one of the owners."

The word mate slammed into her like a punch.

Gwen's fingers twitched toward the mark on her wrist. The skin was raw, reddened, pulsing with heat. She clenched her fist instead.

A mark didn't make a mate.

Taran had done this to *protect* her, not to claim her. She was bound to him in a way she never agreed to. Trapped.

Had that been his plan all along?

Arden's voice broke through her thoughts. "This mountainside, except for state game lands, belongs to the Vasumen brothers. Centuries ago, our people came here, claiming these peaks as sanctuary—to shelter our tribes from those who would hunt us."

Tribes.

She thought shifters lived in *packs* or *clans*. She wanted to ask, to understand, but Arden turned toward her, steering the conversation elsewhere.

"If Taran allows it, I will take you to the shops. Perhaps you would like a new outfit? Or the use of the spa?" His voice was smooth, diplomatic, a distraction.

A distraction from the fact that she wasn't going anywhere.

Not yet.

But before nightfall, that would change.

A truck skidded toward them.

Gwen sucked in a breath, her body tensing as the vehicle barreled straight for the windows. At the last second, the truck veered, tires biting into the ice. Snow sprayed against the glass in a blinding sheet, rattling the panes. Her heart pounded as she lost sight of the outside world.

The lobby doors burst open.

Taran stormed inside, a blast of icy air curling around him. In his arms, he carried a lanky little boy, his limbs stiff with shock.

"Mountain lion at the top of the gulch slope."

"The advanced slope." Arden muttered, already moving.

Gwen's gaze flicked to the doors. Now. This was her chance.

The distraction was perfect. If she slipped away now, no one would notice. The cold mountain wind was a prison door creaking open, calling her to run.

The boy's gaze locked onto hers.

Wide, frightened, and lost.

Something inside her twisted. Her legs refused to move.

"There was a shadow between the rocks," the boy whispered, looking at Arden. "I saw the *bitatelo*."

Taran scowled. "A mountain lion's shadow?"

"I-I th-thought . . ." Large tears formed in the boy's eyes, spilling down his cheeks, and the quiet pain in them put an ache in Gwen's heart.

"I'll fetch Conleth. Stay with this little dude." Taran put the boy in a lounge seat near the crackling fire. "His mother's on her way."

Gwen remained frozen.

She knew nothing about children. The compound wasn't a place to raise one. The few times she had seen a child within its walls, they had been like ghosts. Silent, wary, and quick to vanish.

Yet something in this boy's trembling form pulled her in.

She didn't think.

She moved.

Pain stabbed up her injured leg as she crouched and bit her lip to keep from groaning. Instead, she shifted her weight, lowering herself carefully onto the tile floor beside him.

The boy's deep blue eyes shimmered with unshed tears. One arm hung limp in the makeshift sling, his small fingers curled tightly against the fabric. Broken. She didn't need to touch him to know.

She pressed the heel of her hand against the ache in her chest. "It's going to be okay."

He sniffled, his chin wobbling as he fought to be brave.

Where was his mother?

A presence shifted beside her. Arden.

Invisible feathers brushed against her skin, light as breath.

Gwen inhaled sharply and edged away.

Arden's voice was calm, but firm. "Did you see where the shadow went?"

The boy's gaze darted between them, fear creeping back into his wide eyes.

A shiver crawled down Gwen's spine. His emotions bled into her own, an icy trickle of dread settling in her veins.

"The *bitatelo* chose me," he whispered.

She believed him.

A *bitatelo*—a spirit of the mountain lion. If there is no warrior to possess it, the spirit might only appear as a shadow to the boy.

Arden moved with a quiet precision, peeling back the sling. A dark stain spread across the boy's sleeve. Blood seeped through the bandage, vivid against the fabric.

Blood.

Gwen's stomach twisted.

Her pulse pounded in her ears, a sickening heat rolling over her skin. *Too many spirits. Too close.*

She dragged her gaze away, forcing a slow, steady breath. *Do not pass out. Not here.*

"Where is the *bitatelo* now?" Arden asked, his voice soothing, as if speaking too harshly might spook it away.

The boy shrugged. The slight movement sent a sharp cry tumbling from his lips.

Gwen flinched. Her skin turned clammy at the sound of his pain.

"Don't move your arm," she murmured. "Taran went to get Conleth."

Arden's features softened. "Sunlight can play tricks on the slopes' rocks and trees. It was an accident."

The boy's lip quivered. Gwen offered him a small, reassuring smile. It wasn't so bad. Not the worst.

He could have fallen harder. Could have been buried in the snow. Could have died.

Gwen exhaled slowly, pulling his fear into herself, softening it, shifting it. She reached deep inside for something bright. Healing, warmth, the promise of life beyond this moment.

The cramps in her stomach lessened.

The boy stiffened, his gaze flickering to her face. "Did you have an accident too?"

Gwen blinked.

He lifted a shaky hand and pointed to her cheek. She'd forgotten about the bruise there.

Faded discoloration showed in the window's reflection, the soreness gone.

The way the boy stared at her sent an old prickle across her senses.

Upon impulse, she reached for his hand, anticipating the familiar zing, the shock, the bite of magic that always accompanied touch.

Nothing.

Gwen sagged with relief, curling her fingers lightly around his. "Someday, you'll look back at this and think, 'if I hadn't gotten hurt, I wouldn't have met Gwen.'"

A slow smile spread across Levi's tear-streaked face. "I'm Levi."

"It's nice to meet you, Levi," she said. "I'm Gwen."

The moment stretched warmly between them until Arden's fingers brushed her elbow.

A spark of pain lanced through her skin. Gwen hissed and wrenched away.

Arden's eyes widened. Levi frowned, glancing between them, sensing the tension without understanding it.

Before anyone could speak, a shift in the air sent a ripple through Gwen's bones.

She felt them before she saw them.

Taran and Conleth.

Their dragon spirits rolled toward her, a storm pressing against the edges of her awareness.

Taran's broad frame moved quickly, his dark features set in determination. Beside him, Conleth matched his pace, the resemblance unmistakable in the cut of his jaw and the intensity of his gaze.

A blonde woman darted toward them, her expression drawn and pale.

Levi's fingers curled tighter around Gwen's.

"Mama."

The woman raced to Levi's side.

"Oh, baby, are you okay?" She cupped his face, brushing her fingers through his hair. "What happened? Are you hurt?"

Levi's whimpers swelled into full-fledged cries the moment his mother touched him, his small body trembling under her hands.

Gwen's chest tightened.

The nausea faded, replaced by a deeper, older ache—one she'd learned to bury long ago.

She should look away.

Shouldn't watch.

But she couldn't.

Her mother had once held her like that. She could almost remember the warmth, the press of soft hands, the whisper of a lullaby she'd long since forgotten.

For years, she envisioned her mother returning. She imagined her scooping Gwen into her arms, telling her it had all been a mistake, and taking her home again. All the younger version of herself wanted was for her mother to love her.

Had she?

A sharp sting snapped her out of her thoughts.

Warmth enclosed over her hand, rough, calloused, familiar. Taran.

Her mark burned in response, sending tiny electrical zaps skittering beneath her skin. She gritted her teeth, willing herself not to react, not to acknowledge the way his touch set off something deep, instinctual, dangerous.

"Gwen."

Her name carried in his voice like a tether, pulling her away from memories she didn't want to feel.

"Hey, look at me."

Slowly, she turned.

Her breath left her in a sharp exhale as she met his deep, cherry-brown eyes.

Steady. Unyielding.

For a moment, she almost let herself believe the warmth in his gaze, the quiet promise behind it.

"Please," she whispered. "Don't touch me."

Taran's jaw twitched, but he didn't hesitate. His fingers slipped away, leaving behind a phantom heat.

"Okay." His voice was low, controlled, but there was something beneath it, something raw. "I just wanted you to know you're safe."

Safe.

If only there were true.

She had learned long ago that trusting a man brought nothing but pain.

And worse still?

If he trusted her, if he let her in . . . she would hurt him far more in the end.

She had to.

One way or another, she needed to capture his dragon spirit and get off this mountain. Her brother didn't deserve to die. No matter his mistakes.

The shifter-bloods claimed their spirits came from the Great Hunter. That they didn't receive them until they turned sixteen, and they had lived a part of their lives without them.

Would it really be so terrible to lose one?

At least they'd live.

Peter would live.

Some shifters might view this as liberating; unburdening themselves from their animal spirits.

But deep in her gut, Gwen knew the truth.

No shifter would ever want to lose half of their soul.

Ten

Taran kept pace beside her, his hand hovering near her elbow as if he expected her to collapse at any moment.

He wasn't wrong. Her body was exhausted, but it was her mind that wavered the most.

Ahead, Conleth carried the boy, while Arden wrapped a protective arm around Levi's mother. The woman was still murmuring soft reassurances, her voice thick with worry.

Gwen felt Taran's gaze on her. Twice he glanced at her, assessing, searching. She clenched her jaw. He was trying to understand her, to figure her out. She slowed, moving enough for him to think she followed. Once Taran went inside the medic's room, Gwen paused. Her pulse drummed in her ears. It would be so easy to turn and leave. To slip away unnoticed. Each moment she spent tangled in this world chipped away at her certainty. This wasn't what she expected. They weren't what she imagined from Cedric's descriptions and the few shifters she'd met in the past.

A curvy, dark-haired woman stepped into her path.

Gwen took a startled step back, instinct prickling.

The woman tilted her head, amusement flickering in her warm brown eyes. "I assume they are all in there, crowded around the boy?"

Gwen's pulse slowed, but she didn't lower her guard. She sensed the faintest trace of Ben's dragon in this woman. Another bond she didn't understand.

"You're Kaya," she said cautiously. "Ben's wife . . . er, mate?"

"I sure am." Kaya's grin was easy, like they were old friends. That kind of warmth, uncomplicated and freely given, set Gwen on edge. It felt out of place here. Peter warned her about the shadow spirits prowling, waiting to strike. But to strike a boy? And a shifter-blooded one?

"Are you headed somewhere?" Kaya asked.

Gwen cast a glance at the door where Taran had disappeared. Her heart shouldn't feel so restless. Shouldn't pull in two different directions.

"Air," she said finally. "It's too stuffy in there."

"I can't say I blame you. I'm not big on crowds either."

That took her off guard. Most shifters she'd encountered thrived in groups, bound by their instincts and pack ties—ties that once connected them to their spirit animals. But those ties had broken, and the shifter bloods dwindled in number. Soon this mountain would be filled with nothing more than shadow spirits. She needed to get Peter a spirit soon.

"I'm not good with people," she admitted before she could stop herself.

Kaya chuckled. "Me either. Why do you think I run the kitchen here? I don't have to deal with the guests."

Gwen studied her, wary but curious. She wasn't used to kindness without a motive.

Kaya considered her for a moment, something thoughtful in her expression. "Would you like to come with me? We can grab coffee and stay out of the men's way."

"Do you always invite strangers back to your kitchen?"

Kaya waved her hand dismissively. "Only the ones with dragon tattoos."

Gwen tensed, but Kaya's gaze had dropped pointedly to her wrist.

The mark.

Another reminder of getting herself tangled with a dragon. A forever reminder of Taran once she was gone. Her wrist ached along with the burning ache in her chest.

"Welcome to the family, Taran's mate."

Gwen's stomach twisted. *Family.* She had a family. One she was here to protect. But why, then, did it feel like the ground beneath her had become fragile?

She opened her mouth to correct the assumption, but the burn of the mark made her swallow the truth.

If she told this woman that Taran had marked her only to protect her, would Kaya believe her? Would she help?

Better not to take the risk.

"Please call me Gwen."

Kaya's calm acceptance unnerved her.

Family.

The word coiled in her chest like a living thing, unwelcome and suffocating.

Peter was her family.

Cedric. The hunters. The ones who had taken her in when no one else would. She had sworn her allegiance to them. She had built her entire existence around that truth.

And yet . . .

She turned her gaze, following Kaya's.

Taran had stepped out of the medic's room.

His presence eased something inside her, even as it unsettled everything else. She hated that contradiction, hated the way her chest tightened at the sight of him. He shouldn't affect her like this.

"Taking Gwen to the kitchen. We girls will catch up with you later. Tell Lissette if she or Levi needs anything to call."

Taran's eyes flickered to Gwen. "I won't be long."

And for just a moment, Gwen hated how much she wanted to believe him.

She tore her gaze away, fixing her eyes on the ground.

No attachments. No trust. She couldn't afford either.

"Those crutches must be a pain."

Kaya's voice pulled her from her thoughts. Gwen barely had time to school her expression before Kaya's gaze landed on Gwen's leg, then lingered a second too long on the bruise Gwen wished she could make disappear on her face.

"Not as much as this mark," Gwen muttered, adjusting her grip on the crutches as she followed Kaya.

Kaya frowned. "Your mark hurts you?"

"Didn't yours?"

Kaya lifted her wrist, revealing a familiar dragon head symbol, but unlike Gwen's, a band of fire circled the mark's edges. A complete bond. A real bond.

Not a mistake.

"No. Ben completed the bond almost immediately when he claimed me."

Completed the bond. Gwen's stomach tightened. How many shifter bloods ever claimed mates with blood like hers?

She ignored the sting of her mark and asked, "Did you know?"

Kaya's lips twitched. "Did I know he held the guardian dragon spirit? Or fate chose him for my mate?"

Gwen focused on the path ahead, hating how much she needed these blasted crutches. "Both?"

Kaya's brown eyes gleamed.

"I was there when he got his dragon." Kaya's smile turned soft, almost dreamlike. "From the moment he opened his eyes after bonding with his spirit, I felt it. Like he'd always been mine. His dragon called to my soul, and I knew we belonged together."

Gwen's breath hitched.

She didn't want to hear this. She preferred not to imagine such unwavering conviction. It didn't matter. This wasn't her fate. She didn't want it to be. Taran would never forgive her for what she needed to do to save her brother.

Kaya's gaze drifted to the distance. "He took me to the falls near Frostwood. That's where he claimed me." A mischievous glint entered her eyes. "We could have lingered there for days, entwined, but eventually duty called us back here."

Gwen's brows drew together. *Was that another one of their traditions? The falls. Did they go there only to complete their bonds? Would Taran take her there, too?*

Kaya chuckled, misreading her expression. "We conceived Jade not long after."

"Oh." Gwen's lips parted, but no further words came out.

Heat pooled in her belly, an ache she didn't want to acknowledge.

She clenched the crutch tighter. Thoughts of Taran touching her, holding her, sent a ripple of something dangerous through her.

No.

She was here for Peter.

She wasn't meant to belong with Taran.

Even if, deep down, something inside her whispered otherwise.

Gwen shoved the thought aside, grasping for distraction. "I'm not sure I understand something."

Kaya arched a brow. "What's that?"

Gwen blew out a breath, struggling to ask. "If you were there when Ben was born, wouldn't you have needed to wait until he got older to . . . you know?"

Kaya led her into the kitchen. "Shifters aren't born. They are chosen. When our warriors come of age, they may call upon the Great Hunter to bless them."

Gwen stilled.

Chosen. Not born.

The idea tickled something inside her. She'd spent most of her life under Cedric's rule, knowing she belonged to him, that her purpose had been carved out before she was old enough to fight against it. But the way Kaya said it, like they had a choice . . .

She swallowed with comprehension. "Why don't women have spirit animals?"

Gwen sensed the difference between the females' blood and the surrounding males earlier when entering the resort. Most of the men she'd encountered carried a power humming beneath their skin like a second heartbeat, but not the women. Not Kaya. Not anyone who had glanced her way.

She lowered herself into a seat at a small table, careful as she positioned her crutches within reach.

"I'm sure Taran will explain the curse to you if you ask," Kaya said.

The hairs on the back of her neck rose. What were they hiding from her?

Cedric warned against loose tongues among his men. No one who talked ever lived. Perhaps Kaya deflected her question for good reason. She'd learned, too, that questions could be dangerous.

"Coffee or cocoa?"

"Coffee."

"A woman with matching interests. Tell me you cook, and we'll be the best of friends."

A life where she sat in a warm kitchen, swapping stories over coffee and cookies? Kaya made it seem so easy, so normal. But normal wasn't Gwen's life.

She hesitated before admitting. "No. I never learned. My job at the—"

She almost said compound and stopped. She forced a shrug. "No one ever taught me to cook. Someone else has always prepared our meals, and I carry protein bars when I travel."

Kaya made a face. "Seriously? It's a good thing you're here now. I'm sure Taran didn't select you for your homemaking skills."

Gwen brushed her fingers over the mark on her skin. "No. He shouldn't have."

Kaya set a steaming cup in front of her, along with a small bowl of sugar and a tiny pitcher of cream. She took her own cup and sat across from Gwen. "Don't let the Vasumen men intimidate you. Inside they are all heart."

Heart. It brought little meaning. For years, she'd watched men like Cedric twist that word into a tool to manipulate others for their gain.

Gwen lifted her cup and took a sip. The bitter taste kept her in the now. She needed to stay sharp. Focused. She wasn't here to make friends.

Yet, she wondered if Kaya had the same telepathic ability she witnessed between Conleth and Taran. Their eyes glazed over, and Gwen sensed the change in their awareness. Did telepathic communication function similarly for mates? Could all shifter bloods do it?

Kaya studied her. "What do you think of the resort? Are you enjoying your time so far?"

"My imprisonment, you mean?" The words slipped out before she could stop them, and she curled her fingers around the cup, grounding herself against the flash of regret.

Kaya clicked her tongue. "I know Taran and his brothers—." she paused and shook her head."Even my Ben can be overprotective, but trust me when I say this is no prison."

"Taran won't let me leave."

Kaya crossed the kitchen. Gwen noticed the others working at the far counters preparing food. Two young men washed dishes. None of them carried the presence of a spirit.

Why? Didn't all shifter bloods inherit an animal spirit?

Kaya whispered to a young woman. Soon, she reappeared, cookies in hand. The scent of warm vanilla curled into the air, breaking through the tension knotting Gwen's stomach.

"Ben said the roads through the pass are too dangerous to travel. This side of the mountain rarely sees outsiders. You're the first in a long time."

Which explained why Taran's brother saw her as a threat. "I see."

"The mountain has grown unpredictable lately."

Gwen studied the woman as she nibbled at a cookie, observing her. What else was Kaya holding back? How much had Taran told them about her? "You mean the avalanches?"

Kaya's expression darkened. "The avalanches are one danger. The hunters are far more dangerous. Aluk closed this part of the mountain off from outsiders to protect our people."

Outsiders like her.

Gwen's grip on the cup tightened. Another reason she didn't belong here. She had a mission.

"One can never be too careful. Especially when you must ensure the survival of your family."

Under different circumstances, they might have become good friends. But family came first. Always.

Unable to resist the sweet vanilla scent, Gwen took another cookie. If anyone understood Gwen's dilemma, Kaya might.

Once Gwen's parents discovered she possessed a rare gift passed on through generations of her mother's side of the family, they sent her to live with Cedric.

He'd promised to protect her and keep her secret safe.

She'd been too young to understand the deal her parents made with him. He'd recognized the gift she possessed and made her wield it to his advantage.

You belong to me. The memory of Cedric's voice, steel wrapped in honey, filled her. *From this day forward, you shall be known as my daughter.*

Her pulse quickened.

He trained Peter, treating him like family. But no one dared steal from Cedric. Her heart pounded thinking of Cedric ordering another one of his men to execute Peter.

Her brother's life depended on her. She couldn't forget that.

No matter how tempting this place was. Despite her heart's hopeful whispers, she knew she didn't belong here. Gwen swallowed hard, forcing the thought away.

"Hey, you good?" Kaya reached out and placed her hand on Gwen's.

Fire shot up Gwen's arm. A sharp, searing pain—like claws raking over raw nerves. She jerked back, her elbow knocking into the cup, spilling coffee over her hand.

"I'll grab a towel. Did you burn yourself?"

"No." Gwen accepted the towel Kaya retrieved. A red mark from the coffee formed, but she ignored the burn. It was nothing compared to the ache still crawling over her skin. "Did Taran have Ben send you to interrogate me?"

Kaya's eyes widened, then a flash of something gleamed in her eyes. Gwen held her breath. The other woman laughed. "No. I admit, I have been curious ever since Taran mentioned you were looking for a family member in Sentinel Peak. You're brave to come down the mountain and attempt to cross through sacred grounds to reach your destination. Taran told Ben you came from far above the mountaintop; the change in altitude alone might have killed you."

"I learned in order to survive, one must take risks." Gwen pushed her plate away. "Besides, I stayed well beneath the death zone." Or she hoped she had. The way her body ached, the way exhaustion clung to her bones, told her she might have miscalculated. But she lived, didn't she?

"Sounds like a true mountain woman." Kaya held her mug up in salute. "Back in the kitchen I go. Otherwise, dinner will be late with the crew I've got working back there. They think when I rest, they can, too." She stood up. "Want to join me? There will be hot apple pies coming out of the oven shortly."

"Kitchen inept, remember?" Gwen glanced around the kitchen. "Though I'm not bad with a knife." A diet of hardtack and biscuits dulled a girl's taste buds. The hunters and Cedric seldom brought sweets to camp or the compound.

Taran had taken her rifle. Cedric would question her about the missing weapon, but she'd worry about him later. She needed to check her pack. She was certain Taran had taken her dagger. Knowing she needed to cut through the forest to get to Sentinel Peak, a knife became essential.

"Okay then." Kaya smoothed back a tendril of her dark hair. "Let's get you chopping vegetables. When you finish, I'll teach you to knead bread. Tonight's menu is beef stew, warm bread, and apple pie. Expect hungry guests after their day in the crisp mountain air. Ben and Taran will be hungry, too, after they've been out searching for the mountain lion that attacked Levi."

Kaya snapped her fingers. She turned and shouted at one of the kitchen staff. "Kelby, ensure the drink station has hot water ready for the arriving skiers."

The woman put her thumb up.

Slowly, Gwen rose, not bothering to finish the cookie or the coffee. *Mountain lion?*

Her breath hitched, thinking of the shadow leaping into the boy.

Kaya paused, the grim set of her mouth giving away her unspoken words.

"You find out things fast. Do you and Ben have a telepathic connection?" Gwen asked, genuinely curious.

Kaya's eyes softened. "We do. I assumed you knew all this and forgot you and Taran haven't fully bonded. I'm sure he will explain how our mating bonds work when he gets back. He probably doesn't want to worry you. Ben mentioned how concerned you were about Levi."

Concerned? No.

"I had a broken arm once; I know how painful they are." Gwen tried not to sound like she cared too much about the boy. Getting attached to the child served her no good in the long run. She learned a long time ago that attachment to others cost dearly.

And yet, Gwen offered, before she could stop herself, "Maybe later, I can take him some cookies?"

"Good idea. I'll put together a small plate of peanut butter cookies you can take to him," Kaya said.

A visit to Levi provided her with a reason to inquire about the mountain lion attack. Not because she cared. She had no intention of checking in on him. Maybe later, but not right now.

She hobbled around to the counter without her crutches. Someone laid out a board, a knife, and a stack of carrots for chopping. Close to her reach, a block of other knives awaited her selection. Tempting. Very tempting.

Once Kaya moved on to another station, Gwen eyed the knives. Her fingers twitched with the need to grab one.

Instead, she washed her hands in the sink behind her. Twisting around made her knee throb, but she noticed the sting in her wrist faded to a dull ache. Then she saw it.

Beneath the mark, her veins darkened.

Her pulse stuttered. *What the—?*

Turning back to her task, she cleaned and cut the carrots. Peter loved stew. Their meals typically included rabbit or venison. When they'd first entered Cedric's merry band of hunters, Peter shared his rations with her until she proved her worth and earned her own.

Her throat tightened. She wouldn't think about him. Wouldn't think about what he'd become.

Gwen, eyes brimming, started prepping carrots.

Kaya chatted while they worked, and Gwen listened to how the resort ran all year round, but in the winter, the resort filled to the brim with seasonal residents. "All our rooms in the resort are booked until late spring. Many of the folks return to their homes once the snow has gone. Some stay. Arden works with our youth. He leads hiking trips, and rock climbing is also popular. "

"You mean people who live in Sentinel Peak come here?"

Of course they did. But something about it gnawed at her.

Taran had mentioned the residents leaving. Was this what he meant? Did the medic suggest meeting her in Sentinel Peak because he expected her to fail?

Kaya's brow furrowed. She pulled out a slab of meat and chopped it into cubes. Her head tilted up.

Ben sauntered in, a silly grin on his face. Taren followed close behind him.

The shift in the air hit her instantly. The warmth. The spark.

From the glow in Kaya's eyes and the pink on her cheeks, Gwen envied the couple. The same spark flashed in Taran's gaze, making her belly flip and heat pulse from the mark on her wrist.

Ben leaned close, whispering to Kaya, and Gwen went back to her chopping.

Taran moved closer.

That spark turned to fire, igniting under her skin, as if the mark recognized him before her mind could protest.

Her wrist shot a jolt of heat into her veins, and her traitorous blood reacted.

Jerking her wrist, she sliced her finger with the knife.

Immediately, she dropped the knife, blood spilling from the cut.

Pain bloomed instantly, but before she could react, Taran was there.

He grabbed her hand, covering it with a towel.

Agony shot up her arm like lightning. A sharp gasp tore from her lips, her vision going white at the edges.

She wrenched away, breath coming fast. "Don't—"

Taran's brows furrowed, his eyes flashing. "Gwen?"

She gritted her teeth, forcing air into her lungs. The pain was already ebbing, but the damage was done. His touch lingered, leaving an ache where he contacted her flesh.

His gaze flickered to her hand, and then understanding dawned.

Eleven

For the third time that day, Taran stood inside his brother's exam room.

He hated standing back, watching, waiting.

"The good thing is you don't need stitches." Conleth held out a Band-Aid, his gaze flicking to Taran.

The bloody towel lay discarded on the counter behind Conleth. "Bad news is . . ."

Gwen held out her finger, her lips pressing together.

"The minor cuts always hurt the worst."

Gwen leaned back slightly as Conleth wrapped the Band-Aid around her finger.

Taran stepped closer without thinking.

The need to protect her, to reassure her, was instinct.

He pressed his palm against her back. Just a touch.

She stiffened. Not much. But enough.

Taran pulled his hand away immediately. He forced himself to look away, to keep his expression blank.

She doesn't like to be touched, his dragon spirit reminded.

He'd learned that quickly enough.

At first, he'd thought it was him. That she didn't want his touch because she didn't trust him. But the more time he spent around her, the more he realized she avoided touch with everyone.

Someone hurt her. His dragon rumbled low in his chest.

He didn't know who had done it. Didn't know how long ago it had been or how much damage they had caused. But he knew one thing for certain. *If I ever find out who did this to her . . .*

His dragon growled at the unfinished thought.

Conleth grunted and stepped back, tossing the wrapper in the trash.

You could have cleaned this and gotten *her a Band Aid. We have them in the* first-aid *kit in the kitchen.* Conleth's voice filled Taran's mind.

His brother was right. He hadn't needed to bring her here. But then *you won't have a blood sample.*

My dragon doesn't like her. I think your assumption may be correct. There's something different about her.

Taran's jaw tensed. He didn't care what Conleth's instincts told him.

She's mine. The growl slipped out before he could stop it.

Gwen's gaze snapped to him, suspicion flashing across her face before she glanced at Conleth. "Whatever you two are saying that you don't want me to hear, I can leave."

She shifted her weight, balancing on her good leg, reaching for her crutches.

Taran moved before he could think, his arm coming up to block her way.

"You're not going anywhere without me." The words came out rougher than he had intended.

His mark throbbed, the bond between them pulsing like a second heartbeat. He sensed a strange, inexplicable connection to her. *Mate.*

She was his.

What did it mean for the mark not to heal on her wrist? Did his mate need more time to accept him, accept their bond because of her human blood?

She flinched away from his touch.

Barely. A breath of a movement. But he noticed.

He exhaled slowly, lowering his arm. If she wanted space, he'd give it to her. But he wasn't letting her walk out of here alone.

"Why not?" she challenged.

The defiance in her voice made his lips twitch despite himself. Injured and backed into a corner, she still fought.

"Listen, I'll keep your secret," she said, folding her arms over her chest. "I get it. You all don't want anyone to know about the dragon thing. But if you don't let me go, you are putting yourself and your family in danger. Someone could *die*. I need to get to Sentinel Peak, or else—"

"Tell me."

His gaze flicked to the fading bruise on her cheek. It had turned yellow; the edges softening.

Who hurt you, mate?

Is that why you're searching for someone? Or are you truly a hunter?

"No lies."

Conleth sighed, clearly done with the conversation. He grabbed the towel and the Band-Aid wrapper, shaking his head. "Maybe you two would like to take this out of my office? Seems today is filled with the accident-prone."

Taran barely heard him. His focus was locked on Gwen. The way her fingers tightened around the crutches, the way her throat bobbed as she swallowed. Her heart hammered while a battle raged behind her guarded gaze.

Then footsteps. Quick. Restless.

Conleth glanced toward the door at the same time as Taran. A group of young wolf shifters approached, their presence a faint buzz in the back of Taran's awareness.

But Gwen went rigid.

His dragon growled.

Gwen's grip on the crutches was white-knuckled. Her eyes were glassy, yet sharp. "You think I'm lying to you?"

Taran clenched his jaw. *Careful.* Any wrong move could shatter the fragile ground between them. But he didn't want fragile. He wanted the truth. He wanted her trust.

He wanted *her*.

The silence stretched, thick and charged.

Conleth cleared his throat, breaking the moment as he left the room. But Taran stayed put, gaze locked with Gwen's. He barely moved, but inside, his dragon pushed forward, brushing against her. Just the smallest nudge.

She flinched. Her breath hitched. Something flashed in her eyes. Shock. Confusion. Maybe even fear.

"You can't keep me here forever," she whispered, as if testing him.

Taran ignored the way his dragon spirit wanted to grab, to hold, to keep her. "I realize you're in an uncomfortable position, but if you would tell me, I could help you. Are you trying to find your brother, or is there more involved? Someone else? Another guy?"

One he might have to deal with to keep their mate? Taran steeled himself against his dragon's territorial urge toward Gwen. They have marked her, but she didn't belong to him. *For now.*

Her brows pinched. "Someone else?"

"Husband? Boyfriend?" He should have asked before he marked her. The thought of her with another man was a vise around his chest. *Mine.*

Her lips parted, then she let out a short, humorless breath. "Boyfriend?" Amusement surfaced, a brief spark, then died. Her face hardened. "You think I lied to you?"

Taran didn't answer.

Gwen lifted her chin, defiant despite the vulnerability beneath. "I get you have no reason to believe me, but if you don't trust me, then why should I trust you?"

His fists curled, then slowly unfurled. His control was slipping.

"I suppose that's fair," he admitted. He lifted a hand, fighting the pull to touch her, to anchor her to him. "But you should know—when a dragon chooses a mate, she is the most precious thing in the world to him. We care and protect what is ours. We get one true mate per lifetime, and some of us . . ."

His thoughts drifted to Aluk, to the centuries of grief his brother still carried. "Some of us wait our entire lives for our other half."

A dragon's mate was a precious find for their diminishing bloodline. Finding one's fated mate proved a greater challenge over the years thanks to the curse taking its toll.

Gwen's expression remained neutral. "Well, we *humans* don't have the same luck."

She stepped back, out of his reach.

Turned on her crutches.

Glided away.

Taran stood frozen, pulse hammering. He should have let her go. Let her think she had a choice.

But his dragon spirit coiled inside him, restless.

She was his.

And she had no idea how far he would go to prove it.

Taran led her inside a small boutique named the Koko's Nest, a shop brimming with plush winter clothing, delicate lace, and flowing silks. The warm scent of cedar and lavender wrapped around them, mixing with the faint hum of lingering spirits. Gwen stiffened, her senses keenly aware of the energy woven into the very walls of the shop.

Behind the wood-paneled counter stood a short, pleasant woman with streaks of silver in her dark hair and deep, knowing eyes. Her presence radiated warmth, but Gwen noted the subtle strength in her stance.

"Ah, it's a Vasumen. And who do you bring to my lovely shop?" the woman beamed.

"Koko, this is Gwen. My mate."

Gwen glided in on her crutches, nearly overcompensating and falling at the sound of Taran calling her mate. Her blood pumped a little faster. *Not real. Not his mate.*

She distracted herself by checking out the wooden beams stretched across the ceiling, the woven twig baskets holding garments with careful precision. She forced a small smile, refusing to let the sensation of feathers and flickering spirits unsettle her. Koko opened her arms in welcome.

A shop filled with lace, fur, and velvet unmentionables wasn't exactly the kind of place she ever imagined stepping into. All her clothes were delivered to the compound, chosen by Cedric.

A giddiness stirred in her chest, a foreign, unbidden thrill at the sight of so many choices.

"Pick something out. Whatever you need," Taran said.

Gwen's pulse skipped. Need? She barely allowed herself to want, let alone need. She'd brought a little money. Cedric provided what was necessary and nothing more.

"I don't need anything," she said quickly, pushing back toward the door.

Koko's sharp gaze followed the movement. "Every woman needs something."

She lifted something glittery, luring Gwen deeper into the shop's offerings. A champagne-colored skirt, tiny teardrop rhinestones catching the light like stars frozen in silk.

Gwen shook her head. "I have no use for fancy skirts."

"Ah, a practical woman like me." Koko pivoted, moving with the grace of someone who thrived on understanding her customers. She gestured toward blouses, sweaters, and jeans, her fingers brushing the fabrics like a curator of treasures.

Gwen's gaze snagged on a pair of tall winter boots—white leather with thick fur lining the top, made for warmth and durability, not just fashion.

Koko caught the look immediately. "These?"

Gwen hesitated. "I have a pair of boots. I don't need another."

"Yours are scuffed from the accident. Are you sure?" Taran asked.

She hated his noticing and detested her overwhelming urge to say yes.

She turned away. "I'm good, but thanks."

Taran remained close—too close. His presence wasn't just protective; it was possessive in a way that sent shivers through her. "What about sleepwear?"

Koko's eyes lit up, and the saleswoman took off, her energy infectious. From the corner of the shop, Koko plucked garments from the shelves—silk, fur, flannel. Luxuries Gwen had never touched, let alone worn.

"You're not going to look?" Taran asked, his voice deceptively casual.

Gwen's fingers curled around the handles of her crutches. She could feel his gaze on her, a weight she wasn't sure how to carry. He would buy her anything she wanted. Anything at all—if she stayed.

Dread curled around the flicker of longing in her chest. Once he discovered what she was, what she planned to do, mark or no mark, he would never look at her the same way again.

"I have plenty of clothes," she said, the lie bitter on her tongue.

"True," Taran murmured, "but I don't mind you wearing mine to bed."

The heat of his voice licked up her spine, unsettling in its intensity.

"You won't ever need to worry about being cold." Koko winked.

Taran gave a small jerk of his chin toward the dressing rooms. "Get what you need. It's on me."

His amber eyes swirled—darkening, deepening, watching her with something she wasn't ready to name. Desire? Possession? A silent plea?

Her mark burned in response. She licked her lips. "You'd like that?"

"What man wouldn't?"

Koko pulled out a few more garments, grinning. "Come, you can give us a show, yes?"

"You're not getting shy because of me, are you?" Taran reached for her crutches. The motion was slow, teasing, a test.

Gwen held onto them, forcing a scoff. "Not at all."

She followed Koko, stepping into a private dressing area. The curtain fell closed, sealing her off from the warmth of Taran's presence. Relief and disappointment squeezed her.

Koko hung up two nightgowns, one a deep shade of red, the other lined with fur. Both screamed temptation.

"How do you know my size?"

Koko grinned. "I've been doing this for a long time."

Gwen ran her fingers over the silk; the texture felt foreign, indulgent. She had never worn anything this soft. Never allowed herself to imagine a life where she could.

Her chest tightened. Love didn't exist in her world. Not for her.

Outside the curtain, she could feel Taran's presence, his dragon spirit pressing against her senses. He had no idea what she truly was. What she had to do.

Koko laid a hand on her arm, startling her. The touch sent a jolt of pain racing through her body. Gwen recoiled, breath hitching.

"I'm sorry," Koko said quickly. "So sorry."

Gwen forced a steady breath. "No. I'm fine."

Fine. Such an easy lie.

Koko's expression remained gentle, but a flicker of understanding passed through her eyes. Had she seen the flinch? The way Gwen's body betrayed her secrets?

"Your mate is a good man," Koko murmured. "He is taking good care of you, yes?"

Gwen's fingers tightened around the price tag. Taran was taking care of her. If not for Peter, if not for the truth, she might have let herself believe in the illusion of safety.

She stared at herself in the dressing room mirror, imagining a world where she could reach for him, where her touch wouldn't burn.

Outside the curtain, Taran asked, "Found something you like?"

Jolted from her thoughts, she stared down at the nightgown. The dark red was almost the same shade as his dragon's eyes.

Pick something.

Her fingers trembled. She couldn't afford to like him, but the worst part?

A part of her already did.

Twelve

Back inside his suite, Taran gave Gwen some space. He kept busy gathering a snack for the two of them.

With meat, cheese, and crackers on the table, he made a mental note to thank Kaya for sending someone to stock the refrigerator in their absence. While his hands were steady, his mind churned. When Gwen returned, the deep shadows under her eyes and the wariness etched into her features twisted something in his chest.

She still doesn't trust us.

Yeah, he got that. Even more frustrating was that she didn't feel the pull like he did between their souls.

"Eat." He pulled out a chair at a small table behind the couch, his tone leaving no room for argument. His living space consisted of a two-room suite. A small kitchenette was set to the side of tall windows looking out to the mountain, and shelves of books towered on the far wall. Here, he rarely found a need for digital entertainment.

A single recliner sat nearest to the bookshelves, a worn companion to countless sleepless nights when he stayed here. "Unless you want to sit in the recliner and put your feet up."

Her mouth opened, and he interjected, "Don't tell me you're not hungry."

A quiet growl from her stomach betrayed her. A flicker of something crossed her face—annoyance, maybe. She eyed the food warily before plucking a cracker from the plate.

Her reluctance was both exasperating and endearing. The sight of her—this fierce, stubborn woman—made his dragon spirit restless with eagerness. Fate had given her to him. He wasn't about to let her go, but he also wasn't foolish enough to cage her. A trip to the village shops, letting her see beyond the resort, might prove to her that she wasn't a prisoner. Maybe then she'd see what he already knew: she belonged here. She belonged with him.

But Aluk didn't agree. His brother wanted to lock her away, ensure she wasn't a threat. Why did he have to go running to Aluk about the rifle? His dragon spirit heated in his chest. *Better he find out from you than another.*

Mate or no mate, he knew his brother, knew his alpha. He had to convince Aluk that Gwen wasn't their enemy, while still wrestling with his own doubts. She was holding back a lot more from him than the reason for needing to locate her brother.

"Is this another of your tactics to keep me from waiting to leave?" She snatched another cracker from the plate and eyed his hand, still on the back of the chair.

"No. This is my way of taking care of my mate."

Her lips flattened. "I don't need you or anyone else to take care of me. I learned to survive a long time ago."

"Sure, you did." With a rifle, a dull hunting knife, and an old map.

His mind drifted to the pieces of her past she hadn't yet shared, and when he refocused, she had already taken a seat. She nibbled at the meat, watching him through thick lashes cautiously. "If you're waiting for me to throw my arms around you and kiss you for doing all this for me, you're sadly mistaken."

"One touch."

She sucked in a breath.

Taran hovered his finger near hers on the table. A tether pulled tight, an invisible thread of longing taut between them.

"One simple touch," he murmured, watching her throat work as she swallowed. Her gaze locked on the sliver of space between their hands. A flush bloomed along her cheeks, beautiful and incriminating. But then fear flickered in her eyes, a shadow cast in the depths of her eyes dancing.

His dragon spirit thrashed within, clawing at the confines of his mind. It wanted out. It wanted her.

"Is this all it takes, Gwen?" He inched his finger closer. Her eyes were glued to the motion. "Does one touch between our fingers scare you?"

A battle raged in her eyes, a tempest swirling between surrender and retreat.

His dragon spirit stretched, a beacon in the dark, reaching for her. The need was unbearable. His spirit tore at him, pressing heavily in his chest. Every breath felt stolen. His dragon ached for her, for the bond that should already exist. Holding it back took effort, restraint slipping like sand through his fingers.

Gwen leaned forward, the space between them vanishing into a whisper. He grunted, his hand clutching his chest as his dragon strained inside him.

Her eyes widened.

The chair crashed backward.

She stumbled away, her knee buckling in her haste. "What happened?"

Taran exhaled sharply, his dragon retreating, licking its wounds. He took a step forward, but she recoiled, hands raised. "Don't."

"Gwen. Talk to me."

She shook her head. "I should have known," she muttered. "You can't manipulate me. Niceness toward me will not alter my decision."

Taran stayed still, forcing his dragon spirit to calm. "Good, because I'm not trying to manipulate you. I want you to trust me. You're safe here."

Her laugh was hollow. "You were trying to . . . to . . ."

She huffed, rubbing her arms as if to chase away a chill. Near the bedroom door, she turned back. "You can't seduce me. I'm not the type of girl who falls to her knees and kisses the ground a guy walks on because he bought me a new set of clothes and fed me."

Taran smirked. "I can think of much better places I'd rather have your lips."

Her mouth parted. A flush crept up her neck, turning her ears a delightful shade of red. He chuckled. Good, he had hoped for a reaction from her.

She scowled.

Taran sobered. "Go rest, Gwen. I'll wake you when it's time to go down for dinner."

"You won't try to touch me?"

"I would never hurt you." He rubbed his chest where the ache lingered. "I want to help you."

"You'll fly me to Sentinel Peak?"

"No."

A pause. "If I let you touch me?"

Taran stilled. The offer hung in the air, a dangerous precipice. "That's not how this works."

Something crept into her gaze. Uncertainty. Hesitation? "Then tell me how it works."

Hope fell from her expression when he didn't answer immediately. It gutted him.

"Give me the name of your brother. I will find him. I will help you find your family."

Sia, the beta of the nearby wolf pack, could send word to Rourke, the Sentinel Peak alpha. The wolves who enforced the region were their best chance. But first, she had to trust him.

His dragon spirit rumbled in his chest.

Gwen bit her lip, her brow creasing. Then, without a word, she turned and hobbled into the bedroom. The door softly closed behind her.

The lock clicked into place.

Taran let out a slow breath, one hand pressed against the burning tattoo of his dragon over his heart and the other gripping Gwen's crutches.

Several hours later, Taran leaned back in the armchair at the far side of the large firepit in the lounge. Ben and Conleth sat on either side of him in the circle of seats, looking toward the families socializing in the evening. The warmth of the fire cast shadows on the wooden beams overhead, a stark contrast to the storm howling outside.

Gwen sat with Kaya, positioned closest to the fire and the families with children. A secret smile passed between the two women. He had sensed the change in Gwen the moment she had agreed to accompany him after dinner to the lobby. Something about being here unsettled her, though she masked it well. His dragon stirred, sensing her hesitancy, his frustration gnawing at him. She was his mate, but she was also a potential danger to him and all those who lived on the mountain.

She was human, a stranger to the mountain and their ways. Yet, his dragon spirit chose her. The beast demanded closeness, contact—assurance she would not try to run from them.

Her long hair, loosened from the bun she had twisted it in earlier, cascaded over her shoulder. The sight stirred his primal side. He clenched his fists, suppressing the need to reach out, to bury his fingers in those thick waves and press her against him. But touching her was forbidden. By her own rules, ones he did not yet understand.

"Something has stirred up the spirits in the mountain," Ben murmured, his voice barely audible over the fire's crackling. "Aluk doesn't want to listen, but as the guardians, I need to ensure the queen hasn't escaped."

Taran's gaze sharpened. "You think she's alive?"

"Her soul would remain," Conleth said. "Aluk's dragon spirit is too protective, too haunted. Even if he wanted to, I don't think Aluk's dragon spirit will allow him to listen."

Ben nodded, his attention on Kaya. "He refuses to acknowledge the changes. We have all felt the mountain stirring. This last avalanche is proof enough."

Taran scoffed. "An avalanche is not proof of anything beyond nature. The mountain shifts every winter, and the residents know to seek sanctuary here."

"Something calls to it," Conleth insisted. "The spirits are growing restless. Young Levi claims the *bitatelo's* spirit sought him. That should not happen at his age."

At Levi's age, merging with a spirit animal was unheard of. Traditionally, the rite of passage was performed at sixteen, a sacred ceremony that marked a young man's entrance into their ancestral ways. To claim a spirit before coming of age was unnatural. Dangerous.

"Has the *bitatelo* claimed him?" Ben asked.

"Arden has agreed to take the boy under his wing since Levi's father no longer walks among us."

"Doesn't surprise me. I have seen the way he looks at the mother." Ben drank from a tall mug of coffee.

Conleth rubbed his jaw. "I'll speak with Aluk and hear his thoughts. It might be an isolated incident. We don't know what other surprises the mountain hides."

Ben looked at Taran. "You should inform the other rangers about what happened."

How, when he couldn't leave Gwen? *We can fly this time. She should know how magnificent I am.*

Taran snorted, and the others raised their eyebrows at him. He cupped the back of his neck. "I planned to, but the storm and Aluk's orders delayed me."

Across the lobby, a young girl weaved through those gathered, carrying a stack of s'mores.

"He gave you two days," Conleth reminded him. "I'm heading there in the morning. You have one day left."

Taran reached for the s'mores as the young girl came closer. She yanked it away and narrowed her jade-colored eyes at him. Her hair as dark as her mother's and her quick reflexes learned from her father, Ben's daughter strolled past him. He growled, and Ben took a s'more offering it to Taran. He shook his head, no longer interested. Later, they would hunt—true sustenance for a dragon. But his gut twisted—not in hunger for food. For his mate. Aluk would return soon to check on him, and if the mate bond wasn't complete between him and Gwen, Aluk would take her to the prison in Crag's Cliff. The thought sent rage coursing through his veins, his dragon coiling within him in protest.

"This side of the mountain may no longer be safe for those who seek refuge here."

Conleth clamped a hand on his shoulder. "You should focus on claiming your woman before you become like Aluk. I can't afford to have two brothers with beasts out of control."

Ben kissed Jade on the cheek, and the young girl giggled and took off back toward her mother.

Taran growled. "She barely lets me near her, let alone touch her. Have you tested the sample yet?"

Dark blood or not, Gwen's no-touching rule derailed him. The strange noises she made in her sleep troubled him. He wanted to kiss the silent tears running down her cheeks in her slumber whenever he peered into the bedroom to check on her. Not revealing the door lock never worked since the suite became his, and telling her she couldn't leave hadn't helped him gain favor with her.

"No. I need to fly over to Frostwood and use their equipment there. I plan to leave after we finish here. In the meantime, I would make an effort to do whatever you need to do to claim her. I can see the way you look at her with fire in your eyes. Aluk is the least of your issues. Your dragon will become angry if you don't mark her soon."

Taran rubbed his temples. "Touching her is the problem. How do you claim someone you can't touch?"

"You can't," Ben said, smirking over his coffee.

Conleth's expression turned bored. "You must entice her, claim her in other ways first."

"And will you bring me back to life when she shoots me for trying?"

Kaya came near. Ben gave him a look as he slipped his arm around his mate, pulling Kaya toward him. She leaned down to plant a kiss on

Ben's lips. He smacked her rear playfully. Kaya laughed, slipping away again. She headed back to Gwen, who was sitting near the windows watching the children roast marshmallows.

A small child handed Gwen a roasted marshmallow, and he noted the careful way she accepted it, ensuring her fingers did not brush the child's. A habit. One he had seen before. His dragon rumbled. Another image flashed through his mind. Gwen with a child, their child. Would she even want that? He knew so little about her.

Ben's voice pulled him back. "Do you think something spooked the *bitatelo*?"

Conleth stood, pulling at the sleeves of his sweater. "Arden suspects the mountain lion spirit latched onto Levi out of desperation. It must have been waiting in the shadows for a long time."

"Aluk went to investigate another incident at the prison. He believes it might be hunters, not the mountain," Ben said.

Taran followed Conleth's gaze and found it fixed on Gwen. A growl built in his throat. Since marking her, his possessiveness surged. "She had nothing to do with his."

Except he didn't know that for certain. His dragon hummed a warning in his head to the others. Doubt clawed at him.

"Maybe not directly," Conleth agreed. With his mug of coffee in hand, he tore his eyes from Taran's mate, and a good thing, too, or Taran's dragon spirit might have flared in jealousy. "But her arrival and this happening now can't just be a coincidence."

"And the prisoners at Crag's Cliff, losing their spirits and dying?" Ben got to his feet, too. "Something is going on, and I bet your mate is in the middle of it."

"The two of you need to spend more time in the real world and stop living in ancient times. Leave my mate alone."

"Because you are?" Conleth shook his head. He glanced toward the darkness on the other side of the windows. "I've never known you to be slow, brother."

"I'm not slow," Taran scoffed. "I will not force her. She needs to come to me willingly. I haven't figured out how to get her to trust me." Or fall in love with him.

How did he trust her in return?

"For starters, I'd stop making her feel like a prisoner." Ben licked the chocolate off his fingers. Jade waved, and Ben waved back at her.

"You know why I must keep her here."

"You sure that's the reason?"

"What other reason would there be?"

"I don't know. The curse?" Ben asked, shaking his head when little Jade offered to make him another s'more.

"You spend too much time with my brother," Taran grumbled.

"Someday, when you have daughters, you'll understand. Of course, if your mate ever allows you to touch her." Ben snickered.

Taran's spirit tattoo grew warm against his skin. Gwen jerked slightly. Her gaze landed on her mark, then on him. His eyes heated. Gwen acknowledged his dragon reaching out to her, and something deep inside him responded like a fire struggling against a storm.

Frowning, Gwen stared back down at her mark. Taran left the other men and crossed the lobby toward her. His movements were slow, deliberate, as if afraid one wrong step would make her retreat. The urge to protect her, to claim her, warred with his restraint. He snatched the last sugar cookie from a tray and held it up to her.

"No thanks," she said.

"Are you sure?"

"They're your favorite."

"One of many." How did she know? His *Bodaway Achak,* fire-making spirit, heated within him, a spark rippling through their connection and deepening their bond.

His face must have revealed his astonishment, for she grinned.

"I've seen you eating nothing but those kinds of cookies for the past hour."

"You've been watching me, have you?" He pulled back his shoulders, the realization stirring something unexpected in him. She noticed things about him. Did she realize he noticed everything about her?

"Kaya may have also told me. She knows a lot about the people here," Gwen said.

"We take care of our own." Taran itched for Gwen to trust him enough to let down her guard. He wanted her to see him as something other than a captor. But the wall between them remained. Secrets neither of them fully understood.

He would tear that wall down—if only she would let him.

Thirteen

GWEN SAT IN THE resort's lobby around the stone firepit, families gathered making s'mores and roasting hot dogs, all while the sky darkened on the other side of the tall glass windows. Tiny pinpricks of light dotted over the cabins, across the rocky terrain, and above the treetops. Not one of them beckoned her to make a wish. A heavy weight settled over her chest. She had learned long ago how to swallow her grief, to lock it away where no one could see. She wouldn't cry, not here in front of these families. Across the room, watching but not approaching, stood Taran.

"Gwen." At the sound of her name, Gwen turned. Levi sat near the fire holding a metal stick with marshmallows to toast over the heat. "Can I make you a s'more?"

"Please do," his mother, a petite woman with blonde curly hair, said, "I don't think I could eat another." Her contagious smile drew one from Gwen in return.

"Sure. I'd love one."

On the other side of the lobby, Gwen sensed Taran's watchful gaze. When he caught her looking at him in return, the corner of his mouth tilted up, a small but undeniable smirk that sent warmth curling in her belly. Ben helped a small toddler pull off a blackened hot dog and prepare a bun. His gentle way with the boy caused a familiar ache to resurface. Kaya sat near their daughter, Jade, licking the marshmallow off her fingers.

"Here you go." Levi held out the gooey masterpiece. He still had a dribble of melted marshmallow down his chin. The way he maneuvered with one arm while keeping the other tucked against him amazed her.

Gwen took the treat with great anticipation. She hadn't had one of these since childhood.

"You don't like it?" Levi watched her and waited for her approval. She took a big bite to reassure him. With a thumbs up from her, he turned to grab more marshmallows.

"You've done it now," his mother warned. "You'll be stuffed full by the time he's done."

Gwen, savoring the chocolate, nodded, trying to keep her eyes from rolling back at the pleasure of the sweetness. She forgot how sinfully delicious melted marshmallow and chocolate could be.

"He rarely befriends others, but he seems to like you."

"You're extremely blessed to have a son like Levi." Gwen couldn't resist licking her fingers to savor the sticky sweetness.

"Lissette. And you're Gwen, right?" Levi's mother sat closer to her on the cushioned bench close to the fire.

"Yes." Gwen caught a glimpse of Levi's arm. His scratches appeared scabbed over, and further up near his shoulder, she spotted the dark ink of a tattoo.

Lissette followed her gaze. "He's a brave boy. Levi's been telling me for weeks he felt his father's spirit, but I figured he missed Adam as much as I do. Levi thinks Adam sent the spirit to protect him because of the bad people who harmed his father." Lissette's eyes glistened, and Gwen's throat tightened with the grip of the other woman's sorrow closing in around her neck.

"Merging with a spirit animal hurts at first." Lissette tilted her head, brushing back the moisture there. "I wish Levi would have waited. He won't go through the ceremony like all the other young men when he comes of age. His father would have preferred gaining his inheritance the traditional way."

"Inheritance?" Gwen asked.

"A shifter's spirit doesn't die with them. It lingers, searching for another in the bloodline strong enough to carry it. Traditionally, it's passed through a sacred ceremony—one that bonds the spirit to its new host without pain or distress. When a spirit is taken by force or merges out of desperation, the transition can be . . . difficult." Lissette sighed. "Levi isn't old enough. The *bitatelo* should have remained in the sacred tree until the right time."

Gwen froze. *Passed willingly. A ceremony.* But hunters . . . they ripped them out.

"Levi's father is no longer with you?" Gwen glanced over at the boy. Levi's ripened-wheat-colored hair glinted in the firelight.

"Spirit hunters about a year ago." Lissette inhaled deeply, smiling. Levi approached.

Spirit hunters? Like Cedric and his men. Like her brother. An icy dread wrapped around Gwen's ribs, tightening with every beat of her heart. Lissette's mate likely died accidentally. Cedric and his men didn't kill. They wounded. Slowed their prey, kept them alive. Otherwise, transferring the spirit into the soul crystals became almost impossible. If Levi had his father's animal spirit, then whoever caused his father's death couldn't have been a hunter. Unless—

Maybe in her grief, Lissette misspoke.

"I'm so sorry," Gwen said, meaning every word with all her heart.

"Thank you." Lissette looked thoughtful and her face softened. "My father was a mountain lion shifter, too. It's hard to say why the *bitatelo* came to him this soon."

Something more must have happened for Lissette's husband to perish. The spirit would have returned to the sacred tree, but if the bond had been severed early . . . if the spirit had been torn from one body before it was ready . . .

Levi's spirit hadn't followed tradition. Had his father's *bitatelo*, the mountain lion, stalked him, waiting? Why not until he came of age? Had the boy sought the spirit animal?

She needed answers. And soon.

Spirit hunters harvested spirits, leaving the shifter to seek another or live without one. If a spirit went unused, wasn't it a waste? If her brother's survival depended on taking one, did that make it right? Wouldn't it just end up lost as one of the shadows?

But Levi's wide, trusting eyes followed her. He believed in the sacred nature of his father's gift. Could she look at him and still go through with her plans?

Her stomach twisted. What if she took his and saved him the struggles to come? Lissette said at this age he would have difficulty. She could help him and help Peter.

Levi handed her the plate of s'mores, his grin as wide as the moonlit sky. "Here you go. Three this time."

Gwen hesitated as she reached for the plate, forcing a smile. "Thank you."

"Take the plate too," Levi insisted, thrusting it closer with his good hand.

His enthusiasm tugged at her heart, but his unknowing trust left her stomach in knots. She reached for the plate cautiously, careful to avoid contact, but Levi shifted unexpectedly. Their fingers brushed.

The jolt shot through her like a needle of white-hot pain, sharp and blinding.

Levi stiffened. His wide smile faltered.

The plate crashed to the floor between them.

Gwen's stomach dropped along with it. Levi's gaze darted to her hand, then her face.

"Are you okay?"

His hand hovered awkwardly, as though unsure whether to back away or reach for the plate they dropped.

Her heart hammered. Every nerve was on edge. Gwen bent to retrieve the plate. Levi backed away from her, his brows furrowing.

"That was weird," he muttered, more to himself. "It was like . . . I don't know. My spirit—it kind of tried to push out of me for a second." He looked at his mother.

Her chest tightened, panic flooding her. She forced a shaky smile, hoping he couldn't sense the taint in her blood working its magic under her skin. Taran's mark burned against her wrist.

"Maybe you just need to rest. You've had a big day," she tried to reassure him, assure herself. This couldn't happen here. Not now. Not in front of so many others. What would they do to her?

Levi didn't look convinced. His usual carefree energy muted. The mountain lion spirit inside him rising to the surface. The boy's eyes turning almost pure black.

"Levi." His mother said gently. "I think our new friend is right. It takes a lot of strength and energy to build a bond and merge with your spirit animal."

"Yeah . . . maybe," he said, slowly, glancing at her as if searching for something he couldn't name. Shaking his head, the black cleared from his eyes. He grinned again and grabbed a s'more still stuck to the plate. "Anyway, those are for you. Enjoy!"

"Come now," Lissette said, standing. "I'll read to you for a bit before lights out."

Gwen heard him complain as his mother directed him away. "Just one more minute."

"No more minutes. Now." Lissette instructed him to put his roasting stick with the others against the firepit and to follow her to their room.

Once they were gone, Gwen sat frozen, her hands trembling. The pain from the touch had already faded. What if he had sensed her gift? What if she couldn't control it next time? How long before it happened again without her willing it? Or someone else noticed?

How long before Taran noticed?

Her blood stirred as her gaze lifted, colliding with Taran across the fire-lit space. Heat flushed up her neck. Life was never fair.

Attractive as she might find Taran, Peter's life depended on her finding and extracting an animal spirit. She squared her shoulders as he approached, fully expecting him to march her back to their suite.

Instead, he smirked, glancing at the plate in her lap.

"Are those for me?" He winked, half reaching for the gooey treats in front of her.

Her stomach flipped at the teasing lilt in his voice. He was lowering his guard. Did he trust her now? If sharing her s'mores made him even slightly less suspicious, she didn't mind. Even if they'd drop to the floor, but stayed stuck to the plate.

"Levi made them," she said, lifting the plate. "You're welcome to have them if you'd like."

Her heart did that little flutter thing, and her fingers trembled a little watching him reach down on the plate. He selected one. When he didn't take the other, she asked, "Don't you like it?"

"It's very good." He grinned at her. "You'd best eat the last one before I am tempted to steal it."

Her fingers trembled as she picked up the treat.

Taran took the empty dish from her.

Something in her cracked. Something small but undeniable.

She offered him a bite. "I don't mind if you want to share."

His dark mahogany eyes never left hers as he leaned in just short of the treat.

He didn't touch her. He didn't try.

Taran tilted his head slightly, waiting for her to close the distance.

The heat in her gaze made her throat dry.

With a gulp, she held the treat a little closer. He took a bite, slow and deliberate, his breath warning the tips of her fingers.

"This okay?" he asked.

She nodded, pulse racing.

His lips curled slightly. "You're always so careful not to touch anyone. Why?"

Gwen's breath caught in her throat.

She withdrew her hand, brushing nonexistent crumbs from her fingers, as if the question hadn't landed like a knife in her ribs. "I just prefer not to."

His eyes lingered on her, as if considering her answer, but he didn't push.

The tension coiled in her chest unraveled just slightly.

A brief, fleeting relief.

But how long could she keep her secrets?

Fourteen

NEITHER SAID A WORD while they rode the elevator back up to his suite. Gwen gripped the handles of her crutches. Levi. His father's spirit. The way the boy's eyes darkened, as if the *bitatelo* had reacted to the slight call of her blood at her touch.

She hadn't thought to ask more about Levi's *bitatelo*. How did they know the animal spirit curled up fresh within Levi belonged to his father? Some shifter bloodlines carried more spirit animals than hosts, waiting for a vessel to claim. Could it be his father's, or was it another lingering, untethered soul?

Biting her lower lip, she remembered every spirit Cedric ordered her to extract. A small shard of their essence imprinted in her DNA. If her brother's survival depended on taking one, didn't it make sense? Wasn't she just ensuring it lived on?

A tall, golden-skinned man with brown hair haunted her memory—a prisoner headed to the shifter facility run by the government. Like most prisoners, they sent her to extract the spirit until their time served ended. Had Levi's father been among those souls? Then, it wasn't his father's spirit he inherited.

Had she played a part in the boy's loss?

It's not a loss when he gained a spirit where one may have wandered in the shadows.

Back inside the suite, Taran gave her privacy to prepare for bed. She lingered near the bed, staring at the massive size. Did he plan to claim her? Did that mean what she thought it did? Every muscle in her body tensed, but he drew down the covers for Gwen and tucked her in.

"Sleep well." He reached toward her, then hesitated, his hand pulling back at the last second.

For a fleeting moment, she wanted him to touch her. Hold her hand. Brush a fingertip across her cheek. Anything.

"Taran."

"Good night, Gwen."

She gazed up at the ceiling. What had she been thinking? She hadn't. That was the problem. The longer she waited, the hard her mission became. She had wanted him to *touch her*. Staying here any longer than necessary wasn't an option.

Gwen lay and bide her time.

Taran claimed her to protect her, but every time she looked into his eyes, she saw a yearning there all too familiar? Could it be Taran was as lonely as she?

She scoffed. He was free here on this mountain. He could go where he pleased and be with whomever he wanted. Not her. Anyone but her. But the way he looked at her made her wish differently.

If only her blood were not tainted.

Peter.

Taran's mark on her wrist burned as a constant reminder she didn't belong here. Another reason she needed to leave. Her heart still thrummed from him tucking her in and how careful he was not to touch her. And earlier, when she fed him the s'more.

He asked permission.

He. Asked. Permission.

What was wrong with her?

She dressed again in her cargo pants, boots, and long-sleeved shirt. Noticing the new hoodie he had bought her, she took it and slipped it on for extra warmth. He had wanted to get her something silky, something soft, but she refused. There was no need for such things at the compound. Besides, she wouldn't be here long enough to need them.

Yet questions lingered in his gaze when he looked at her.

Guilt lassoed her gut.

She didn't want to feel comfortable here. She didn't want to see Kaya's kindness or the way families held their children close. She didn't want to think about couples wrapped in each other's arms, or what it would be like to have such a bond.

Some gift.

Her fist curled. The curse of her mother's people tingled in her veins.

Gwen pressed her hand against the soul crystal tucked inside her bra. Time was slipping away, and with every hour, Peter edged closer to death. She had no way to contact Patch. No way to confirm he was still alive. But if he wasn't . . .

No, she refused to think otherwise. He had to be alive. He always found a way to survive.

He had survived for her.

A lump formed in her throat. Her mother handed her over to Cedric without hesitation, bargaining her away like she was nothing more than a piece of property. But Peter—Peter wouldn't let her go alone. He had followed, sacrificing his own freedom for the chance to protect her. Peter made sure she wasn't used as a pawn between Cedric and her mother for some other purpose.

He had given up everything for her.

And here she was, lingering in the safety of having Taran's mark while Peter lay somewhere out there, suffering.

Her hand curled into fists at her sides. Mark or no mark, there had to be another way to save him. Staying here meant leaving her brother to die. And that wasn't an option.

She could choose Taran, his brother, or any other shifter in the resort.

Her gaze flickered to the couch outside the bedroom, where Taran lay sprawled, his arm draped over his eyes. His bare chest rose and fell in a steady rhythm. The tattoo of his dragon spirit glowed against his skin—the same design as her mark.

Her gaze glued to the motion, following the lines of his abs. Were all dragon men so hot they didn't mind sleeping without covers? She remembered his warmth in the cabin. The way it drew her close, but at a distance to keep from physically touching. Like an itch, she wanted to touch him now. Her buzzing veins dared her, yearning for her to brush against his skin, feel his spirit, and crave its closeness.

She waited another hour, listening to his breathing, watching for the deep rhythm of sleep. When she was sure he wouldn't wake, she moved.

She wrapped her knee tighter to stabilize it—she couldn't risk getting past Taran on crutches. The pack he returned to her sat by the door. Her rifle was still missing. He had taken it along with the map and her dagger. She would have to do without them.

Taran's snores filled the quiet space. The mighty dragon had a roar, even in his sleep.

A small, bittersweet smile tugged at her lips before she pushed forward.

She stepped toward him, her heart pounding like a drum against her ribs. Just a little closer. One breath away.

He smelled of fire and pine. Like warmth. Like something dangerous she couldn't afford to want. Her fingers twitched at her sides. If she touched him, if she let her skin brush against his, her gift would stun him long enough to capture his dragon spirit.

She let her gaze go over him one last time. She didn't want to hurt him.

She closed her eyes, willing herself to turn away.

Carefully, she leaned in to inhale his dangerously addicting scent. It enveloped her senses, stirring emotions and forbidden thoughts of wishing there was another way.

Her gaze fell on his lips. Full and puckered in his sleep, she continued to lean toward him and caught herself before she woke him. His dragon's spirit coated her skin like a gentle caress. Beneath the mark, her blood hummed, and it spooked her.

Time to go.

Gwen's lips grazed across his head, a fleeting touch that sent shivers racing down her spine.

Taran stirred, murmuring faintly.

Panic seized her chest. She pulled away, her lips tingling from the brief contact.

An inner voice urged her to stay. She was safe with him. He protected her. A stranger. He called her his mate. Deep down, a large part of her wanted to believe him. But taking a risk on Taran might cost more than her brother's life. Every second she lingered, she risked Cedric discovering her missing. He'd send his scouts to track her. It was only a matter of time before they'd find her. Find him.

And Peter would be dead.

With one last glance at Taran's sleeping form, she grabbed her pack and slipped out of the room, her heart heavy.

In the lobby, the fire had burned down to embers, flickering shadows stretching across the walls. The hush of the space only amplified the pounding in her chest. She hesitated, scanning for signs of anyone stirring. The stillness should have comforted her. Instead, it felt suffocating.

Was she really doing this?

The door was only a few steps away.

Her fingers tightened around the strap of her pack, but doubt gnawed at the edges of her resolve.

If she stayed, Taran might help her.

Maybe there was another way.

But there wasn't.

Peter didn't have time for her to hesitate.

A shuddering breath escaped her lips as she entered the night.

The crisp air stung her cheeks, carrying with it the faint scent of pine and fresh snow. She exhaled, watching her breath swirl in the cold. The scents of the mountain would haunt her for the rest of her life. Every time the wind shifted, she would remember Taran.

She had to do this for Peter.

Her knee protested as she moved, but she pressed forward. The sooner she left, the safer Taran and the others would be.

Then she saw him.

A man pulled up in a snowmobile; his spirit animal's presence commanding even from a distance.

This was it.

She could still walk away. She could turn back, seek Levi's spirit instead. What if she woke Taran and hoped this mate thing was real? Would he help save her brother?

She imagined Peter's eyes. The way they had always looked at her with a fierce protectiveness, even when they were younger. He gave up everything for her. She couldn't fail him now.

Before she lost her nerve, she stepped forward.

The sight of his wolf spirit filled her with a mixture of awe and trepidation.

"Is there something wrong?" the man asked, pulling down his ski mask.

Gwen's stomach twisted.

For a fraction of a second, she saw him as a person. This wasn't Cedric. The man wasn't a hunter. He was someone's brother. Someone's son.

But Peter was hers.

Her hands shook. She clenched them, forced herself to move.

Gwen grabbed the man and yanked him toward her.

She planted her lips on his.

Shock rippled through his body, vibrating down into her bones.

She gasped as the mark on her wrist seared. Heat flooded her veins. The wolf spirit howled in her head in protest, clawing against her hold. The man's fingers dug into her arms, claws shredding through her jacket. She winced, but held on.

His resistance was fleeting.

A sharp inhale.

A shuddered exhale.

And then . . . surrender.

The moment his spirit detached, guilt roared through her.

Wetness ran down Gwen's cheeks.

She helped lower him to the ground, pressing a trembling hand to his shoulder. His eyes were wide, unblinking, his mouth parted, stunned.

"You're in shock, is all," she whispered. "You'll be okay."

She wasn't sure if she was reassuring him or herself.

The wolf spirit coiled inside her, fighting against the prison of her blood.

"I'm so sorry," she choked out. "I need this one. Please understand."

The words felt hollow.

The man didn't speak. Just stared at her, his expression frozen somewhere between confusion and pain.

The snowmobile engine idled behind her. Suddenly, it seemed too loud, too real.

If she didn't leave now, someone would come.

She stumbled toward the vehicle, her pulse thundering in her ears.

Adrenaline drowned out the pain in her knee as she climbed onto the snowmobile and gunned the throttle. Snow sprayed beneath the tires as she tore down the trail.

Tears blurred her vision. She sobbed, her chest burning as the stolen spirit twisted inside her, pressing against the fragile edges of her control.

It wasn't supposed to feel like this.

She pulled off the trail, heart hammering. The darkness of the trees swallowed her whole.

With shaking fingers, she unzipped her coat, fumbling for the soul crystal. It burned against her skin. She pressed it to her lips, shoving it into her mouth before she lost control completely.

The wolf spirit surged, slamming into her, tearing her apart from the inside.

She doubled over, a heave wrenching from her throat.

The crystal tumbled from her mouth. She caught it before it hit the snow.

A sob racked through her, violent and raw.

How many more times could she do this before she lost herself completely?

Tears dripped onto the crystal. She pressed it against her chest, inhaling shakily.

"I'm coming, Peter." She zipped up her jacket, steeling herself against the cold. Against the guilt.

Against the truth that no matter how much she told herself this was necessary . . .

She had just stolen a life.

Would Taran be the one to hunt her now?

Gwen shoved the thought away.

Gripping the handles of the snowmobile, she revved the engine and sped into the night; the shadows cloaking her.

Fifteen

FRESH SNOW SWIRLED IN the air, the cold biting through the insulation of Gwen's gloves. The mountain still had it in for her. At this rate, she'd be frozen like a Popsicle before she even reached Sentinel Peak.

What if they blame Taran?

Her grip on the throttle eased, the snowmobile slowing beneath her.

Peter. His skin was ashen, his hand clutching her arm, flashed through her mind. She clenched the handlebars, squeezing too hard. The machine lurched forward, speeding across the snow, the wind stinging her cheeks.

She wouldn't look back. Not when Peter needed her.

She let the trails lead her away from Avalanche Ridge, farther into the deep, uncharted parts of the forest. The trees thickened, their towering forms swallowing the light. Shadows stretched long and menacing in the darkness, shifting like living things.

Every instinct screamed for her to keep going.

The further she veered off the trail, the darker the woods became. She swore she saw hulking shapes moving between the trees—glowing eyes, gleaming fangs. Her heart bounded in her chest as she scanned the forest, searching for anything unnatural lurking in the gloom.

Peter. She had to find him.

Gritting her teeth, she forged ahead, weaving between the trees. The snowmobile's headlights cut through the dark, but something inside her warned against stopping to check the map. She continued until she had to weave around trees and make her own trail to forge ahead.

Then, with a sputter and a lurch, the engine cut out.

"No!" She smacked the tank between her legs. Nothing. She rocked forward, willing the machine to move. Still nothing.

Biting back a scream, she jumped off, yanking up the seat to check inside.

No gas can.

"Well, at least I won't starve to death," she muttered, shoulder her pack.

With no other choice, she pressed forward on foot, switching on her flashlight. The beam barely cut through the oppressive darkness. Every sound—branches rattling, the wind whistling through the trees—sending a chill down her spine.

Then came the whistle. Low pitch. Long.

She stiffened, the memory crashing into her like a tidal wave.

The slap of leather. The slow, measured steps outside her door. Cedric.

Panic clawed up her throat. She ran.

The woods mocked her, their shadows twisting.

A figure stepped in her path.

Gwen skidded to a halt. "No. Please, no."

A sob tore from her throat. She stumbled back; her pack catching the brunt of her fall.

The figure moved closer.

Terror surged through her. She scrambled backward, slipping in the snow. "I had no choice."

A darker shadow rose behind the figure. It grew, stretching, expanding—until the unmistakable shape of a dragon loomed over them. She whimpered. "Don't do this. Please don't do this."

The shadow dragon peeled away from the figure, slithering toward her like a living mist. Warmth radiated from it, wrapping around her like an unseen embrace.

She trembled. "Please."

"Gwen."

The dragon spirit rumbled, its voice deep and resonant, vibrating through her body.

She reached out, fingers brushing through the strange, shifting warmth. The spirit's presence sank into her, cradling her in an unexpected sense of peace.

Ahead, the figure still approached. Taller now. Smaller. Hands raised in surrender.

"I'm not going to hurt you."

Her heart slammed against her ribs. That voice.

"I'm not going to hurt you."

"Taran."

Curling deeper into the dragon's shadow, she whispered his name.

"I'm here." His voice was steady, but she tensed as he stepped closer.

"You need to calm down," he murmured. "My dragon thinks you're afraid of me."

She was.

Against her warm flesh, the soul crystal cooled. It took her several blinks for her vision to adjust, and she was grateful for the forest's dim light. Shadows masked the fact that he lacked clothing, but his dragon's spirit lingered between them, a coiled presence vibrating with protective energy.

"What's happening?"

Taran hesitated. "My dragon thinks it's protecting you."

"How?" Panic reached its way up her throat. "Your dragon can't leave you. It's supposed to be inside you!"

His dragon spirit rumbled, a sound like distant thunder rolling through the trees.

"We are connected. You and me," he said, his voice rough. "My mark. Mine to claim. Our bond makes us one, *solanu*—my soul mate."

Gwen struggled to her knees, the pulse of his dragon spirit radiating outward, pushing him back another step.

"I'm not going to hurt you," he repeated. "You don't have to be afraid of me."

Did he know? He couldn't know, could he?

His dragon would know.

"I feel you," he choked out, voice ragged. "Like claws scratching, but good." He sucked in a breath.

Gwen gripped the trunk of a nearby tree, hauling herself upright. She raised her hand.

Taran let out a guttural sound—somewhere between a groan and a growl. "More. Yes, *solanu*. Move leftward a bit, would you?"

Panic twisted in Gwen's gut. "This—this shouldn't be happening! How is this possible?"

Her hand sought the mist again, hesitantly stroking it in the direction he murmured. A flicker of his movement caught her eye in the faint sliver of moonlight breaking through the canopy of trees. She froze.

Her actions made him *quiver.*

"*Solanu,*" Taran rasped, urgency lacing his voice. "I can't be separated from my dragon spirit for much longer. The more time we remain here, the more vulnerable I become. Send my dragon spirit back to me."

Desperation crackled in his voice, mirroring the growing fear in her chest.

She didn't understand.

It didn't work this way.

Her gaze dropped to her hand, her cursed gift racing through her fingertips, her blood alive with power.

She *felt* his pain. It sank into her, deep and unrelenting.

A new resolve hardened inside her.

Gwen closed her eyes, forcing herself to calm. The dragon spirit clung to her like a heavy blanket, warming her against the bitter cold. Her mark *itched*. The sting was long past, but the sensation lingered.

Taran pressed a hand to the glowing mark, the faint outline of it expanded across his chest. "T-tell it to return t-to me," he stammered, his teeth chattering. "T-tell it y-you are safe with m-me and unharmed."

Without his dragon spirit, his body was losing heat too fast.

Her throat tightened. "If I give you back your dragon, you'll let me go."

"N-never."

His answer was swift, but something shifted inside her.

She pressed a hand to her chest. "I don't know how."

Tears spilled over the cold of her cheeks. Her lungs rattled, her instincts battling for control. Cedric's voice whispered in her thoughts, instructing her how *her gift* should be used.

She *should* take his dragon. Claim its strength and power.

That's what Cedric would want.

But she wasn't Cedric.

"Taran is good," she whispered. "Taran saved me."

A sharp exhale. Then Taran crumbled.

"Taran?"

Gwen shoved through the hazy mist and stumbled through the snow to reach him. She fell beside him. His dragon spirit cast over them with a buzzing tingle of warmth.

With gloved hands, she cupped Taran's face. "I've never given a spirit back to its guardian. It won't listen to me. How do I—"

"Like this."

His hand rose, fingers tangling behind her neck.

And then—his lips fused to hers.

A quake rippled through the air.

Electricity crackled around them. Soft at first, his lips barely moved against hers, tentative, testing.

Gwen gasped as the spirit slipped away, the connection between them blooming bright. She sank into Taran, her body responding as he deepened the kiss. His grip tightened, his mouth tracing across her cheek to her ear. A deep, satisfied rumble vibrated through his chest.

Her mark cooled.

Her blood froze.

Taran pulled her closer, his breath warm against her skin.

His voice was quiet.

Dark.

"Tell me you are innocent."

The warmth of his lips lingered, even as ice curled through her veins.

Innocent. The world coiled around her, pressing in like an iron band tightening around her ribs. Taran's breath fanned against her cheek, but the way he held her—*the way he asked*—sent a shiver down her spine.

She wanted to tell him the truth and wanted to let herself believe that the safety she felt in his arms wasn't a lie.

Before she could answer, the night shifted.

A whispering chill ghosted over her skin.

The pulse of the soul crystal at her throat quickened.

Taran's breath came hard and uneven, his dragon spirit settling back into him like a missing piece snapping into place.

Gwen trembled, her lips parted, her breath mingling with his in the frosty night air. He should have been satisfied. His dragon spirit settled back inside him again, and she hadn't fought him when he kissed her. But her reaction wasn't what he expected.

She'd gone still.

Not the kind of stillness that came with surrender.

The kind that came with fear.

His dragon growled low in his chest. Not at her, never at her, but the weight in the air between them. An ache, like a punch to his gut, radiated in the place where his dragon spirit tore from within him and slowly weaved back into his soul.

An icy wind rushed between them, followed by a howl carried over the trees.

His dragon went rigid beneath his skin.

Wolves.

His grip on Gwen loosened as he turned his head toward the sound. Another howl followed, closer this time. He needed to take her back before any of the others found her.

Beneath them, the snow pulsed with something darker than the night itself.

Taran inhaled. His dragon flared inside him.

Shadows.

Not just any shadows—lost spirits. Black as ink, they slithered from beneath the trees, seeping out of the ground like mist.

Something around Gwen shifted. He felt it in the air, an energy crackling.

His dragon roared.

He stepped in front of her, shielding her as the first set of glinting eyes emerged from the tree line.

Protect. His body pulsed with heat as scales rippled beneath his skin, the shift threatening to take him fully.

She shouldn't have run.

Our mate is in trouble.

She shouldn't have left the safety of the resort.

Four giant black shadow wolves formed around them.

He shifted, wings unfurling, fire rising in his throat as the wolves closed in. His dragon pulsed with fury, but the shadow spirits weren't after him. They wanted *her.*

Gwen.

Unable to speak in this form, he lowered himself, muscles coiled, silently commanding her to climb onto his back. His tail flicked, keeping the wolves at bay. If she hesitated too long, he would grab her and fly, whether or not she liked it.

But she wasn't looking at him.

Her eyes remained locked on the largest of the wolves.

Taran snarled.

The wolf stepped closer.

Gwen swayed.

Taran lunged.

The wolf leaped.

A strangled sound came from Gwen.

He swung his head around, but found only his mate.

Where is the wolf?

Anywhere. His dragon growled.

A shudder wracked her body. Her pupils blew wide, breathing hitched, limbs trembled as if something cold slithered against her skin.

His dragon rumbled low in his chest, pushing his thoughts toward her. *I will protect you. Do not be afraid.*

Gwen's head snapped up, lips parted like she might say something. Her breath came too fast, too shallow.

And that scared him more than anything.

Three more wolves remained around them, quiet, watchful. His dragon swung his tail wide to send them leaping back. He gathered her into his claws and unleashed fire on the other wolves. They evaporated, and he left several tree branches lit with embers.

Another howl rang out.

Don't worry, solanu. He didn't know if their bond ran deep enough for her to hear him. *I will protect you.*

Below, the village lights flickered like scattered stars. Men were gathering, shouting, unaware of the spirits lurking just beyond the trees.

Taran forced his attention forward, his wings cutting through the night air. He needed to get Gwen away from the wolves and whatever had just happened in the snow.

The wolf's presence had vanished, but something else lingered, like a ripple in the air around Gwen. A filament of something clung to her. *The wolf spirit she possesses. There's still time to fix this.*

The moment they landed on the pad behind the resort, Taran let her go.

Gwen hit the ground hard, scrambling back.

His body burned as he shifted, dragon scales retracting, claws folding into fingers. The shift was rougher than usual, his fury making it jagged, raw.

"Don't run," he growled.

Her eyes glowed for a moment—blue, unnatural—before the golden flecks bled through, swallowing her humanity. Hiding it.

His chest tightened.

Aluk justifiably wanted Gwen confined. She was a hunter. Taran brushed it off, believing there was more to her than what they thought. He'd wanted to believe it.

Because she was his mate.

And that made him a fool.

His fingers curled into fists, his dragon spirit thrashing against his ribs. She was his mate. *His.*

But she was also a threat to his people. She'd forced another man's spirit to leave him. She'd almost taken his.

But she didn't.

His hand snapped out, locking around her wrist.

Gwen sucked in a sharp breath, struggling against him. "Let me go!"

Taran yanked her forward. "What did you do to the night guard?"

Gwen twisted violently, fighting his grip. Her free hand flew toward his face.

Taran caught her wrist midair, his fingers tightening just enough to stop her swing, but not enough to hurt her. "Did you steal his spirit, too? Or just knocked him out?"

She lashed out again. This time with a kick. He stepped into it, absorbing the impact, leveling his gaze with hers. "Have you not done enough harm for one night?"

She stilled.

Something feral flickered in her expression.

"I did what I had to do."

"Who sent you? If someone is making you do this, tell me now."

She glared at him, unblinking.

Taran ground his teeth, dragging her toward the resort doors. His stomach twisted, nausea rising like bile in the back of his throat. In the soft glow of the lights along the back side of the resort, Taran tried to read her expression. Her scent changed from the forest. Fear no longer wafted from her, but a thick, heady desperation mixed with wolf.

"I can't help you if you don't tell me who sent you? Who put you up to this?"

He waited a long moment, but when she didn't answer, he dragged her along. His dragon spirit tattoo itched oddly. Jumbled thoughts of guilt and loyalty flowed through his mind. *Her* thoughts.

Once inside the resort, he pulled her past darkened shops and toward the spa entrance. Shoving her forward, she stumbled inside the waiting room of the resort clinic. Ben stepped forward, his dragon spirit burning in his eyes.

"You found her."

Taran blocked the exit with his body, arms crossed, his fury still simmering beneath his skin.

Gwen's pale face gutted him.

The guilt he sensed rolled off her thick enough to choke on.

"Aluk's on his way," Ben continued. "Conleth is in with Lye. His spirit has been *torn* from his soul."

Taran's muscles locked.

His dragon went still.

Gwen pressed her hands against her chest, shaking her head. "No . . ."

Taran lowered his chin. "Do not lie."

She hesitated.

And that hesitation hit like a punch in the gut.

She'd done it.

She yanked a spirit from a man's soul.

From another *shifter.* From someone who had trusted their bond with their animal, someone who had never feared losing it because it was supposed to be forever.

Taran barely heard Ben tossing him a pair of sweats. He caught them without looking away from Gwen.

Conleth stepped out of the exam room. His expression was dark. "What did you do to him?"

"I—" She shook her head, fingers curling into her jacket sleeves.

Taran stepped closer. "Did you take his spirit?"

"I don't see what the big deal is," she said, lifting her chin defiantly. "He can get another one."

The room went silent.

Ben let out a low growl.

Conleth stiffened.

Taran's fury snapped like a whip through his veins.

What did she say?

He took another step toward her, heat rolling from his skin, his dragon spirit *furious.*

"What the *big deal* is?" Taran's arms shook with his restraint. "Woman, who told you we can just 'replace our spirits'?"

A crease formed across her forehead. Her gaze darted toward the others. She was searching their faces, trying to read them. Trying to *understand.*

Taran's stomach sank.

She wasn't lying.

She believed it.

A sick sort of dread curled through him.

Taran exhaled, slow and sharp, like an open wound. His dragon spirit keened within him.

Stealing a spirit wasn't just *theft*.

It was murder.

It meant the shifter would never be whole again. That they would slowly wither as the bond between their soul and their spirit unraveled. His people had a name for it—they called it wasting illness.

It meant she had left the security guard, Lye, to die.

And she had no idea.

Taran's dragon lashed inside him, torn between the instinct to protect his mate and the truth that she was a danger to them all.

Had she taken Lye's spirit the same as she'd lured his dragon from him?

Wanting her was a mistake.

"Who told you these lies?" he demanded to know.

Gwen's expression faltered. She pressed her lips together, jaw tightening. But she didn't answer.

Taran's stomach coiled tighter. His dragon pressed against him, itching to force the truth from her.

"She's hiding something," Ben said.

Conleth's voice cut through between them. "He is dying, woman. If you do not return his spirit, his soul will fade without it," Conleth said.

Gwen hugged herself. Her gaze flickering between them, her fingers curled into her sleeves. "H-how do I know y-you're not the ones lying?"

Taran's dragon spirit ached in his soul.

She sounded uncertain. Afraid.

Not the fear of someone caught. The fear that came when a truth you believed was suddenly crumbling beneath your feet.

Ben took a step forward, his voice like flint. "Because if you do not return his spirit, *hehewuti,* then not even your mate can save you from your fate."

Taran narrowed his eyes at Ben. He'd challenged her. A low growl rumbled in Taran's throat. He stepped between them before Ben got any closer, his dragon's presence flaring like heat in the air.

"She has dark blood," Conleth muttered, keeping his distance, but watching Gwen from the corner of his eye. His tone was flat, but Taran knew his brother well enough to hear the astonishment underneath. "She can't be your mate. It's why the mark doesn't heal against her skin."

Taran's hand rose to his chest, fingers scratching over the spot where his spirit tattoo pulsed like a second heartbeat.

He knew his mark should have sealed against her skin the first time they touched. The dragon's bond recognized mates.

Yet, Gwen still felt like his—like a tether had wrapped around his heart and refused to let go.

"Show me your tattoo," he said.

Slowly, Gwen removed her glove and pulled back her sleeve enough to reveal the mark on her wrist.

The mark should have been a deep, permanent red, but hers looked faded, the edges glowing faintly like an ember struggling to stay lit.

Worse, beneath the mark, dark veins ran under her skin.

His gut churned.

"You called her a *hehewuti,*" he said, the word tasting foreign and *wrong* in relation to *his* mate.

A cursed one. A death-marked spirit thief.

Gwen flinched.

She pulled her sleeve down, but before she could cover it, Taran's hand shot out, catching her wrist. She gasped, a sharp inhale between clenched teeth.

Her pulse thrummed beneath his fingers, quick and unsteady. His dragon roared inside him, torn.

Mate. Threat. Protect. Destroy.

The contradictions clawed at his ribs, shredding through every ounce of control he possessed.

He could not ignore what she'd done. What she *was*.

And yet — "Would you have stolen my dragon spirit tonight, too?" he quietly asked.

Pain shone in Gwen's wide eyes as she looked at him.

"Please," she rasped. "Don't touch me."

A strange invasion, like claws reaching within him, pierced beneath his tattoo.

He let her go. His dragon snarled in his head.

Conleth tilted his head, studying her. "Is that how you do it?" he asked, his clinical brain always researching and curious. "Touch?"

Gwen rubbed her wrist, fingers trembling. She didn't answer.

Ben's voice sliced through the silence. "Who sent you here to hunt us?"

"No one." Gwen wiped a bead of sweat forming on her brow, her skin even paler under the bright lights inside the room.

She lies. Ben said in Taran's mind.

Her heart says otherwise. His dragon interjected. And he could feel the unsettling truth in the bond between them. A bond he created with his mark, with his kiss, and once it formed, he would go mad without her.

"I'm not a hunter," she insisted.

Ben let out a quiet, humorless laugh. "You're not a hunter? But you stole Lye's wolf spirit. Do you have a buyer waiting for you in Sentinel Peak? Or are you meeting up with more hunters trying to poach on our brothers?"

"I wasn't going to sell it," Gwen whispered, taking a step toward Taran.

His spirit coiled, caught in the war between lashing out and pulling her in. He hated it. His body reacted before he could stop it. Even after everything, he had no choice but to protect her. *Are you sure she doesn't lie?*

"Then what was your plan?" Conleth asked.

Gwen's breath came out shaky.

She looked at Taran.

Not Ben. Not Conleth.

Him.

Maybe his dragon spirit was right. Why take a man's spirit without intending to take it for herself or sell it? Had she taken it by accident? By touch?

But she ran.

He shook his head, trying to understand. He knew she was hiding something. She wasn't human. She was one of *them*. Had they sent her to endanger them? Imprisoning her in Crag's Cliff no longer seemed a threat, but was inevitable to protect everyone on the mountain.

And that scared him more than anything.

Sixteen

Gwen took off her gloves against her better judgment. Heat flooded her body again, a searing wave starting from her core and spreading outward, burning through her veins like wildfire. She clenched her fists, her breath coming in quick gasps as she fought the flutter of her eyelids, forcing herself to stay present.

Inside her, the wolf spirit prowled, pressing against the edges of her soul, testing for weakness. The shadow spirit had latched onto her in the forest before Taran pulled her away. Too late. It had already crept inside, curling its claws into her, wrapping around her like smoke, with sharp teeth hidden in its depths.

A shudder wracked her frame as the wolf lunged for her soul. Uninvited.

Her stomach lurched, and her hands trembled as she forced a shield between them. Pressure built in her chest, heavy, as if the wolf sought to drown her from the inside out. Cold sweat slicked her spine, warring with the unnatural heat pooling beneath her skin.

"My brother will die without this spirit." She unzipped her coat, fabric sticking to her damp skin. A sharp pain lanced through her skull, as if the wolf clawed at her mind in retaliation.

Taran narrowed his dark amber eyes. She felt his dragon through his gaze.

"He's ill, and if I don't get him another spirit soon—" A sob climbed its way up her throat.

Inside her, the wolf spirit twisted, snapping its teeth in frustration, but it wasn't alone. A separate weight pulsed against her chest, coiled inside the crystal nestled against her heart.

Lye's wolf.

The one she had stolen.

Nausea rose, causing her to take deep breaths. The second wolf's spirit was fighting her, too. Not as a violent force, but a pulsing ache that refused to be ignored. The crystal burned against her skin, its presence growing heavier, as if accusing her of what she'd done.

Conleth's voice cut through the haze. "Spirit Hunter. You're the reason this mountain is cursed. Our alpha ran your kind off centuries ago."

Ben's words followed, sharp and unforgiving. "How do you even exist?"

Gwen barely heard them over the wolf's relentless howling inside her. The beast scraped its teeth down her spine, pressing harder, pushing, demanding. Her pulse roared in her ears. Every muscle in her body strained to keep her upright as the foreign spirit battered against her shield.

Taran said nothing.

His silence slashed deeper than their words.

The retreat of his dragon's presence, the absence of his warmth, let her gutted.

"I shouldn't," she whispered, slipping off her jacket, suddenly too hot. "My mother tried to hide me. My brother Peter . . . He's going to die if I don't help him."

She forced another breath into her burning lungs and peeled off her coat. It felt suffocating, clinging to her. But the relief was fleeting.

The crystal around her neck pulsed, and the wolf inside her snapped its jaws, enraged at the barrier she held against it.

Conleth stilled. "Your brother is Peter? Peter Riley?"

She nodded, barely holding back a moan as the pressure inside her mounted. "McLeod. Peter Riley McLeod. Cedric took us in. We wouldn't have survived. I wouldn't have—" A sharp pain laced through her ribs, cutting her off. She doubled over, cradling her stomach as the wolf spirit inside her twisted violently.

Taran moved before she hit the ground. HIs hands gripped her arms, firm but careful. "Gwen."

"We don't have time for this." Ben moved, eyes blazing. "Give me the crystal."

She clung to Taran's forearms, fingers digging in, searching for something solid as her body betrayed her. The electric snap of his touch should have sent agony lacing through her, should have burned like it always did.

But it didn't.

Ben bared his teeth. "Lye is *dying*, and you're hoarding what belongs to him. If you don't take it from her, I will."

Taran snarled at Ben, then looked back at her. "Give it to him, *solanu*. Without it, Lye will die. See what it's causing."

Gwen found it hard to believe them. She'd seen Taran's dragon spirit leave him and return. Lye's spirit hung inside the crystal. Her brother's last chance gambled between Lye's spirit and the wild one trying to possess her.

Her hand closed around the crystal. "No."

Her body was a battlefield, torn between instincts she didn't understand and the wrenching in her gut at her actions.

Ben lunged.

Gwen had no time to react before Taran shoved her behind him in a blur of movement. The sheer force of it sent her stumbling. Her back slammed against the wall, air leaving her lungs in a rush.

Ben's hands were already up, fire crackling between his fingers, his dragon present in his eyes.

"Stand down," Taran growled.

"Then give me the crystal. We're wasting time," Ben laced his words with the dominance of his dragon. She felt the compelling force of it deep into her bones.

"This isn't the way." Taran's jaw clenched.

Ben let out a harsh breath. "Then what is?" He turned back to Gwen, stepping closer, his dragon's heat radiating off him in waves. "If you won't hand it over, I'll take it from your corpse."

"Ben," Conleth warned.

Gwen's fingers dug into the crystal as the wolf inside her howled.

Taran kept his body angled between them. "Gwen. Give him the crystal."

She met his gaze.

"Peter," she whispered.

Invisible teeth sunk into her side, biting, a reminder she had another option. It was a risk, one where no one else would have to die. If they indeed spoke the truth. Deep within her, something whispered for her to let go. *No.* "My brother . . ."

"Is already dead," Conleth said, cold and final.

A surge of anger, hot and blinding, threatened to drown her grief.

Ben's taunting words fueled the flames. "Did you take his spirit, too?"

"No!"

Rage gave her strength. Gwen shoved Taran back as she lunged for Ben. A snarl ripping from her throat. Primal. Raw. Not entirely human. Before she reached him, steel bands wrapped around her, yanking her against his chest. She thrashed, kicking, sinking her claws into Taran's arms.

Ben took a step back, nostrils flaring. His dragon flickered beneath his gaze, swirling with gold and red. His lip curled. "Her scent is off. I recognize it, and yet it's not Lye's wolf."

Gwen snarled at him, her nails sinking into Taran's arm.

"Stop it," Taran ordered, shaking her just enough to rattle the wolf inside her. The spirit recoiled for a heartbeat. "Release Lye's wolf spirit."

"If Rourke and Sia don't kill her for her this offense, you know Aluk will lock her away."

"Ben." Taran's chest rumbled against her.

"She's a danger to everyone here and herself," Ben said.

"*Solanu*, you must give Lye his wolf spirit back." Taran didn't move to take it from her. He waited.

"Who is Rourke?"

"He and Sia are the alphas of the two wolf packs on the mountain. They're our enforcers, and it's against their pack you've committed a grievous crime," Conleth said, patient and calm as ever.

"Return the spirit to Lye," Taran said.

Gwen's resistance faltered. "I-I can't." She flopped her head back against his shoulder, the wolf's howls echoing in her mind. "Peter . . ."

"I don't know your brother." Conleth's voice softened slightly. "I don't know what happened to his wolf. For the amount of time you've been here, it's too late for him. Don't punish Lye for fate's choice. He has a son. The spirit you stole is his family's legacy."

Conleth was right.

Lye's life was ebbing away.

She had not one but two wolves in her possession now. The shadow one tried to slip into her soul in the forest and it refused to leave her.

She might still have a chance to save Peter.

"Give us the spirit!" Ben shouted at her, his eyes turning gold and red with the impatience of his dragon.

"Ben, leave," Conleth instructed.

Ben opened his mouth but closed it at Conleth's deep glare. The mated dragon shifter turned on his heel and strode away.

"Lye doesn't have much time," Conleth said.

Taran tensed. "She has to touch him."

No! The wolf raked its claws through her gut, and Gwen hissed with pain.

Not you. The other one. The one she trapped in the crystal resting snug against her heart. Gwen gritted her teeth, waiting for the burning sensation to pass.

I am stronger. Let it go.

Taran snaked his arm around Gwen's waist, lifting her effortlessly. He carried her into the next room. The sight of the man lying there reminded her of her brother's fate, his skin almost white as a ghost. The man's eyes remained closed, and his chest rose and fell in slumber.

A heavy silence hung in the air between her ragged gasps for breath. She became aware of his hand sliding under the hem of her shirt. His hand touching the bare skin above the hip.

Surprise. Delight. Awe ran through her system.

She had spent her whole life bracing for agony, for the electric stab of contact that burned like fire against her skin. How was it gone now? And in its place, a dangerous kind of wonder curled in her stomach.

Taran's touch doesn't hurt me.

There was no time to dwell on it.

A bigger ache formed alongside the wolf, trying to get at her soul. The emptiness within the wolf shifter, Lye, pulled at her.

Opposite of the vibrant life force that thrummed within her, his will to live slowly drained.

This is what it means to lose your spirit.

An icy shiver crawled up her spine.

"Touch him," Conleth said from behind them.

"It doesn't work like that."

"How does it work, beautiful?" Taran's lips were close to her ear, his breath warm, his voice a seductive whisper. A shiver raced across her skin at his nearness, at the shear intimacy of it.

"We need you to pull the spirit out of the crystal and direct it back to him before the sickness takes him," Conleth said.

Sickness?

Gwen tensed, her muscles coiling like a live wire.

The wolf inside her snarled.

Not Lye's wolf. The one inside the crystal. It stirred, restless, sensing the one it wanted to reunite with.

"He has wasting illness?" Her throat tightened.

Taran didn't answer fast enough. Instead, Conleth did.

"He'll die," she whispered. Her chin wobbled, and before she could stop them, tears blurred her vision.

"I believe we've already established that," Conleth said.

Taran's gaze held hers, softening, almost hesitant. "Your brother has wasting illness?"

Gwen could only nod. The tears slipped free, trailing hot paths down her cheeks.

"I'm sorry, *solanu.*"

The name twisted inside her, too close to Cedric's voice, too close to everything she wanted to escape.

"Lye needs his wolf to survive. This isn't the cure for your brother. Release the wolf spirit and direct it back into the man."

Her fingers clenched, covering the space where the crystal lie snug beneath the fabric of her clothes.

It's not inside me, she wanted to say, but decided against it.

Her pulse pounded.

The soul crystal throbbed against her chest, pulsing in rhythm with her hammering heart. Fear coiled around her throat like a vice.

"May I?"

She gave him a slight nod to go ahead.

Taran moved without hesitation, dipping his fingers beneath the neckline of her shirt. A jolt, intense yet painless, shot through her from his touch.

Heat.

A shattering awareness she couldn't afford to feel.

Her breath hitched.

Then, in a single motion, Taran plucked the crystal from where it rested against her skin.

She needed to save her brother.

But not at the cost of another man's life.

He turned, laying the crystal against Lye's chest.

"Now what?"

Gwen swallowed hard. The answer burned in her throat, but she couldn't quite make herself speak.

Because this moment—this terrible, pivotal moment—wasn't just about saving Lye.

It was about what she had *felt.*

And *that* terrified her more than anything.

Conleth stepped in front of her. "I've got it from here."

Taran grabbed her arm, dragging her out of the room. The sudden movement sent a wave of dizziness crashing over her. Her limbs felt unsteady. Her breath came in ragged pants. Disoriented.

In the waiting room, a large man with the spirit of a wolf approached them, his anger swelling around him. His growl vibrated through the air. The wolf inside her stretched, rose, filling her at the threat.

"We found the snowmobile and a woman's scent." His gaze locked onto her, sharp, piercing. His nostrils flared. "You."

Gwen's stomach twisted. A sour, acidic wave of nausea rolled through her. She clutched Taran's forearm, fingers pressing into his skin as if anchoring herself could stop the inevitable reckoning.

"Conleth is reviving Lye. We recovered his wolf spirit." Taran slid his arm under her knees as he lifted her into a bridal hold. The sudden movement sent her heart slamming against her ribs. "My mate is ill."

The wolf shifter stepped closer, but something in his movements changed subtly, almost imperceptibly. His posture remained rigid, his hands clenched into fists, but his breath hitched. His pupils flared wide, then shrank again. He inhaled, slow and deep, his brow furrowing. "You smell . . . wrong." His gaze bounced between her and Taran. "Not just human. Not just dragon-marked."

"Step aside, Rourke."

The muscles in Rourke's jaw worked as if he were biting back a reaction he didn't understand.

It wasn't her he was responding to.

It was the wolf.

Inside her, the spirit rose, watching, waiting. Gwen resisted the instinct to shrink back. The hairs on her arms rose, a strange, primal awareness prickling over her skin. This man was an alpha, but her wolf didn't cower.

Rourke's gaze glinted, just a flash of hesitation. Of confusion.

Then, as if snapping himself free, he bared his teeth. "You plan on taking her from here? I recognize her scent. I know what she did."

Taran's grip tightened. "She did what was necessary in order to survive."

Rourke scoffed. "She stole a spirit. That's not survival. That's—" He cut himself off, his nostrils flaring again. His stare bored into her, deeper this time, searching. His lips curled back, his fingers twitched at his sides, betraying a sliver of uncertainty. "What *are* you?"

"Mine," Taran said, as a cool tendril slipped though the mark on her wrist.

An unspoken challenge crackled between them.

"If she's—"

"You're out of your jurisdiction," Taran cut him off and pushed past him.

"Once the others find out, do you think jurisdiction will make a difference?"

"When did wolves gain dominion over dragons?" Taran shot back.

Rourke growled.

Gwen turned her face into Taran's chest, burrowing into the warmth, the steadiness of him. Inside her mind, the wolf stirred, pacing, restless. A low keening echoed through her skull. A sound filled with something she didn't understand. Loss? Anger? A hunger that wasn't hers?

Her breath came in a pant. The world tilted.

Behind them, voices blurred into the storm brewing in her head.

"Taran," Conleth called. "Lye's waking. Where are you going?"

Taran's steps never faltered. "To do what Aluk told me to do two days ago."

Ice prickled down her spine. Gwen tipped her head back, forcing herself to meet his gaze. A stony glint burned in those dragon-slit eyes, a cold, merciless resolve that sent dread spiraling through her veins. His jaw flexed. His heat pressed against her, steady, unwavering.

Pain spiked behind her eyes, sharp and punishing. The wolf inside her pressed against her soul, waiting for a moment of weakness. Restless. The darkness crept closer, winding around her mind like smoke.

As they went down the hall, Ben stood, arms crossed, and glared at them.

There was no way for her to get to Peter now.

"Kill me and get it over with," she pleaded.

Seventeen

TARAN'S DRAGON RUMBLED DEEP in his chest, an ancient, restless sound that vibrated through his ribs. The scent of her should have filled him with warmth, with the same grounding certainty that had once soothed his dragon's restless nature. But it was fractured now. Wrong. His dragon still fought for her, warring against the restraints of Taran's will.

She is ours. Mine.

But Taran sat trapped in his own mind while the dragon flew them further away from the resort.

Why, after all this time, had his dragon chosen *her*?

His spirit rumbled, the answer curling through his thoughts like smoke. *Cursed.*

By the time they reached his territory, his dragon loosened its grip, retreating to the depths of his mind. They landed near the cabin, and Gwen trembled in his hold. Whether from the cold or the consequences she feared, he didn't know.

Her body radiated heat, yet her teeth chattered. How could she run from him and steal another shifter's spirit? The question dug at him, dragging behind it a gnawing doubt he couldn't shake.

Without bothering with clothes, Taran swept her up in his arms and carried her toward the cabin. Feverish warmth seeped through his arms. He could feel the way she tensed, bracing for whatever came next.

At the door, he set her down, none too gently, and shoved her inside before the cold seeped into her bones. Taran crossed the threshold. He slammed the door behind them. The force sent a dull thud echoing through the cabin. The sound quickly became swallowed by the mountain silence.

He grabbed her by the arm and pulled her toward the couch, ignoring her sharp cry of protest. She barely had time to stumble before he pushed her onto the cushions.

His dragon hissed.

Fire burned in Taran's gut. Two days. That's all it took for him to lose his head over a woman. He wouldn't make the same mistake again.

He turned away, needing distance. Tossing wood into the hearth without care, he inhaled for a moment and exhaled flames. The fire caught instantly, crackling to life, but it did nothing to temper the chaos inside him.

"T-Taran?"

Her voice curled around him like a thread pulled too tight. He glanced over his shoulder.

Curled up on the couch, she appeared smaller than before. Pale. Fragile.

"I believe you'll find I'm more merciful than my brother."

She paled even further. Her lips lost what little color they had left, her breath shallow, pupils blown wide with something he refused to call fear.

"What m-makes you t-think I won't r-run from you a-again?"

The lingering scent of Lye's wolf clung to her like an offense. He wished for the warm vanilla, soft, rich, intoxicating scent that once had wrapped around him like an unspoken promise. Now it was tainted, shadowed, and festering with the reminder of her betrayal. His dragon recoiled, furious. *How long before that stench stopped taunting him?*

Taran rolled back his shoulders, forcing the tension from his muscles. Turning on his heel, he stalked to the trunk across the room by his bed. He yanked on a pair of jeans; the scrape of denim against his skin welcomed. She took a wolf spirit under his watch.

He swore under his breath.

"Taran," she whispered again.

"Because you're in no condition to run," he said finally. "Your best chance, should you try, is to hope the mountain claims you first."

Gwen's lips parted, her pupils swallowing the color of her irises. A tremor wracked her frame, but not just from the fever burning through her. Outside, the wind howled against the cabin walls, a spectral wail that sent his dragon's hackles raising. *The mountain hears you.* His dragon said. *It waits.*

"And if it d-doesn't?" She shivered, clutching the blanket around herself.

The mountain had claimed stronger warriors than her. It swallowed men whole, their lives torn away before they could even cry out. If the shadow spirits found her, they'd rip into her like scavengers to a fresh kill, desperate to live again.

A storm of longing and betrayal warred inside him. The pull of their mate bond was undeniable, no matter how much she refused to acknowledge it.

Taran curled his hands into fists against the need to touch her.

"I will."

Her eyes widened. "You w-would force me?"

She brought her knees to her chest. A sharp pang sliced through him. His dragon pushed the memory of their kiss to the forefront of his mind. The forest. The kiss. The way she had looked at him before she knew he knew what she was.

Blood pounded in his ears.

If she had wanted to, Gwen could have taken his dragon spirit. She could have traded the wolf for his dragon. Why hadn't she?

Her blood.

It called to his dragon. And to Lye's?

Taran clenched his jaw.

She had stolen the wolf guard's spirit but returned it. The choice meant something.

Didn't it?

His lips curled, but the smirk didn't reach his eyes. "You think I couldn't make you stay if I wanted to?"

A sharp, invisible thread yanked at his chest, tightening around his ribs the moment she denied their bond. His dragon lashed out, slamming against the walls of his mind in protest.

A low growl rumbled in his throat before he could stop it.

Every part of him—his body, his soul, his dragon—knew what she was to him.

But she refused to see it.

Or maybe she was afraid to.

"Not y-your m-mate," Gwen whispered. "Can't b-be."

Liar.

From across the room, he felt the bond tugging at him, tightening around him like a noose. *Say it again.* He wanted to dare her. *Say it, and see if I let you go.*

"Tell that to my dragon."

Even he questioned the sanity of his ancestorial spirit.

He grabbed a blanket off the bed and tossed it at her, forcing himself to put space between them.

Her pulse thrummed wildly at her throat. She curled away from him, but not before her breath hitched as he took a single step closer.

"You weren't s-supposed to e-exist."

A bitter laugh scraped from his throat. "Then neither should you."

Her pallor was too pale, her breath coming in slow, controlled draws. The scent of her was wrong. It still carried hints of vanilla, but beneath it, something festered—old and tainted. His dragon hissed with unease.

She was worse than she let on.

"My people have existed for centuries," he said. "We found this mountain first."

He watched her pull the blanket tighter.

"A-and now . . . you'll put m-m-me in a p-prison."

Taran winced.

She *deserved* worse. She tried to kill one of his people. She'd *hunted* them, taking what was never meant to be hers.

He should have left her for Aluk.

Raw pain slashed through his chest, white-hot and violent.

Mine! His dragon roared in protest. The beast slammed against the edges of his control, talons dragging through his ribcage as if trying to claw free and reach her. Taran pressed a hand over his heart, breath coming too fast, too hard. He grit his teeth, holding against the attack. *Protect!*

"Think of this place as more like a safe house than a prison."

He needed his dragon spirit to calm down.

I brought her here to keep her safe.

Gwen pulled the blanket up tighter, curling on her side. A tremor wracked her body, not just from the shock or the cold. Something was wrong. "W-what does it m-matter? Y-you know w-what I am, w-what

I can d-do . . ." Her teeth chattered. Sweat slickened her skin, but her lips were bloodless. "Y-your alpha is g-going to k-kill m-me."

"Despite what you've done, I won't let him." Taran rubbed the glowing sigil etched over his heart and around his shoulder, his warrior's mark pulsing with heat, the burn of his dragon's will echoing beneath his touch. Gwen gasped. Her own mark glowed in response. A deep red pulse spread through the lines etched into her flesh.

His dragon settled somewhat, its possessive rumble vibrating through his ribs. She was his. Whether or not she accepted it.

Gwen sank deeper into the couch. Her eyes closed. "I'm d-dead, anyway."

The wind howled through the cracks in the cabin walls. Taran's dragon bristled, sensing more than the cold.

"No one is going to kill you." Not while he harbored this stubborn spirit inside him.

Cursed.

I know. Taran wanted to shout. *She tried to kill one of us.*

She is trying to save one of her own. Wouldn't you have done the same?

Taran spun on his heel, hands on hips, head hanging in argument with his dragon spirit.

I wouldn't kill.

Neither did she.

She would have.

It was not her intention.

Taran's shoulders slumped. The truth of it sat heavy in his chest. Moving to stand in front of her, he blurted out bitterly, "I would offer you my body heat, but you might try to steal my dragon again."

She wouldn't. Has she not proven herself to us?

You went to her?

To protect against the shadow wolf.

Taran's pulse spiked. *A shadow wolf?*

Taran ran his gaze over his mate with a new set of eyes. His dragon let out a slow, warning growl, his talons pricking beneath his skin.

Gwen's lip curled. She opened her eyes, and for the briefest moment, something else looked back at him. Not Gwen. Not entirely.

Taran's dragon rumbled, a deep, primal command shaking the walls of his chest. "Gwen. *Solanu.*"

"What?" She curled up, panting like she'd run a marathon.

"Where are you hiding the soul crystals?"

She shook her head, bending her neck, stretching and sniffing. Her movement was unnatural, her muscles twitching as if something inside her fought for control. "No more crystals. O-only one ch-chance. Mountain fall s-shattered the rest."

His chest swelled. His mate was fighting. Against the shadow wolf. Against herself. He'd been too carried away, too enthralled by her in the forest, to notice it.

But his dragon spirit had. *Protect. Mine.*

Yes, we *protect what is ours.*

Without another soul crystal, how would he pull the wolf spirit from her?

"And your hunter friends? Are they in Sentinel Peak? Are they waiting for you there?" He needed answers. He needed to fix this before it was too late.

He knew no other way to get a shadow spirit to evict itself from his mate unless he returned her to Conleth or Arden.

Arden, the shaman of their people, spent his time preparing the youth to embrace their heritage. Taran had spent years training under him, learning the rituals, the stories of those before them. Along with his brothers, Taran had listened to the warnings, and the lessons of why they could not afford to let their spirits fall into the wrong hands.

Like the hunters. Like Gwen's kind.

Taran sensed Aluk arriving back at the resort. He blocked his mind from Aluk as his dragon shifted uneasily at the thought of his oldest brother learning what he'd done. Taran had flown around the back side of the mountain to avoid his alpha.

To protect his mate.

"I told you." Her fingers dug into the couch. When had her nails become so sharp? "I came here alone. My brother is d-dying."

"Dead." Taran's words were final, but not cruel. He needed her to focus on staying alive. "Again, I'm sorry. Once blessed with a spirit, we can't live without them. One life, one spirit. One cannot live without the other."

"My brother is human." Her chest heaved, her breath coming too fast. "He's not a bad guy. He's made mistakes."

She gritted her teeth. Sweat beaded across her forehead, but beneath the sheen of fever, something darker webbed along her skin.

Taran moved closer.

She growled.

His dragon flinched. The wrongness of it scraped against his senses.

"It's not fair. Other people need spirits to protect them, too. Why should your kind get to hoard them all from others?"

Taran's neck muscles tensed. His dragon flared to life, rage licking at his veins. *Hoard?*

The memory burned hot in his chest—memories passed down, tales of hunters who killed to rip spirits from his people's bodies, leaving them to die as empty, hollowed-out husks of what they once were.

"Your kind are the thieves," he growled. "You steal what isn't yours and wonder why it destroys you."

"My brother isn't a thief." A feral, inhuman noise escaped her lips.

Taran's dragon reared back. *It mustn't take over.*

"You know nothing about me or my family."

"Does he share your gift?"

"No."

Canines dropped down from inside her mouth as she pulled back her lips in an animalistic snarl. She uncurled from the couch. The blanket slipped away. Her pupils shrank, locking onto him like prey. "No one else possesses this gift. It's why Cedric values me above the others." Her breath hitched. "He'll come for me when I don't return. He will never let me go. I can never be yours."

Taran's dragon bristled. *We shall see.*

Once they dealt with the wolf inside her, once Aluk didn't want to kill him, he'd seek this Cedric and ensure the man never went near his mate again.

"Can you release the wolf within like you released my dragon?"

Aluk would lock her up at Crag's Cliff for sure. No one would get to her. Not even him.

Never again.

His dragon spirit reared inside him, startling him. *Again? Cursed.*

The veins along her neck darkened, twisting like black vines beneath her skin.

"No." Her voice turned gravelly. She lifted her chin and rasped, "I'm not letting this one go."

"But you will." Taran knelt in front of her. His dragon prowled beneath his skin, waiting. "For me."

Claim.

"I'm not yours to command." Shadows crept across her face, her features glimmering between human and beast, the darkness of the wolf threatening to swallow her whole. How had he not seen this sooner?

Calm. Must keep calm for the sake of our solanu.

Terror coursed through him. If she lost control, he might not be able to bring her back.

"But you want me, don't you?" Taran asked, his pulse pounding. He kept his voice steady, willing his dragon to surface. "I can feel you, *solanu,* because you are my mate. I feel your pain. This shadow spirit within you wants to consume you. It will take your soul until only the spirit remains. You will cease to exist."

She shook her head in disbelief.

"It has no bloodline, Gwen."

"Peter." Tears streaked her face. For a moment, her eyes changed—her gorgeous blue and gold flecked irises breaking through. "Soul crystal."

"You must fight it." Taran reached for her, hesitated, his hand dropping at the last moment. He was afraid—afraid of bringing her more pain. Afraid he'd already caused her too much. "You can't help Peter if the wolf anchors its spirit within your soul. Once they meld, they can't be separated."

At the mention of her brother, Gwen's eyes regained a glint of recognition. Jealousy twisted in Taran's gut, but he shoved it aside. She loved her brother—that love kept her fighting. He wanted her to fight for him, too. She already did. At the resort, the way her gaze searched for him when she thought he was gone. She cared for him, too.

Taran held her gaze. "He has a soul crystal?"

"Yessss." Her voice slithered with something inhuman. Her eyes flashed, the wolf lunging back into control.

It might work. It meant having to sacrifice one of the lost shadow spirits, but could save his mate. The dark spirits never returned from the shadows.

Claim.

Not like this. Taran gritted his teeth, gripping the sleeves of her jacket. Her eyes hardened, the struggle raged inside him. "We need to get the shadow wolf out of you."

A snarl ripped from her throat.

"I will help you get to your brother," he said, "but on one condition."

She froze. The color darkened again in her eyes.

"Anything." Desperation burned in her swirling gaze. She seized his wrist, her grip tight, trembling.

"Fight, Gwen. Do not yield to the wolf."

She yanked him forward, her lips crashing against his. Taran stiffened. He tasted her—warm, wild, intoxicating. And he tasted the spirit within her.

The wolf fought him, pressing for dominance against his dragon. Taran wrenched back, holding her at arm's length.

"Mine," she said, growling.

His dragon rumbled, deep and possessive.

"No, Wolf." He allowed his dragon forth. His eyes burning. "She's mine."

Eighteen

Before Taran questioned his sanity, he scooped Gwen up in his arms.

She snarled and snapped at him. His dragon pressed at his skin, alert. His gaze locked with the shadow wolf's spirit inside her. The feral wolf spirit pushed back, resisting his dominance, but it was a pitiful fight against a dragon.

Taran carried her to the bed, dropping Gwen onto the mattress. She rolled, trying to escape, but he caught her around the waist, pulling her back. Gwen kicked at him, a strong instinctive reaction, but she hadn't realized something yet.

Her knee didn't hurt anymore.

The shadow wolf was healing her.

Taran let her struggle for a moment, grabbing her hands and binding them with torn strips from the bedsheets.

"I always imagined us doing this a different way, *solanu*," he teased, though his chest ached at the sight of her fighting for control.

A deep growl rumbled in her throat.

Taran cupped her face, relishing the feel of her skin against his palm. He wanted to touch her without fear, without the wolf between them. He ran his fingers along the curve of her jaw, his thumb resting lightly against her cheek.

"Stay with me."

Her narrowed eyes gleamed with the darkness. The wolf still lurked inside her, waiting for a moment of weakness.

"Fight it, Gwen," he urged. "Do not let the wolf sink into your soul."

His dragon reached for her, extending their bond. For a second, he thought he sensed the wolf hesitating. A flare of Gwen surfaced in her expression, raw. Vulnerable.

"N-need P-peter," she gasped.

"Tell me where we are going."

Before she could answer, his senses flared. A presence. Someone was coming.

He glanced toward the ceiling. "We've got company. Don't move."

He reached the door as someone landed outside. Taran swung open the door. He expected one of his brothers to show up but peered around his cousin, half expecting one of them behind him to be his alpha.

"Aluk wants to see you. He would have come himself, but he's dealing with the wolf tribe. Bring your mate." Ben stepped inside, but Taran didn't let him get far.

He grabbed a pillow from the couch and tossed it at Ben. "Cover yourself."

Ben smirked, holding the pillow in front of him. "You shouldn't have taken off. I told Conleth you wouldn't take her to the prison."

Taran's jaw tightened. He glanced over at Gwen, her body tense, her face drawn in battle with the wolf. He saw her slipping. Time was running out.

"You didn't come on Aluk's orders," he realized.

Ben sighed. "No. But you need to bring her back. Aluk has to decide what happens now."

"I'm not taking her back to the resort." Taran grabbed Gwen's bound hands, pulling her to her feet. She leaned into him, her body trembling.

Ben studied her, her gaze sharp.

Taran's chest puffed out; a familiar protectiveness flared. Ben might have Kaya, but Taran didn't like the other man looking at his mate.

"Then I'll take her for you." Ben made a move to step forward, but Gwen growled, and Ben halted. His brow furrowed. "Is that a wolf? You let her take another spirit?"

"It possessed her in the forest. It's one of the shadow spirits."

"Doesn't matter. Aluk will get it out of her and lock her up. She's a danger, Taran. You can't see it because of the mate bond."

Taran's grip on Gwen tightened. "And you've had it out for her the moment she took Lye's wolf." He narrowed his eyes. "What happened to believing the mountain brought her here? That she's a means to breaking the curse?"

Ben exhaled through his nose. "Aluk's offer is the only chance you have of saving your mate. No one else has a spirit strong enough to compel a guardian spirit."

"No!" Gwen gasped, leaning into him. "P-Peter."

"Did she call you Peter?" Ben lowered the pillow.

"Pillow."

Ben rolled his eyes. "You're not thinking straight." He gestured at Gwen. "The wolf will consume her."

"You are the one who needs to think," Taran snapped. "Twice now, a spirit has pre-ceremonially merged with a person. If you know so much about the curse, then help me save my mate or get out of my way."

Ben's dragon flared in his eyes.

Taran's dragon pushed forward, itching to rise. But shifting indoors would hurt Gwen. And bring this entire cabin down around them. He alone would take the roof off.

Gwen groaned, her knees buckling.

Taran caught her, pulling her into his arms before turning toward the door.

"Where are you going?" Ben demanded.

"To find her brother and get this mutt out of my mate." Taran nuzzled her, his nose twitching at the wet dog scent coating his mate's skin. He stepped outside, the cold air biting his skin. Coming to his cabin had been a mistake. Gwen shivered against him. "Don't run, *solanu*. I need to shift. Flying is the only way to get you there."

Ben followed him. "You're going to help her steal our heritage?"

Taran ignored him. Taran set Gwen down on her feet. He discarded his pants, then tossed them around her while wrapping his pant legs around her like a scarf. "I need you to hold these."

Ben scoffed. "Taran, this is insane."

"Not crazier than a man pursuing a dragon spirit that rejected him."

Ben's eyes glowed. "Still jealous, cousin?"

Taran snorted. He closed his eyes, letting his dragon spirit rise. Heat rolled through his veins. Muscles stretched, bones cracked, wings erupted from his back — Gwen snarled, twisting to flee.

Ben lunged, grabbing her. "She's a threat!"

Taran roared. The trees shook.

Ben shoved Gwen towards him, lifting his hands in surrender.

She's one of them. She's a spirit eater. Ben said through their dragon bond.

I know what she is. Taran lowered his head to Ben's level, growling. *You no longer believe she was called here to break the curse?*

Ben's eyes darkened.

Aluk will come after you. The wolves are demanding justice.

You are quick to run to my brother and seek his praise when not too long ago I remember you begging for my help.

Ben glared at Taran, his chest heaving with the grumbles of his dragon spirit. *You want to bring this up now?*

Taran widened his eyes in question.

Ben rolled his shoulders. *Fine.* He dropped the pillow, crossing his arms. "I'll give you a few hours' head start."

Taran wasted no time.

He clutched Gwen against him, his wings beating hard as he lifted into the sky.

The woods below murmured secrets of those entering the Great Hunter's realm. Deep in the mountain, hidden within the core, energy pulsed, dark and seeking. Centuries passed since the fae cursed the shifters for imprisoning their queen. The mountain stirred beneath him; the trees wavering with the winds.

The mountain rippled toward the peak, calling another avalanche to life.

Taran flew faster.

He would not leave Gwen's fate to Aluk. Or to the mountain.

Inside her, a battle raged—a violent clash between the wolf and the power pulsing through her blood. One force sought to consume the other. Gwen had never experienced anything like this before. She had always enticed spirits, drawing them out so she could direct them into soul crystals. But without a crystal, the wolf's essence seeped deeper, coiling through her veins like a spreading infection.

Her skin burned, and her muscles ached. Her own power fought back, rejecting the spirit like a body rejecting a virus.

I am far more powerful, the wolf whispered, its voice a low growl inside her mind. *With my strength and your blood combined, you would be a far greater warrior than all the packs roaming this mountain.*

Gwen curled tighter against Taran's warm scales, seeking refuge. The wind barely touched her in his grasp, his talons forming a pro-tective cage around her. Not trapping—protecting.

Why was he shielding her?

He should have left her at the resort or taken her straight to their prison. Instead, he was helping her, holding her, protecting her. Even after she'd deceived him. Even after she'd lied.

A dragon's mate must be cunning, brave, and strong.

The thought wasn't hers. Gwen clenched her teeth and shoved it away, but the wolf howled, its voice slicing through her mind like claws. Pain exploded behind her eyes. She gritted her teeth, forcing herself to focus. Peter. She had to hold on. Her brother needed this spirit.

My brother is the one you want, she whispered inwardly. *He's a scout and a tracker.*

The wolf prowled at the edges of her consciousness, its glowing white eyes blending with her own vision.

Does he share your blood?

Her body seized. The spirit didn't need her to answer. It already saw the truth in her memories. The pressure in her skull intensified. She tugged at the bounds around her wrists to distract her from the pain, as if flying in his clutches wasn't enough.

Without me, hehewuti, you can never touch him. It's part of the curse.

Curse. Someone mentioned the curse earlier. Gwen's stomach lurched as the altitude dipped. They were descending.

Ask him what they did to your people. The wolf's voice coiled tighter, filling her head. *Ask him why the Great Hunter closed the gates of the eternal forest, blocking its guardians from entering.*

A shadow formed in her mind, a massive, dark wolf stalking just beyond a ring of flames. Its red glowing eyes stayed locked onto her. The wolf snarled, baring teeth as sharp as obsidian.

She gasped.

Taran's dragon presence washed over her like a wave, blanketing her in warmth. *Why?*

The wolf lunged toward her, but the flames rose in front of her, blocking its path. She stepped back in her mind. Darkness curled around the edges of her vision, threatening to pull her under.

Gwen. His voice sounded in her mind, both familiar and foreign, part dragon, part man. He gathered her into his arms.

She panted, breathless, trapped in a race she couldn't win. The wolf chased her, urging her to surrender.

Run to the dark. Give in. Let me take control.

"Taran!"

A circle of flames erupted around her, but instead of heat, it cooled the fire burning beneath her skin. The wolf spirit prowled just beyond, pacing restlessly.

You are a coward to hide behind the flames of a dragon.

"I need to know where to go." Taran's voice drowned out the thoughts of the wolf. "Gwen? Speak to me, *solanu*," he urged.

She licked her lips despite the cold. "Rockview Pike," she shouted. "The old ranger's station. It's a few miles north of Sentinel Peak."

Had he heard her?

"Your brother is a forest ranger?" he asked, the question floating in her mind.

The wolf's presence pressed closer, testing the boundary of the flames in her mind. The darkness pressed at her insides, growing stronger. "Hurry." She pleaded, "Please hurry."

Not long into their flight, the sky rumbled a warning. Taran flew low, gliding just above the treetops, using the dense canopy for cover. The mountain lay still beneath them, its silence unsettling. Moonlight glistened off the snowy peaks, and in the distance, a fine mist of rain drifted in the wind.

His dragon snorted with irritation as the drizzle thickened, droplets turning to ice along the membranes of his wings. The temperature plunged. *Must keep mate safe.*

With each beat of his wings, ice formed, melted, and refroze, constricting his movement. Pushing forward was too risky. With a sharp dive, he aimed for the shelter of the mountain. *Lair.*

Taran skimmed low over the snow, releasing Gwen just before he hit the ground several yards away. The impact sent a shock through his legs. Ice coated the surface, the snowfall now turning to sleet. He whipped around, growling.

Gwen landed with a roll, her bound hands limiting her movements. He shifted mid-stride and reached for her just as she pushed onto her knees. He caught her by the arms, lifting her to her feet.

"What happened?" she asked between breaths, shivering against the cold pelt of rain.

"We need to find shelter." He took her by the arm. The gleam of the wolf's eyes decided for him. He kept her wrists tied. "Come on, I know a place."

He pulled her along carefully, keeping pace with her unsteady steps. Her landing on the frozen earth had unsettled him more than he liked to admit. Seeing her shiver sent his dragon into a frenzy. *Move faster. Keep her warm.*

The path wound up the slope, snow crunching beneath their feet. His dragon preened the closer they got to their lair. A hum of satisfaction threaded through Taran's mind. Visions of furs piled high in the cave flashed in his thoughts—memories his dragon clung to.

Ice coated his hair, water dripping down his face. Halfway up the trail, he reached over and pulled Gwen's hood up. Her arms trembled. Her breath was unsteady.

"We're almost there."

His dragon urged him to pick up speed, but Gwen wasn't built for this kind of endurance. He forced himself to slow, ignoring his beast's impatience.

The entrance loomed ahead, narrow and shadowed. Gwen hesitated. "A cave?"

"It's safe." He caught the rasp in her voice. A shiver ran through her. *Is she sick? Or is that the wolf?*

He stepped behind her, guiding her in. The tunnel walls widened as they moved deeper, and the tension in his dragon bled away.

Gwen stopped, tugging at her bound wrists. Her teeth chattered. "W-what is this p-place?"

Taran strode toward a ledge, dipping his fingers into the oil pooled in a carved basin. With a thought, he sent heat through his palm. The oil ignited, light flickering across the cavern.

Gwen stood in the center of the space, gaze sweeping over the towering rock ceiling, the scattered remnants of his dragon's hoard glinting in the dim glow.

"It's not much," he said, rubbing a hand over his jaw. "But it belongs to my dragon."

Gwen turned, brows drawing together. "Yours? It—it seems ancient."

Taran exhaled, crossing the space between them. "It is. The knowledge of this place stays with my dragon." He met her gaze. "And my mate."

Gwen's heartbeat stuttered. "A safe haven," she murmured. Her eyes flickered with some unreadable emotion. "Has it been here since the Great Hunter released the dragons?"

Relief unfurled in his chest. She understood.

He pulled her closer, the cavern walls shimmering with veins of crystal. "This place is a secret," he said, his breath warm against her ear. "But more importantly, it's ours now."

A sharp inhale. "No one else knows?"

"Only my brothers."

"You come here often?" she asked, voice softer now.

"Often enough." He gestured toward the flames. "Come, warm up."

His dragon rumbled in approval. The moment he let go of her, a possessive need clawed at him. *Not the time.*

"We need to find Peter," Gwen said.

Taran's jaw tightened. He reached around her wrists, undoing the bindings. A pulse of energy jumped between them, lighting the markings on her skin. A soft gasp escaped her lips, and the sound sent a protective surge through him.

"We'll wait for the storm to pass," he said. "I can't fly in this weather."

She rubbed her wrists, still holding her arms close. "How long?"

"A few hours. Maybe till morning."

"Or it could p-pass quickly."

"Not likely." The petrichor in the air warned of a longer storm. "Too much moisture in the clouds. It'll keep freezing over."

He pointed toward the alcove near the fire where furs lay stacked for sleeping. His dragon hummed at the thought of Gwen resting there. *Mate.*

Not the time.

"You should get some rest."

Gwen hesitated. "But the wolf—"

"My dragon can hold it back. For now."

She tilted her head slightly. Her irises darkened, darkness seeping in like molten metal. "Dragons doomed us. Betrayed the tribes."

Taran reached for her jacket zipper, dragging it down. "Know your place, wolf."

A low heat radiated down his arms as his dragon flared inside him. His tattoo burned—the bond between them reacting to the two spirits wrestling for control. Gwen's face paled, dark veins threading across her skin.

"You can't touch her," the wolf inside Gwen rasped. "Her fae blood is too tainted."

Taran's vision blurred with dragon fire. "Get out of my mate."

Her gold flashed in her eyes. Then she grinned.

A wicked, knowing grin.

Her voice dropped to something darker, something ancient. "*Nimitqwa ktelo.*"

Taran's breath stalled.

What once was, will be again.

Nineteen

Taran's eyelids drooped, his chest rumbling with a sound that sent vibrations through the air. His dragon spirit pushed into her—not like before, not summoned by the pull of her blood. This time, it shoved the wolf back, keeping the aggressive beast at bay.

He stood before her, unashamed, firelight flickering across the ridges of his bare body. The glow of the trapped flames within the stone walls caught in his amber eyes, making them burn like molten gold.

Heat flushed through her, blooming beneath her skin, winding deep inside with a need she wasn't sure she had the strength to resist.

Nimitqwa ktelo.

The wolf within her recoiled, stepping back, its grip loosening just enough for the pain to ease. But it wasn't surrendering. It huffed inside her mind, pressing against the edges of her soul. *Without me, he can never complete the bonding ceremony and claim us as his true mate.*

Gwen turned her head away. "There is no 'us.' You can't have this body," she muttered, her legs wobbling beneath her.

Taran's hands caught her before she could fall. His grip was firm. "Tell the wolf, *solanu—You. Are. Mine.*"

Gwen's breath stilled. Her gaze locked onto his, a shiver rushing through her, filling every inch of her with longing. *For him.*

"Taran," she whispered, knowing this might be the first and last time she felt his touch. But then logic slammed into her, squeezing her heart.

This is you. Not me. You can't have him.

The wolf growled in frustration, flooding her veins with its essence, clawing for control. But Taran's gaze pinned her in place. His presence alone was enough to keep the beast from taking her.

"Keep your eyes on me," he commanded, his voice rough with authority. "Back down, wolf."

His growl vibrated against her, sending a shudder through her body. The wolf whimpered and slunk back into the depths of her mind.

Relief washed over her, but her knees nearly buckled again.

Taran caught her and held her firm.

"What do we do now?" she panted, her body caught in the battle between the wolf and this new pull—something deeper, something impossible to ignore. She stepped closer into his warmth, unable to help herself.

Taran's jaw flexed. "We keep you warm and wait."

Her pulse skittered. "What if I don't want to wait?"

Taran stilled. A muscle ticked in his jaw. Then, slowly, he lowered his head, his breath brushing against her neck. His lips skimmed just beneath her ear, sending a shiver down her spine.

Her heart pounded as the bindings on her wrists loosened, slipping away.

Peter.

The name crashed through her desire, a sobering reminder of why she was here. Why couldn't she let herself have this?

"We have to find Peter," she breathed, stepping back. "Something must have happened."

Taran pulled away. Her gaze flickered to his lips, watching them part as if he wanted to argue. Her breath hitched. The heat in her belly curled tighter, but shame slid in alongside it.

Peter needed her.

They had come so close.

She needed to keep her focus.

Inside, the wolf lay down, ears pricked forward but still watching. Waiting. Taran's dragon might have subdued the beast for now, but the wildness still simmered beneath her skin.

So did the want.

Her blood pulsed beneath her skin, charged with something she didn't know how to fight.

"You won't know until we get there," Taran said. "Don't let your worry weaken you. The wolf spirit in you is strong."

She swallowed hard, nodding. She just needed to hold on. Long enough to get to her brother.

She hoped Peter had kept his empty soul crystal. Otherwise, she feared what the transition might do to him. *It's not your choice.*

Her fingers curled into fists.

Taran's dragon tattoo flared with heat beneath her palm, grounding her. She clung to the sensation.

"What about your brother?" she asked, trying to distract herself—from the way his shoulders flexed, the carved muscle of his chest, the sheer presence of him.

"Aluk will come for us." His voice darkened. "The wolf alphas will demand retribution for what you've done. I can't protect you if we stay here."

"So, we run?"

Darkness flashed in his eyes. Pain.

Guilt twisted in her gut. She had hurt him by running, even if he hadn't said it outright.

The wolf rose inside her, its instincts twisting through her like smoke. *Mate. Mark. Claim.*

Before she realized she'd moved, the space between them vanished.

No. This is me. Not the wolf. Not the spirit trying to take over.

But then the wolf's hunger surged, a pulse of heat flooding her veins. Before she could stop herself, she pressed her forehead against Taran's shoulder, breathing him in—pine, ash, something distinctly *him*. It awoke something buried deep inside her. She never wanted to forget it.

A low whine built in her throat. Her lips brushed his skin. *Not me. The wolf.*

Her tongue darted out, tasting the salt on his neck before she could stop it.

Taran's arms tightened around her. His muscles went taunt.

"Gwen," he rasped, his voice a deep growl.

The wolf stretched inside her, pleased, pressing against her control. Take him. Let him claim us.

No.

The pull to be closer, to feel his touch, was intoxicating. The wolf pushed her forward, guiding her hands, urging her to press her mouth to his jaw. She kissed along the rough scruff, her lips tingling from the contact.

Taran trembled. With his hands flexing against her waist, his restraint was a thin wire she could snap if she just—No. She was still in control. *She had to be.*

"*Solanu* . . . what are you doing?" His voice was thick, rough.

She knew what she was doing. And she didn't.

The wolf thrashed, snarling to take what belonged to her. The need inside her tangled with the beast's desires until she didn't know where she ended and it began.

Her hands lifted to cup his face, but her fingers shook. She tilted his head, aligning their mouths. A rush of courage surged inside her. Was it hers? Or the wolf's?

"This might be our last chance," she whispered. "I—I want this."

Do you? The question rose, but she crushed it before it could take root.

Rising onto her toes, she brushed her lips over his. A spark shot through her veins, igniting something beyond her control.

The wolf exhaled in triumph, sinking its claws deeper into her soul until it yelped, singed by the fiery shield that flared to life inside her.

No.

The blaze spread, sending the wolf back. The beast snarled, lashing out, but Gwen gritted her teeth and shoved the wolf further into the recesses of her mind.

Not this time.

Taran stilled. A growl rumbled from his chest.

For a heartbeat, she feared she had pushed too far.

Then, his arms crushed her against him.

His mouth claimed hers, but not with instinct-driven hunger. Not with the dominance or the wild demand of a predator. This was Taran. Steady. Fierce. Restraining his strength even as his grip tightened around her. He kissed her with a quiet intensity that sent a gentle rush coursing through her—not from the wolf, not from its restless need, but from something deeper. Something hers.

The wolf snarled, thrashing, trying to rise.

Gwen shoved it down.

No, you *don't own this. You don't own me.*

Caution pulsed. She felt compelled to withdraw. To flee.

But she couldn't.

Wouldn't.

Her fingers traced his chest, slipping lower. Taran shuddered at her touch, muscles jumping beneath her fingertips.

Then he caught her wrists.

Broke the kiss.

The wolf inside her whined, but its cry was distant now, smothered by the fire Gwen had ignited within herself. Dragon's fire.

Gwen blinked up at him, her breath coming in ragged gasps. "Why?"

Taran exhaled hard, his grip tightening for a moment before gentling. "You should rest."

Slowly, the kiss-induced fog in her brain cleared.

"What about you?" she murmured.

"I'll watch for the weather to break."

"In dragon form? Outside?" Heat still hummed beneath her skin. "Won't that make it easier for them to find us?"

A muscle ticked in his jaw. "If I hold you, I'll want to do more than kiss you." His thumbs brushed over her pulse and made it jump. "And I won't risk hurting you."

"You're not hurting me." She glanced down at his hands—broad, calloused, strong. Safe. A sharp ache laced through her. She knew what he meant, but he didn't believe her. "It's the wolf."

His expression turned guarded. "Another reason this isn't a good idea."

"No." She grabbed onto him before he could pull away, fingers curling around his waist. "This is exactly why it's a good idea. Don't you see?" She searched his face, willing him to understand. "The wolf is suppressing the magic in my blood. Once it's gone, I may never be able to touch you like this again."

His dragon-slit eyes locked onto hers.

"You can hold it back?" he asked carefully.

"It's like you breathed fire inside me," she said. "And the wolf can't get past it." She didn't want to leave him. No matter what happened. She wasn't afraid. "I want to be your mate, Taran. *Claim me.*"

Taran went rigid. "You don't know what you're asking."

She lifted her chin. "I do."

Slowly, he lifted her wrist, pressing his thumb over the mark. It flared to life, burning hot beneath her skin.

"This is you." He looked her in the eye. "Not the wolf?"

She nodded, pulse thrumming beneath his touch. "Your dragon spirit is holding it back. Without you, I'm not strong enough."

His eyes darkened, sending a delicious shiver through her.

"You don't have to give yourself to me to keep my protection," he murmured. "Claimed or not, I stand by you."

His fingers brushed over the mark on her wrist, tracing the design unique only to him.

"We'll get through this," he murmured. "Together."

"I know." Gwen leaned in, pressing a feather-light kiss to his cheek. His skin was warm beneath her lips, the scent of pine and embers clinging to him like a promise of safety. "But I've spent my whole life being wanted for the wrong reasons—the gifts in my blood, what I can do for others. Never just . . . me." Her fingers curled against his chest, her palm absorbing the steady thrum of his heartbeat. "You should run. Ben was right. Hand me over to Aluk. Let him lock me away before I ruin anything else."

Taran's grip tightened, his fingers flexing around her arms, grounding her. His next word rumbled low in his chest, more felt than heard. "Never."

She took a sharp breath, air catching at the back of her throat. His vow settled over her, pressing into the spaces where doubt had lived for too long.

"Do you have any idea what it's like to be afraid to touch?" Her voice wavered, barely more than a whisper. "To crave something you can never have?" The words burned in her throat. She had buried them for so long, refusing to let herself feel the longing that now unfurled inside her. "I've wished for this. For you."

Taran lifted a hand, fingers brushing over her cheek, trailing a path that left her skin tingling. "I'll hold your hand anytime."

"No." She swallowed hard, her pulse thrumming at the base of her throat. A simple touch wasn't enough. Not now. Not when the ache inside her stretched too wide, too deep. "Please, Taran. Claim me. I have no right to ask, but—"

His amber gaze locked onto hers, searching, questioning. The space between them felt impossibly small. Time slowed, waiting for him to decide.

"This would make the mark on your wrist permanent."

"Yes."

His eyes flashed. A war between restraint and desire erupted in gold and red sparks in his eyes.

Slowly, deliberately, he lowered his mouth to hers.

The world stilled.

His kiss coaxed rather than claimed. Each touch unwound another knot inside her, teasing loose the fear she'd carried for too long. Heat rose, low and quiet, beneath her skin. Not magic. Just him. Here. And he wanted her. Not her skills. Not her gift. *Her.*

Taran drew her closer, his arms wrapping around her like a shield against the rest of the world. She sighed into him, fingers threading into his hair, holding on as though she could carve this moment into eternity. His comforting warmth banished the chill of the cave and everything she had ever been told she could not have.

A murmur of her name escaped him, soft as the rain outside, but it settled into her bones, rooting deep. His hand guided hers, pressing her palm over his heartbeat, his dragon tattoo heating beneath her fingertips.

She could have stayed there forever—wrapped in his warmth, in the quiet promise between them. The fire crackled, casting golden light over them, as something deep inside her answered.

Mine.

The voice stirred in her mind, familiar yet different.

Not the wolf. Not Taran. His dragon.

Her fingers tightened in his hair.

She was his. And he . . . was hers.

Twenty

Taran adjusted his position beside Gwen, careful not to jostle her. Every second counted. Soon, they would force the wolf from her body, and her blood magic would reclaim her sense of touch. But what then? When he could no longer hold her without pain? When Aluk came for them and imprisoned them both?

Taran's fingers ghosted over her shoulder, memorizing the warmth before it was gone. He traced the delicate lines of her skin, burning the sensation into his memory. Would her love survive past the fire of their bond? Would she still want him when the fire no longer kept the wolf contained?

Inside, his dragon stirred, a low growl vibrating through his chest. *Love knows no bounds.*

But Taran wasn't sure.

Time, a ticking clock, quickly fled from him. The wolf inside her fought against the fire of his dragon spirit wrapped around her soul. It sapped at his strength, like an ache in his muscles to feed it through their bond. Until they located Peter, the wolf would continue to attack and wear her down. He'd rather hand her over to Aluk and evict the wolf than lose her completely, but her brother would die, and for that, he was certain she would never forgive him.

Gwen's breath, soft but restless, stirred the air between them. The flickering fire cast dancing shadows across the stone walls.

Her body tensed.

"Don't move," he whispered. His touch remained featherlight at her waist, not wanting to think of never holding her like this again.

"I'm hurting you." She moved away, but the sudden loss of her body close to his made his chest tighten.

Far from it. He ached for her. The worry in her eyes pierced deeper than any pain ever could.

Their gazes locked. *No matter what happens, I am yours.*

She reached for him, sliding her fingers into his hair at the back of his neck. "Kiss me."

Taran didn't hesitate. He leaned in, his lips brushing against hers in the gentlest of caresses. A sigh slipped from her as her arms wound around his neck, pulling him closer. How much time did they have left?

Her heart beat against his, the rhythm syncing, a fragile melody against the looming storm.

"Would it always be this way?" she whispered, her grip tightening.

No. Time slipped through their fingers like melting ice. Its roaring current dragged them toward a precipice. The wolf. Peter. Aluk. Each threatened to sever the fragile thread holding them together.

He couldn't voice the words that would burden her with the chilling reality. So, he kissed her again with a fierce possessiveness born of impending loss. He pressed her closer, imprinting the feel of her against him, a silent scream against the future waited. This touch, this fleeting connection, was his only language, his desperate attempt to pour every unsaid promise, every agonized fear, every ounce of his affection into her before the chance vanished from him.

He pulled back, forcing himself to meet her gaze. His thumb brushed her cheekbone, savoring the warmth, the impossible softness. "I'm told it gets better as time goes on."

"How do you know?" she whispered.

"Ben."

Aluk rarely spoke of his mate, the love and loss he carried like a wound never fully healed. Dragon shifters weren't like the others. When they lost their mate, they didn't just grieve. They withered. Their souls intertwined too deeply to survive the severing.

"I want to hold on to you forever." Tears glistened in her eyes. "Once the wolf is gone, I'll go back to the way I was."

A gut-deep ache of torment tangled with a surprising, profound contentment struck him. A familiar yet strange, pull tugged at him. His dragon offered no memories from the past, leaving a terrifying void in his mind. No stories surfaced, only suffocating silence. How could their people have allowed them to separate them from their mates?

A sharp pain flaring in Taran's soul. His dragon spirit held fragments of the past, glimpses of the fae's wrath, of a battle they lost, of a curse etched into their blood. Now it showed him. They chose to uphold their promise to protect their gifts, and the fae queen had cursed them for it.

No one will take our mate from us.

Taran agreed. Whatever had brought Gwen down this mountain, she belonged with *him*.

"How long has it been since you could withstand another's touch?" he asked.

"The last person to touch me was my mother." Her eyes glimmered with sadness. "Before she told me to run."

"Why?"

She took a deep breath before answering. "My stepfather would have killed me. Peter tried to protect me, but couldn't always be there."

The helplessness in her voice coiled tight around his ribs. "How old were you?"

"Twelve."

Taran's dragon snarled. "And your stepfather? What is his name?"

"I've forgotten his name." Her frown deepened as she pressed a palm against his chest. "It doesn't matter anymore."

Like hell it didn't.

Her touch burned through him, the weight of time pressing against them both. They couldn't stay here.

"We have to move," she said. "Peter is counting on me."

Taran cupped the back of her head, pressing his lips to her forehead. "You don't have to do this alone anymore."

He wanted to promise her forever, but reality loomed like a storm on the horizon. The wolf spirit inside her fought for control, flecks of gold flashing through her eyes. Black lines pulsed against her skin, a poisonous mass of veins marking where the shadow spirit clung to her.

And it was winning.

Taran's dragon growled. *Time is slipping away.*

"Once we find your brother and handle this business of the wolf, nothing changes," he vowed.

But he knew that was a lie. Everything had changed.

He glanced toward the back of his lair. "There is dried meat in the chest. Eat while I check the weather."

She smirked. "Don't you want to help me?"

"If I helped you, mate, it would be back down on the furs."

His dragon rumbled its agreement.

She rolled her eyes but smiled. Her wolf, however, bristled at him, prowling behind her gaze, the beast unwilling to yield. The glow of her tattoo changed, once an angry red, now pulsed blue that mirrored the rhythm of his heartbeat. The dragon spirit melded between them.

His mate. His *solanu.*

"Without Peter, I couldn't have survived all these years. I can't let him die." She grabbed her clothes and dressed quickly. Three days. It hadn't been nearly enough.

"I have to find him."

Taran froze. His dragon stretched its senses. The mountain was too quiet.

"What is it?" Gwen asked.

He reached into her mind. *Solanu.*

Her voice came back, but it wasn't Gwen. *You can call me Aswigini, for I am an ohunko.*

Taran's muscles tightened.

Ohunko.

His dragon rumbled, ancient memories stirring like embers in a dying fire. The *ohunkos* had once walked these lands as warriors, their presence a whisper of judgement and justice. They did not simply exist—they enforced balance, wielding power to protect their people. Then they had vanished, their bloodlines severed.

Nimitqwa ktelo. What was would be again.

Taran stole a glance at Gwen. Her face was serene, her eyes soft. Unaware. His mate did not know the power she harbored. No idea of the danger.

He reached for her mind again—*Gwen.*

Nothing.

The wolf blocked him.

His dragon growled.

"Taran?" Gwen rose and went to him.

A chill slithered through his veins. *You are one of the original guardians of this mountain, whose dark heart taints you.*

Gwen wrapped her arms around him. "What is it?"

Taran rested his chin on top of her head, inhaling the scent of her, feeling the steady thrum of her heartbeat against his. He smoothed down her wild hair, combing his fingers through the silken strands. *Mine.*

You're welcome, dragon. Enjoy her while you can.

His grip on her tightened. *You will not have her.*

But deep inside, dread chased him. If the *ohunko* had truly returned, if Gwen carried its spirit, then Taran might not have a choice.

He might have to turn his mate over to his brother.

To save her.

To save them all.

Outside the lair, the wind howled, a mournful sound that rattled the ice-crusted trees. The mountain was restless. It knew. It always knew.

"There's no one here." Taran's voice pulled her from the shadow wolf's void ensnaring her. She turned her face away from the comfort of his warm chest to gaze into the dark, abandoned ranger station. With the enhancement of the wolf inside her, she noticed the difference from her human sight. The clarity and precision made her blink.

Taran's dragon spirit enveloped her, keeping the wolf from surging forward unexpectedly to possess her, and possess her it would.

"Are you sure this is the right place?" she whispered, afraid to wake the sleeping beast inside her. She fought to contain the wolf spirit, preventing it from trapping her in her own mind. It fed on her fear and curled its essence into every memory and doubt she carried.

"This is the only ranger station within miles of Sentinel Peak."

On her feet, Gwen's gut seized with panic. "No. He's supposed to be here. He promised." Gwen reached up, stuffing her hands in her windblown hair. The wolf inside her chuffed with glee. A growl escaped her.

Taran turned, walking across the open space.

Gwen rushed to the first office, the door missing and cold air trickling inside through the slits in the boarded window. An old desk and a dusting of snow on the floor greeted her.

Taran opened a door, then entered the next room.

A faint smell halted her.

"Can you scent your brother?"

"Scent him?" She tilted her chin up, closed her eyes, and focused on the familiar smell. The moment Gwen inhaled, the past surged forward like an avalanche. Peter's arm around her, his laugh, and a wicked grin.

"Do you know your brother's scent?" He strolled out of the small room across from her, walking away with unlaced boots on his feet and pulling his arms into a long-sleeved tan shirt. Taran's muscles rippled with the movement of his arms. She licked her lips. *Want.*

"Where did you get that?" She pointed to his chest.

He paused, those dark eyes of his turning amber and a smirk on his face. "You mean this?" He tugged on the shirt, leaving it hanging open.

The wolf inside her rose its head, sharing her sight and liking what they saw. Gwen wrapped her arms around her waist, hoping to stop the surge of heat flushing her skin. "Yes, the clothes." She nearly choked. The whole time, they had been traversing the woods with him unclothed, but when the man donned a shirt, her pulse quickened. Warmth flooded her cheeks, her thoughts back to lying on furs and Taran's body pressed against her.

"Sniff this." He held out another shirt toward her.

"You want me to smell a shirt?"

"Human noses aren't sensitive as a shifter, but the wolf in you might help you recognize it."

"I don't know what my brother smells like." She took the shirt and inhaled.

The wolf came awake. "T-Taran?"

"Let the wolf work with you. What does it smell like?" he asked.

"You." She handed back the shirt. "Do you always keep spare clothing tucked away in places for when you shift?"

"I do. This was my station before the winters got bad on this side of the mountain and I moved to the cabin."

"You were a ranger?" she asked.

"I still am."

"Oh."

"Sniff." He held it out to her again.

"I told you; it smells like you."

"This isn't my shirt, *solanu*, nor is it my bedroll laid out in there. Is it possible this belonged to your brother?"

A dose of frigid cold traveled through her veins. How did she not know her brother's scent? A flutter of panic erupted in her chest. She failed to form words, and her vision was slightly blurred with tears. Inside her, the wolf seeped into her veins. It heightened her senses, including the smell. The familiarity of the light smell she detected frustrated her more. A small sound rose from her throat. Peter. She recognized the bergamot orange under the pine scent.

Humans pay so little attention to these things, the wolf dismissed from within.

"Peter is sick." And all the other shifter crystals he'd worn over the years changed his scent. She should have memorized her brother's unique smell, but the last time she saw her brother, Gwen had focused on his gaunt face and the receding light in his eyes.

"He can't survive much longer without an animal spirit. We need to find him." Tears rolled down her cheeks.

Taran brushed them away, the wolf pressing through her sight, blocking her from him again. "If these are your brother's things, he couldn't have gone far. Do you know if he came alone?"

"No, he would have come with our medic. He's a friend of Peter's." Whose gaze always lingered on her a beat too long.

Her brother held Patch in high regard, but something felt off about the man or the mountain lion spirit of his soul crystal. Either way, Gwen couldn't shake the eerie sensation she got thinking of Peter's friend. He worked for Cedric, like the rest of them.

"You trust him?"

Gwen shook her head. "I don't have a choice. He's my only option of helping Peter."

She placed her hand over her mouth, her eyes wide. *We will hunt him and make him pay for the death of your blood brother.*

"We don't know if he's dead."

Had Taran heard the wolf? It didn't matter. "We have to find him. I'm so selfish. The storm has passed, and here I am wasting time." More tears slid down her angry face.

"No time has been wasted. We could not have left any sooner," Taran assured her. "What you've done is far from selfish." He kissed the tears on both her cheeks. "You are brave, courageous, and strong. All the qualities my dragon spirit and I have come to love in you."

"You love me?" She hiccupped between the tears.

"Would I allow you to touch me otherwise, *solanu*?"

"And when the spirit is gone from me, and I can't touch you anymore?" she whispered. "Will you love me then?"

"Always."

Gwen swallowed hard. "Taran, I . . ."

She saw Taran's eyes dull and his muscles tense. "We need to find your brother and get the wolf out of you. Did the medic tell you anywhere else? Where did you last see your brother?"

Taken aback by his abrupt change in demeanor, Gwen tried to force the pang of hurt away for later.

"West." She dug her hands into her hair, clawing at the roots. The wolf inside her mind thrashed, mirroring her rising panic. Its snarls echoed in her mind, fueling her fear. But Peter's face, pale and scared, pushed through the haze. She had to find him. "There is a camp west of the compound."

She turned in frantic circles, trying to stay one step ahead of the wolf racing inside her mind. Each spin made the room tilt, but the wolf refused to stop. "We have to find him."

"Could he have gone back there?"

"No!" The word exploded from her, raw and choked. Tears welled in her eyes, blurring her vision. She wouldn't let Peter die. No way.

"You need to focus and stay calm to keep control of the wolf. Otherwise, you are no good to Peter."

She pushed past him. Gwen dug through the pack. Her fingers were numb despite her gloves. Socks, a flask, and a rolled-up pair of military-grade cargo pants tumbled onto the ground. Her heart lurched when she spotted Peter's phone.

Her fingers trembled as she swiped the screen, the familiar lock screen lighting up. A photo of her and Peter from years ago, smiling, unbroken. A single line of text was typed across the image. An address in Sentinel Peak.

Bile burned in her throat. "Cedric."

Taran nudged aside the fabric of the bedroll and lifted a leather cord with an opaque soul crystal tied at the end.

She snatched it from his hand. The moment her fingers closed around the crystal, a cold pulse shot through her palm, spreading up her arm. Gwen clutched the soul crystal to her heart. "It's too late."

Cedric had found Peter.

Twenty–One

"And you know this from the necklace?"

Her chest heaved. Each breath ragged. Gwen spun to face him, her pulse hammering. The crystal dug into her palm like a vise, sharp edges pressing into her skin. *Breathe.* "It's Peter's."

Taran's gaze fell to her clenched fist. "Then you can use it for the shadow wolf inside you."

A sickening shudder rolled through her. She forced her fingers to unfurl, revealing the crystal resting in her palm. "Not with the stain of the prior spirit's essence."

The wolf surged up, a heat flaring through her limbs, a foreign strength making her fingers tighten against her will. Sweat prickled along her brow, icy trails running down her temples. She fought against it, but beneath her palm, the crystal cracked.

A sharp, eerie howl reverberated inside her skull.

Taran's hand closed over hers, prying her fingers apart. "Don't."

But it was too late. Wisps of dark essence slithered from the fracture like dying embers. Her wolf's cry turned guttural, enraged.

"I didn't mean to. I—" Her throat tightened. Tears blurred her vision.

The wolf within howled mournfully in her head.

A bitter laugh escaped her. "It's a test."

"What?"

She squeezed the broken soul crystal, ignoring the string of jagged edges biting into her palm. "He's testing me."

Realization struck cold and sharp. *Cedric knew about Peter. He always knew.* Her stomach lurched. "The medic has been reporting to Cedric."

Taran's head tilted, sharp interest flashing in his dragon-red eyes. "Tell me about this, Cedric. You've mentioned him before."

He kneeled in front of her. Gwen's shoulders bunched, the wolf rising in response. A growl rumbled in her throat.

Taran's pupils slit, his body tensing like he was preparing to hold her back if she lost control.

But she was already lost.

"It doesn't matter. I failed. Peter's gone, and Cedric knows what he's done. What I've done."

Taran's voice softened. "Talk to me, *solanu*. What else have you done?"

The air thickened. The walls seemed too close. Too tight.

"You know what I've done." The wolf prowled around his fiery shield inside her, seething. Hungry. "I took a man's wolf spirit and almost killed him to save my brother." And now—"

She swallowed hard, bile rising in her throat. "I'm harboring a feral wolf inside me, hoping it will tame once I give it to my brother. But now Cedric has Peter, and my brother is a dead man."

Taran's eyes glinted like dark rubies. "You don't know that."

The wolf snarled in her head, unconvinced.

Gwen closed her eyes, horror weighing her down. "By now, Cedric knows the truth. I can't save Peter."

The crashing reality made her nauseous.

"Where is Cedric? You mentioned a compound."

She flinched. "They'll kill you."

Images of Taran filled her mind. Taran and his brothers, captured. Their spirits ripped away, and the bodies left as husks.

She hugged herself against the ripple of fear coursing through her body. "As soon as Cedric realizes what you are, he'll take your dragon spirit for himself. And then—"

The rest of her words filled her mouth like poison, too bitter, too late.

She lifted her gaze, meeting Taran's. "He'll send the others to hunt your brothers."

"Or he'll be the one to die. Have you little faith in me, mate?"

Gwen fought back a surge of panic. *No, you don't understand.* "You don't know the power Cedric has."

"And he wields this power over you?"

"He owns me," Gwen whispered, raw and broken. "My stepfather *sold me* to him." The admission was like tearing open an old wound, bleeding in front of Taran. "It's why my mother told me to run." Tears slipped down her cheeks. "It's not her fault, none of it."

"And Peter?" Taran asked.

Gwen closed her eyes, huffing, remembering his stubbornness. "He stayed close. Made himself useful. Valuable. He wanted to be near me. Protect me."

The wolf snapped its jaws, a surge of rage rushing through her. A growl ripped from her throat. *No, not now—*

The fire he placed inside her wavered. Her vision darkened at the edges. A red haze seeped into her thoughts. The air thickened, heavy with threat.

A crash.

The ranger station door splintered inward, hinges groaning in protest. Gwen dropped to a crouch, her wolf's instincts sharpening, preparing to fight.

Taran lunged in front of her, shoulders squared, teeth bared in warning. A massive figure filled the doorway. The sunlight behind him created a halo of dust motes around his imposing form. Power radiating off him seared like a burn to her skin.

Alpha.

Gwen sucked in a sharp breath. Her wolf stilled.

"Stand down, guardian."

The deep, commanding voice slithered through her veins, compelling, ordering.

Gwen almost *obeyed.*

Her wolf bucked against the dominance, but the pressure was suffocating, like being trapped beneath an avalanche. *Nice try, wolf.* She shoved it down, regaining control.

Taran cursed under his breath. "So much for a few hours' head start."

She met the intruder's gaze. His dark hair. Eyes like dark wheat. Raw, untamed power.

Her stomach turned to ice. "You're the dragon alpha?"

Aluk's gaze locked onto hers.

Heat surged beneath her skin. Her wolf lifted its hackles, a defensive growl vibrating in her chest. A pressure pressed against her skull. A command. *Submit.*

She curled her hands into fists. *No.*

"You've been claimed."

The alpha's words sent a ripple of awareness through her. The mark on her wrist flared to life with a tug, pulling her closer to Taran.

He stepped closer. Taran growled.

"Calm, brother," the alpha murmured. "I see you're not the only one with dibs on this female."

Gwen's knees nearly buckled under the weight of his presence. A primal sensation rippled through her, pulling deep inside her. Her wolf whined, ears flattening, body lowering slightly. Her wolf wanted her to sink to the ground, to *submit*.

No. A violent shudder ran through her.

Gwen forced herself upright, clenching her fists. *I am Taran's. Not his.*

And yet—something inside her disagreed.

Her gaze snapped to Aluk, to the raw authority in his golden eyes.

A foreign ache spread through her chest, not hers, but the wolf spirit. An ancient longing, something outside of her memories, curled tight around her heart like a phantom presence.

The wolf wanted to go to him.

To submit. To belong.

Why was this happening? She had no bond with Aluk. Her loyalty, her heart, belonged to Taran.

And yet, the wolf spirit inside her was responding to Aluk's dragon like — like it *knew* him.

Aluk's gaze swept over her, nostrils flaring. "How long has she been harboring this wolf spirit?"

"It came to me in the woods." She needed him to know she hadn't stolen it. That she didn't belong to it. That it wasn't hers.

Aluk's eyes narrowed. "Not long, then. Good."

Gwen had a sinking feeling that this had just gotten so much worse.

Taran squared his shoulders, standing between them. Gwen wasn't sure she heard him over the pounding of her heart and the frantic pacing of the wolf inside her.

"Her wolf reeks of old blood." Aluk was watching her too closely for comfort. "You shouldn't have taken off, little brother. We could have settled this back at the resort and saved time and trouble for many of us."

"For you," Taran said.

Aluk's gaze swept over the room before settling on Gwen. "Brother or no brother, I am still alpha, and my word is still law."

Taran's shoulders squared, his dragon flashing in his eyes. "And what law have you come to enforce?"

"Your mate attempted to kill one of our people and steal his wolf spirit. Did you think Rourke would let this go simply because you claimed her?"

Fear knotted in Gwen's stomach. She needed to get to Peter before the wolf pack alpha got to her. "I didn't have a choice. I need to save my brother, then I'll leave, and you'll never see me again, I swear."

Taran's body jerked, his face turning towards her.

She meant it. Once she returned to Cedric, he'd never let her out of his sight again. She would never see Taran again. Her lungs tightened, an ache blooming in her chest at the thought, but if this kept her brother alive and Taran and his brothers out of Cedric's knowledge, what other choice did she have?

"Spare me the justifications," Aluk said. "Your actions endangered this entire mountain community. You broke the law and must pay for your actions."

Taran took a step forward. "There are things you need to know first."

"I've had reports of a rogue wolf spirit and a dragon harboring her." His tone turned cold. "We need to get the wolf out of her."

"No!" Gwen snarled.

The wolf inside her lunged, furious at the threat. A sharp, piercing pain lanced through her skull. Her vision blurred, the world spinning. *No. No. No.*

She pressed a shaking hand to her forehead, waiting for the dizzy spell to pass. The wolf would not take her. She needed to hold on to it for Peter. For herself. She wouldn't lose her soul to the wolf. Fire crackled inside her, reminding her of the bond she shared with Taran. How long could he hold the shield there?

"No one is taking my mate anywhere." Sweat beaded across his forehead. His eyes glinted, gold and fire changing between human and dragon.

"Don't challenge me," Aluk warned.

Taran's hands curled into fists. "She's my mate, Aluk. My. Mate."

Aluk lifted his chin. His eyes darkened, changing from molten whiskey to black. "I know what she is."

"You told me to claim her within three days, and I have."

"Yes, when she was nothing more than a hunter, but now she is possessed by one of the *ohunko*." Aluk frowned, deep creases burrowing between his brows.

Heat flooded her veins. Unfamiliar, wrong. She wanted to shake it off, but her body, the wolf inside her, wanted to move closer to Aluk.

No. She wasn't his.

But the wolf inside her wasn't fully hers, either. Holding the spirit, trapping it within her, was the only way to save Peter.

"As her mate, I can choose to take her punishment," Taran declared.

Gwen's pulse pounded beneath her mark. Taran stood between her and whatever judgment Aluk passed. A lump rose in her throat.

"She can't be your mate. She's one of *them*. Her presence here puts this entire mountain at risk."

A deep growl rumbled from Taran's chest. Gwen felt his dragon's ire, heat rolling off him in waves. It curled around her like an unseen shield.

But the wolf inside her bucked against it. Panic rushed up her throat. If she lost control, if the wolf took over completely—*I have to find Peter.*

"There are other ways," Aluk said. "But first, we need to ensure it's contained."

Gwen's hand trembled on Taran's arm. "No. You can't. There's something you don't understand."

Aluk tilted his head, studying her like a puzzle he was close to solving. "And what don't I understand? You have fae blood. You extracted a man's animal spirit, and now an *ohunko* controls you. The guardian is not of your blood. If it possesses you, it will use you to become the assassin it once was. Is that what you wish to become? A killer?"

Protector. Her wolf rumbled.

"I need this wolf spirit to save my brother. He has the wasting illness."

"He's human," Aluk said, his tone edged with warning. "To take the *ohunko* inside him will crush his soul. He won't be your brother, but an empty vessel for the guardian spirit to use. Either way, he's dead."

Heavy silence settled over the room.

Is that true?

Gwen pressed her lips together in a hard line.

Now, who is the one that doesn't understand? asked the wolf.

I'm only holding onto you to save my brother!

Except without me, you will never feel the touch of another again. You're blocking my magic.

Your mate can only hold his fire inside you for so long. Even now, it weakens. With me, you can touch him, *and I can help you control the power in your blood. Long ago, your kind and mine were one.*

Smoke choked the air. The scent of burning wood and moss filled her lungs.

Her wolf slipped into her vision, locking the dragon alpha in with her. A broad chest provided support against her back. Scents of pine and ash surrounded her. Her gaze never left Aluk . . .

She leaned against a tree. The bark bit into her back. Feathers tickled against her shoulder. Deep in the woods, streams of light filtered through the leaves above. Scents of warm moss and rotting bark gave way to the stench of something stronger. She followed it, running through the forest. The gentle thump of a quiver bounced between her shoulder blades. Smoke covered the sunlight, darkening the light between the trees. Burning scents assaulted her nostrils.

Fear and a sense of duty propelled her forward. Her body heated, a sheen of sweat and the prickle of the animal inside her sent small bumps over her skin. She tossed her quiver. Her stomach tightened, her lungs expanded, and in a painful snap, her bones rearranged; the scorching heat of claws raking through her made her scream. No sound left her lips. In a fluid motion, she continued, her vision sharper. Through smoke and fire, she distinguished silhouettes on the mountain. Screams. A woman's, not hers.

She broke through the forest, leaping toward the ring of men. Their long silvery hair and odd robes caused her heart to pound faster. They cornered the woman, driving her back toward the opening in the mountain.

The roar of a dragon made the earth rumble. Three hooded figures stood off to the side, their hands emitting light through the burning embers and their mouths moving, and she snarled, leaping toward them. Suddenly, something struck her; pain rippled through her body. Darkness.

She gasped, jerking back into the present. Strong arms steadied her. Taran.

She blinked, disoriented, her breath coming fast.

"Solanu. Are you okay?" Taran's voice cut through the haze.

Aluk's voice chilled her. "Never look me in the eye again."

"It's the wolf."

Would Peter be able to control the spirit within him?

You must understand the past to fix the present, Nimitqwa ktelo. You. Not this Peter you hope to exchange with me.

"Do whatever you want to me," she pleaded. "First, let me save my brother. You can't let Cedric win."

Her heart thudded frantically.

A storm brewed in his eyes.

"You wanted to catch the spirit hunters," Taran said. "The wolves are already gathering for a hunt."

Aluk's eyes dulled, as did Taran's.

The wolf inside her sat back, easing the tension within her.

Aluk exhaled slowly. "Tell me everything you know," he finally said. "If your information proves valuable, perhaps a compromise can be reached."

Twenty-Two

GWEN HELD UP THE phone, the address glowing on the screen. "He'll be waiting for me here."

Aluk's fingers dragged along his rugged jaw, his gaze steady, unreadable. "It's most likely a trap."

She braced herself, pulse pounding as the seconds ticked by. Every moment he didn't drag her away was a small victory.

"Echo Forge Road—the old clinic." Taran murmured, leaning close.

"Stepping foot in Sentinel Peak, let alone the clinic, is the wolves' territory. It means risking possible exposure," Aluk said.

"I can't leave Peter there to die!" In her mind, letting Cedric condemn her brother to death was a more dire consequence. "Cedric will figure out I've gone if he hasn't already. He'll come after me, and I won't be able to get to Peter before it's too late. You don't understand how dangerous he is."

"And what about the rest of us?" Aluk's voice deepened, his dragon brushing the edges of his words. "If the hunters discover we exist, war will break out. We will defend ourselves against those who seek to erase our heritage. Including the human government. If they realize what we are, they'll eradicate us."

Gwen pictured the devastation. The woman in the mountain. Trapped. No escape. Her wolf stirred, uneasy. "There has to be a way."

"We don't shift," Taran said.

She frowned. "Can't shifters sense each other?"

"True shifters, yes," Aluk said. "Those who control stolen spirits don't have the same instincts we do."

He still hadn't told her no. The slight tilt of his head made her hope he was at least considering it.

Taran added, "Their perceptions are dull. They can't shift like us. While their senses are heightened, they lack the ability to detect another shifter."

Gwen latched onto the idea. "Then don't shift. Cedric and his men won't know. Everyone around here knows the wolves roam these mountains. They won't suspect otherwise. Unless they mistake you for a mountain lion."

"I'm not a cat," Taran muttered, irritation flickering across his face.

"One thing in our favor—the wolves are riled," Aluk said under his breath.

Taran's head snapped toward him. "You think Rourke is going to allow her in his territory?" He turned to Gwen. "He took claim of the entire town, since the government forced many of them from their homes."

Cold crept into her bones. If the wolves wanted her dead, they might keep her from reaching Peter. Cedric and his hunters became the least of her worries.

Aluk exhaled and scratched at the growth on his chin. "If we're going after hunters, I'll have to contact that shifter again." He motioned with his hand. "Kelly, whatever-his-name-is."

"Send Ben," Taran said.

Gwen placed a hand on his arm. Beneath her palm, his muscles remained tight, his dragon restless. She smirked as irritation flashed across Taran's expression at the mention of Kaya's mate, Ben. His own doing. But the memory of Taran forcing Ben to hold a pillow in front of himself made her bite back a laugh. She couldn't wait to tell Kaya.

If she ever got to see Kaya again.

A lump formed in her throat, and she forced it down. She had to save Peter. Her only choices were the shifter prison or Cedric's grasp. Nether option was survivable.

"Or I could send you." Aluk looked at Taran.

Gwen pressed a hand to Taran's chest. "Send whoever you want, but we're wasting time. The wasting illness, remember? My brother is dying."

"There's still the matter of the wolves. Sia is pressing for retribution," Aluk said, looking at her.

"Let them have their retribution—whatever it takes to get to the clinic and save my brother!" Gwen panted, ire bursting forth from within her. The wolf inside started pacing around in her head.

A growl rumbled deep within Taran's chest. Across from him, Aluk's eyes flecked with a mix of gold and red, his dragon pressing against his control. The two locked eyes for several minutes, jaws clenched, muscles tensed in a silent exchange. Taran's shoulders slumped, his gaze dropping to the floor.

Gwen saw no other way. If it worked, Peter would live. Taran and his people would be safe. Unless Cedric secured the compound, the wolves would get their justice.

Inside her, the wolf crouched low, displeased. *I'm doing this for my brother.*

You won't be able to touch your mate.

It won't matter if my brother is dead.

"We need a plan first," Aluk said.

"You'll help me?"

"Do not mistake my assistance for letting you go. Once the spirit hunters are dealt with, there's still the matter of the crimes you've committed against the people of the mountain."

"Of course," she murmured.

Taran wrapped an arm around her shoulders, pressing a kiss to the top of her head. She melted against him, savoring the fleeting comfort of his nearness.

Never again, the wolf taunted in her head.

"I'll deal with the wolves and meet you at the clinic," he said. "Don't do anything until I get there. We don't know how many hunters we're dealing with."

"It would be better for me to go in alone," Gwen argued. "Cedric won't believe any other story if I show up with someone. I left the mountain by myself. He'll expect me to return the same way."

"I don't like it," Taran said, his hold tightening.

"Me either, but she has a point," Aluk admitted. "And we can't risk exposing our dragons."

"They don't know dragons exist," Taran countered.

"My point." Aluk's gaze bore into her. "If you run, I'll roast you."

From behind her, Taran growled. "Don't threaten her."

Aluk stepped back. "Figure it out. I won't be long."

Hours later, they walked down Echo Forge Road.

The cold seeped through Gwen's boots, numbing her toes long before they reached town. Without knowing where Cedric's lookouts were stationed, shifting had been too great a risk. They had to walk.

Sentinel Peak felt abandoned, as if the town itself had been drained of life.

A rusted swing set creaked in the wind near the clinic's deserted playground. Sunlight cast long, jagged shadows over the deep snow, ice glazing the broken windows of the off-season medical facility. The old clinic loomed ahead, its eastern wall buried in drifts of snow, brutal winds gnawing at its weakened structure.

Dread fisted in her gut.

The wolf stirred. *Let me out. I can help you.*

Not out. Shift. Possess. Protect.

Something made the wolf on edge.

An unsettling silence hung in the air.

"I don't like this," Taran murmured.

Gwen's heart hammered against her ribs.

"I'm coming with you."

"No. Peter's in there and Cedric will have men posted."

"There's one on the roof." Taran gripped her shoulders, turning her just enough to see the long barrel of a rifle peeking over the edge of the building.

Her stomach twisted.

"Probably a lookout. He's seen you now. He'll report it."

"It doesn't matter." Taran's grip tightened briefly before he let go. "Once you go inside, I'll disappear. It'll look like I'm gone. Remember the plan."

They'd gone over it on the way here, though Taran had fought her every step. She could feel his unease, the rigid control he kept over his instincts—his need to protect her.

Several times, her wolf had whispered, *Let me help you. Let me shift. Let me rip them apart.*

No.

Her merging with the wolf, a complete surrender to its spirit, could not be undone.

Peter needed forever.

Not her.

She forced her hands to unclench.

I'll walk in alone, find Peter, and give him the wolf.

Once her brother walked free, Taran would handle the rest.

This has to work.

The wolf inside her snarled. *You rely on the dragon too much.*

He's my mate.

Dragons are all about their law and order. Mate or no mate, you cannot make a dragon change its ways.

Meaning?

The wolf refused to answer her.

"It's going to be okay," Gwen said, the words more for herself than Taran. "Cedric won't hurt me. He needs me."

"I need you."

Taran's raw confession had a lump lodging in her throat. She ached to reach for him, to offer the same comfort he craved, but the wolf spirit inside her was a constant, inescapable reminder of the prison she carried within. Even if she survived this, even if Cedric didn't drag her away, what kind of future awaited her? What could she offer Taran when she didn't even know if she'd still be herself?

Tears welled up, blurring the image of his face, now etched with desperation.

"I need you too, Taran," she whispered. "But you must let him take me. Peter comes first. Remember the signal."

A sob escaped her. Leaving him like this felt impossibly harder than they'd planned.

"I don't like this." His hands came up warm against her chilled face. She leaned into his touch, memorizing the feel of him. This might be the last time she ever could. Her body reacted instantly, instinctively, reaching for him in ways she couldn't allow.

"Kiss me."

"Is it you asking or the wolf spirit?"

"If the wolf had taken over, do you think I'd ask?"

Taran smirked, but his eyes were anything but amused.

She pulled down the scarf covering the lower part of her face. His gaze dropped to her mouth, his irises darkening. She licked her lips, ignoring how chapped they felt, watching the spark ignite in his eyes. This might be her last chance.

"You're bold." His voice was hushed. Rough. "You already smell like me, or else I'd deny you. How do you plan to explain having my scent on you to Cedric?"

"You said spirits in the crystal can't sense other shifter presences."

"True, but wolves, like dragons, have a great sense of smell. If any of them host a wolf spirit, they'll know."

Truth.

"Cedric carries a bear spirit, but some of the others are wolves and mountain lions."

"Then we'd best be quick." He yanked her against him, giving her no time to gasp before his lips claimed hers. Slow. Deliberate. Each second carved into memory. His tenderness almost undid her, the aching gentleness behind every second unraveling another layer inside her. He tasted of hope. Like a future she wasn't sure she'd ever have.

She wanted to promise she'd return. If only she could ask him to wait for her, but she didn't know what awaited her inside that clinic.

The shield around her soul ignited higher.

Taran trailed soft kisses to her nose, her cheeks—each one another goodbye.

When he finally pulled away, she licked her lips, trying to hold on to the taste of him, the scent of him, the way his gaze made her feel like she was the only thing that existed in his world.

Her heart twisted painfully.

She pulled the scarf up, and turned towards the clinic.

Leaving him behind.

Taran stayed behind a snow-covered building, watching Gwen make her way toward the clinic. A knot of tension tightened in his stomach. His gaze fixed on her, he watched her slowly approach to the old structure. The clinic's windows stared back at him, resembling the empty eyes of a lifeless body. A layer of frost clung to the shattered remains of its sign.

Taran's muscles bunched, every instinct screaming at him to move as Gwen reached the darkened glass doors. He needed to get inside. His mate underestimated the power of the *ohunko*, the guardian spirit she harbored.

Above, on the roof, the sun glinted on the end of a rifle barrel aimed at Gwen. Frustration burned through him as he circled around, skirting through the vacant houses. It took every ounce of control not to shift and take the sniper out of the sky.

Aluk had better not take long to speak with the wolf alphas and bring the pack for backup. *No time to wait.* Taran studied the rooftops, mapping a silent path forward. Ice and snow made the terrain treacherous, but he adjusted, his body heating and the path clearing as he moved forward.

One objective. One threat at a time.

He scanned the rooftop of the building adjacent to the sniper's position. *Clear.* He scaled the back wall of the clinic, landing lightly behind the ventilation shaft. He avoided patches of ice and tested spots before putting down his full weight, not wanting a sound to give him away. His dragon stirred, prickling against his skin, sharpening his senses.

Taran waited. The guard changed his position. Tilted his head. Then Taran struck.

He drove his shoulder into the man's chest, knocking the wind out of him. The sniper fought back, wrenching his rifle tight, but Taran let go, catching him off guard. The weapon clattered onto the roof, spinning down the slope. Taran's fist connected with the sniper's jaw. Bone met bone in a sickening crunch. The man crumpled, and Taran caught him before he hit the ground.

Unconscious. But not dead.

Taran stood still for a moment.

The sniper breathed evenly.

The wind whistled.

No alarms went off. Good.

He slid down the roof, catching the edge before swinging himself inside through a broken upstairs window. Silent. Unseen.

I'm coming, mate.

Twenty-Three

Knowing Taran watched from a distance did nothing to stop the chill creeping into Gwen's fingers. The night air bit through her gloves, but the cold inside her had nothing to do with the weather. From the rooftop, she could almost feel the sniper's red dot ghosting over her heart, but the ache lodged deep in her chest hurt worse than any bullet ever could.

She always thought "instalove" was a trope reserved for romance books—something fictional, exaggerated. Yet walking away from Taran felt like someone was driving splinters into the cracks of her breaking heart. She blinked hard, forcing back the sting behind her eyes. The scarf covering her face wasn't waterproof, and she refused to let tears soak into the fabric.

The darkened glass doors of the clinic groaned as they swung open. Two men stepped out, their faces hidden behind masks. Gwen didn't need to see them to know them. The essence of their soul crystals gave them away, slithering over her skin like oil. The wolf stood up inside her, irritation wafting through her stomach like bad heartburn. She rubbed her chest—not so much from the wolf, but the slow, gnawing ache settling in her ribs.

Once she saved Peter, she'd never get to return to Taran again.

The threat of shifter prison meant nothing compared to the emptiness that stretched ahead. The absence of his touch, his nearness, the way his eyes darkened when he looked at her.

"Cedric's waiting," the taller man said.

Gwen glanced back, catching the movement of the other man stepping closer. The stale air inside the clinic reeked of old paper and something faintly metallic—blood, maybe. The cracked tiles beneath the dusty welcome mat peeked through, the faded word barely legible.

As they passed the reception desk, the cold hum of dormant electronics filled the silence. A waiting area loomed to the left, where a carpeted nook with armchairs and scattered magazines tried unsuccessfully to fake warmth. Nothing about the place felt inviting. Darkness swallowed the hallway ahead, impenetrable.

Her wolf adjusted to the lack of light instantly, sharpening her vision. The others didn't struggle either, their stolen spirits gave them that advantage.

Footsteps echoed behind her, too close. She felt the weight of the man's animal spirit pressing against her, its presence coating her skin like a greasy film. The wolf snapped to attention, pulling at the others. An alpha's presence drew a response, whether they wanted to give it.

"Her scent is off," the man behind her muttered.

"Quit whining," the taller man snapped. "If you don't like it, stop breathing. She's been stranded in the wilderness for days. Not like there's a mountaintop hot spring anywhere around here."

He turned, eyes glinting in the dim light—feline, predatory. Gwen swallowed the nausea crawling up her throat. Someone had died for that spirit. Some families were now empty-handed, missing the blessing stolen by hunters.

"If anyone needs to bathe, it's not me," she said coolly, hoping to redirect them.

The taller man snorted. "Thought you were smart, having Wingman and Zorro drop you down the mountain. Found nothing, did you?"

Codenames. Always codenames. Even after all these years, she couldn't bring herself to remember the names of all Cedric's men.

"You nose blind? She reeks of wolf," the first man grumbled.

"At least she didn't come back empty-handed."

Gwen's patience thinned. "Where is Peter?"

We find your blood and release him. Then we take out these two and return my brethren to the Great Hunter.

One thing at a time. Gwen steadied the wolf with a thought. Even her own heart lurched. A familiar scent hit her—bergamot and dark earth. Her pulse kicked harder.

The frontman froze mid-step and raised a hand. "Stop."

The hunter behind her grabbed her shoulders. Gwen twisted, baring her teeth in a low growl.

"Let her go."

Cedric's voice cracked like a whip.

The hunter recoiled. Cedric's arrival caused him to stumble aside. Gwen turned her head slowly, a cold drip of dread sliding down her spine.

He hadn't changed. His long white hair was pulled into its usual man bun, silver strands catching the dim light. Scruff clung to his jaw like frost, a permanent fixture. He leaned in close enough for her to see the way his nostrils flared.

He inhaled. Deep.

"Ah. So you brought your brother a wolf."

He extended a hand, palm up. "I'll take the spirit you're carrying, darlin'."

Gwen stepped back, shaking her head. In the hall's darkness, she used the wolf's enhanced vision to study him more closely. His irises were still that familiar icy blue. Sharp and emotionless. Calculating.

"Come now," he said, voice dipping low with warning. "You don't want to make me angry."

He lowered his chin, gaze hardening as he pushed his will toward her like a rising tide. The oppressive force of his alpha-bear spirit bore down on her chest.

"Give me the wolf."

The wolf inside her bared its teeth. Gwen clenched her jaw, forcing herself to blink. Her body trembled. Not in fear, but in restraint. The wolf wanted out. It tried to slip closer to her soul.

Do not provoke him, she warned. *We need to get to Peter.*

This ohunko *thief is not worthy. He defiles every spirit he touches.*

Cedric moved closer. "Daughter."

The word scraped down her spine.

Not by blood. Not by choice. Cedric had taken her in, yes. But not out of kindness. He adopted her for protection. He gave her a home, and he did it for the secrets in her veins. Her fae blood. To him, it was a resource. To others, a shield. He purchased her for less than a farmer bought a cow and proclaimed to all she belonged to him. As his 'daughter,' she became untouchable. Hidden. Sheltered. Used.

Never again.

The wolf growled low, agitation turning to fury.

"Father," she said, tasting ash.

Where was Peter? She needed to reach him. She needed to pass the spirit before it cursed her. It wasn't the weight of the wolf that wore her down—but the guardian vying for her soul. Without Taran and his dragon to help hold the shield, she was slipping.

"I am sorry." She lowered her gaze to his boots. "I should have told you, but I knew you wouldn't approve. I wanted to prove to you I could do this on my own."

Her voice hitched, breath trembling.

Cedric raised a hand and waved the hunters off.

They obeyed.

The pressure in her chest lessened slightly, but not completely. The wolf guardian remained braced, crouched, ready to spring.

"I don't have any soul crystals," Gwen said. "They broke when I fell coming down the mountain."

She cast a quick glance at Cedric, searching for any sign of acknowledgement or understanding. Nothing. Only the eerie glow of the bear spirit's presence behind his pale blue eyes.

"I lost your rifle too," she added. "I'll find a way to replace it."

The wolf inside her bristled, pressing sharp claws against her mind, radiating fury at the way she tempered her words. She clenched her fists. *Not now. We have to get to Peter first.*

Cedric folded his arms, the motion broadening his already imposing frame. The power of his bear spirit thickened the air around them, pressing against her like an unseen force.

"You wished to prove your independence?" he mused, voice like slow-breaking ice. "Or did you wish to please your brother and fall for another of his selfish schemes?"

The wolf rumbled a warning. A slow, chilling trickle of its essence bled into Gwen's veins, an icy thread creeping outward. How much longer could she hold on without Taran's dragon pressing its dominance over the wolf? It was growing bolder.

And she was slipping.

"I'm sorry." Cedric's gaze bore into her, heavy and suffocating. "I have to give the wolf to Peter. I don't mean to disobey you, but I can't let him die. He's my brother."

Tears burned down her cheeks. *Taran is outside. Peter is waiting for me to save him.*

And the wolf—it prowled in front of those dying flames, shielding her soul.

Cedric tilted her chin up with two fingers, then cupped her cheek.

Gwen stiffened. Her shoulders locked—then, strangely, the tension eased.

She didn't flinch.

His head tilted in consideration. He spread his palm fully against her cheek.

Pull away. The wolf screamed at her. *Move. Don't let him touch you.* But she didn't.

Instead, she leaned into it.

A slow burn ignited in her chest as the wolf stirred beneath her skin, clashing with the bear spirit's lingering energy. Yet no pain came. In the past, Cedric's touch meant punishment. But the wolf inside her dulled that curse.

His power over her was waning.

Cedric studied her, something glimmering in his expression. Fascination, perhaps. "My touch does not hurt."

He lifted his other hand, cupping her face fully. Gwen's pulse stuttered, fire and ice colliding under her skin.

"It's the wolf," she whispered.

"You don't need a crystal, daughter." Admiration touched his voice. "I have always known you were more special. Your human blood may have diluted your powers, but it gave you something most hunters will never have."

His grip tightened. "Can you shift? Do you have control of its abilities?"

"No," Gwen kept her voice low. "I've kept it trapped since I took it." She left out the truth. That the wolf didn't want to be trapped. It wanted to merge with her. Permanently.

A sharp realization struck her.

Would it do the same for Peter?

Her whole life, her blood had been a curse. But this—this was something else. This was power. A gift. One she couldn't share with her brother.

Elation and gratitude flooded her veins.

Inside her head, the wolf chuckled.

Cedric lifted his hand and motioned to the nearest hunter. "Get me a crystal."

Gwen's lips parted in a silent gasp.

He studied her as if he could see past her skin, into the very essence of her being. "I can feel it in you. The way your blood carries the wolf's essence. It's powerful—like an alpha." His lips quirked. "Almost as superior as Gorak."

The crystal hanging from Cedric's neck pulsed red. Gorak. The bear spirit inside Cedric's crystal. Its energy pressed outward, thick and oppressive.

A slow, creeping revulsion crawled up her spine.

Crush the crystal. Release him! Gorak is one of the ohunko, *as am I.*

Gwen wrapped her arms around herself. "Is Peter alive? May I see him?"

Cedric's eyes flashed, the red glow overtaking the ice-blue. Gwen didn't dare move.

Then his gaze softened, the creases in his brow smoothed. The bear spirit receded.

He released her.

Only then did she realize how numb her body had become in the cold hallway.

"Come." Cedric turned and motioned for her to follow. "We shall discuss you and your brother's disobedience and the cost of your actions."

Twenty-Four

ARE YOU WITHIN RANGE, brother?

Taran's mental call echoed, unanswered.

He landed softly on the old linoleum tiles. His dragon prowled beneath his skin, alert, ready.

Movement. To his right.

A hunter near the door appeared poised about to leave. Shock registered on the man's face as Taran lunged, catching him before he could raise a weapon. He cornered the hunter, delivering a knockout blow to the side of his head. The man crumpled.

Taran dragged the unconscious hunter to the bed in the corner, using a length of cord from the guy's belt to tie his hands and ankles to the frame. Not elegant, but secure. The hunter would live. His dragon growled, rumbling in his chest.

Can't have him warning the others.

He cracked the door and listened. Voices echoed faintly from the floor below. He slipped into the hall and edged around the stairwell's corner. Two hunters in black leaned back against the wall. The sharp tang of disinfectant lingered, stinging his nose. This place once served Sentinel Peak's families. Those without spirits and lacking fast healing once came here for care. Now, it reeked of ghosts and men who didn't belong.

He paused, his gaze lingering on a worn photo near the stairwell of a woman cradling a baby wrapped in a snowflake-patterned blanket. A strange ache tugged at his chest. Children born to shifters were rare now. The winters grew harsher, and few females remained untouched by the fae curse. He never imagined himself a father. Until Gwen. She changed everything.

He'd burn the world and this clinic down if he needed to ensure no harm came to his mate.

A snarl.

Instinct flared, and Taran spun, taking the brunt of a charging body. Claws sliced his shoulder. Mountain lion.

His dragon surged, heat rising under his skin, begging to be unleashed. Taran shoved back, slamming the attacker into the wall.

Footsteps pounded below.

He tossed the spirit thief down the stairs, tangling him with the two hunters charging upward. One stumbled to avoid the pile. *So much for stealth.*

"Element of surprise is overrated," he muttered and reached out telepathically for Aluk. Still no response. He swore.

Stubborn wolves.

We can't expose you.

The spirit thief's cat claws had torn his arm, but he was healing already. The gun drawn by another hunter glinted under the light in the stairwell. Taran launched himself, sending them both to the lower landing. The others scrambled to follow.

Three against one. For a human, it might've been a death sentence. But he wasn't human.

He pinned the first man, ripping the glowing crystal from his neck. It pulsed like a living thing. With a single motion, he smashed it to the floor. A wail, feral and ghostlike, rose as the white mist of the freed wolf spiraled toward the wall and vanished.

Taran stood breathing heavy. Another hunter charged, helping his friend up, then pointed his gun. Taran tensed.

"You'll want to be careful with that," Taran warned. "It's against the law to trespass."

The hunter sneered. "You think this is your territory, wolf?"

Taran gave a dry chuckle. "You think I'm a wolf?"

The spirit inside him growled.

The hunter held his gun up higher. "You're not lean enough for a cat. Bear, maybe?"

A retching sound came from behind. Withdrawal. The freed spirit left its former host hollow and sick.

Taran grinned. Sure, he'd play the bear for them. "I think you're out of your element, spirit hunter."

He counted the figures moving in. Six now. One retreated. Two flanked him.

"I think you owe my friend a new animal spirit," the hunter said.

Aluk's voice filled his mind. *Rourke is sending his enforcers. Where are you?*

Inside. Trying to reach Gwen.

More footsteps. More guns. Another hunter, eyes glinting with cruelty, inhaled.

"There are more. Shoot him before he warns them." The man on his side panted and winced between words.

"It's a good thing our spirit handler has returned." The man leaned in, his eyes flashing like a cat, and he inhaled. "His scent matches hers. The boss won't like you messing with his daughter, shifter. Around here we ask a girl's father for permission first."

Taran froze.

The man was no father.

"Good," Taran said. "I've been meaning to have a word with him."

A gun jabbed his ribs.

"These are iron bullets coated with milk thistle," the hunter said. "It'll burn your spirit out."

Taran's dragon rumbled laughter inside him. *Let them try.*

He played along, letting them guide him through the hall.

"Grizzly? Nice." The sickly hunter trailed behind them.

The one leading Taran called over his shoulder, "You might have lost a wolf, but it looks like you gained a grizzly man. We'll have to change your name to Grizz."

Taran resisted the urge to roll his eyes. His muscles tensed, and he curled his fingers into fists. He walked between them up the hall.

Six men. One is tied in the bed upstairs.

How did you get in?

Top story window. Hunter on the roof. I let him nap. I've been captured. I'm hoping they'll lead me to her.

A sharp prod hit him in the spine. "Try to call for help again, and we'll see what color your insides are."

Without the spirits controlled by the crystals, the men posed no threat to him. Cowards.

His dragon inhaled deeply. Gwen was nearby.

Her scent. Her magic. The faint pulse of the wolf spirit was still inside her.

Down the darkened hallway, a figure emerged. Tall, with long silver hair and eyes like glacier melt. Shadows warped around him.

"What is this?" the man asked.

"Butcher here lost his wolf," the man in the back said, holding up Butcher. The spiritless hunter moaned.

Taran tensed. The man's scent, his presence—familiar. Foul.

Not human. Not shifter.

Fae.

The same face Gwen had described, now cloaked in glamour and lies.

"I thought you swept this place?"

Cedric. Inside, his dragon snarled. While on the outside, Taran's lip curled, not in a snarl, but in a humorless, predatory smile.

"You look like a cat caught in the wrong fight," Cedric said, his accent thick.

Taran bared his teeth. "Says the man with the spirit of a bear hanging from his neck and the glamour of fae blinding these humans from your true identity. Tell me, did you kill the fae whose magic you stole, or did you trade for it?"

"Fae powers can't be traded or inherited. They're born, and when they die, they return to nature." Cedric's smile was razor-thin. His eyes turned red. The crystal pulsed.

Taran's dragon stilled. *Ohunko.*

The beast inside the crystal caused it to glow red beneath Cedric's chin. *Another one.*

That made three of the sacred guardian spirits. They protected the various clans, packs, and thunder. This one was trapped, hanging inches from Cedric's throat. Is that what his mate intended to do for her brother? To trap the wolf?

Taran had only seen one merge with a human—and that one was sealed inside Ben. The others were all thought lost or mad with vengeance, corrupted by the centuries they'd spent under the fae's spell. A spirit like that, once twisted, could tear a soul apart.

Cedric stepped closer. "My father was a fae. He gave me enough blood to survive, and just enough to use their magic."

"Then you don't need the guardian's power. Release it."

Cedric's smile widened. "You'd like that."

Taran's heart pounded. He had to keep the wolf from devouring his mate's soul. Keep the bear contained, but out of Cedric's control. If the *ohunko* were here . . . If they merged from the shadows . . .

The curse. *There are fae on the mountain.*

"You have no business here."

Taran didn't trust his brother's dragon. The alpha spirit within Aluk was unstable.

Rourke and his men are on their *way, Aluk too.* Conleth's voice filled his mind.

"I am the shifter agent in charge of this territory." Cedric tilted his head and grinned. "And these men? They're here under my authority."

Taran blinked. Agent Kelly.

That's how Cedric tracked their movements. He controlled the transports. The permits. The records.

"Kelly," Taran said, his voice a harsh growl.

Cedric's essence reeked of dark, smoldering smoke and rotting earth. "You touched my daughter. Her scent is all over you."

"She's mine," Taran growled.

He didn't just mean the bond they had forged, but the woman who trusted him with her pain, who flinched at anyone's touch but leaned into his words. Gwen wasn't Cedric's to claim. She had never been.

The crystal around Cedric's neck thrummed with rage.

Taran's dragon flared in response.

"No one has ever touched her before now," Cedric said, his eyes narrowing. "Not even I."

"Good. You keep your hands off her."

"Ah, but today, I laid my hands on her cheeks and felt her cool flesh and the wetness of tears. It was a gift."

Taran clenched his fists. The temptation to shift burned under his skin.

"And the wolf—quite a bonus." Cedric went on. "I don't like you touching what is *mine* without permission."

You don't own her.

"Where is Gwen?"

"Cuff him," Cedric ordered. "Then find the others. There's never just one in a clan."

"I don't have a clan," Taran said.

"Your kind always does." Cedric went into the next room.

A hunter returned with cuffs of iron.

Twenty-Five

Gwen dropped to her knees beside Peter's cot, the sour scent of sickness clinging to the damp air. Peter lay still, his skin a mottled shade of ash, like the embers of a fire long gone cold. The rise and fall of his chest barely stirred the threadbare blanket draped over him.

Across the room, Patch, the medic, hunched at a rickety table, one eye swollen nearly shut, a dark bruise curling along his jawline like a brand. A jagged gash split the skin just beneath his cheekbone.

Gwen's throat tightened. "Cedric did this to you, didn't he?"

Patch didn't look at her. His silence said enough.

She reached for Peter's hand, her fingers trembling. His skin felt paper thin, like it might crumble beneath her touch. "Peter."

He flinched slightly, lashes twitching. Slowly, his lashes fluttered, and eyes once the color of sun-drenched fields, now faded, jaundiced, and glassy with pain, greeted her. His hair, once a deep chestnut, had grayed at the ends, the way dying leaves lost their color before falling. Her brother aged before her eyes, slipping further away. Her eyes stung looking at him. She tried to swallow the lump forming in her throat.

"Gwen," Peter's voice cracked like thunder in a quiet storm. His eyes locked onto hers, wide and wild. "You shouldn't be here."

"I brought you a wolf," she whispered, curling her fingers tighter around Peter's hand and pressing it to her chest, where her heart beat like a war drum.

Peter's breath rattled. "You . . . filled one of the crystals?"

"We don't need a crystal. It's in me. I can use my gift to give it to you."

She closed her eyes and inhaled, searching for the tether of power braided into her blood. *Go to Peter.* She pictured him before the illness, grinning, whole. *He has shifter blood. He's strong enough.*

The wolf inside her growled, low and unmoving.

He is not worthy. The wolf's voice coiled through her mind like a chilly wind. *His blood means nothing. He drifts too close to the Great Hunter.*

Then take my strength. Just go to Peter.

I am ohunko. *I choose. You cannot barter with legacy. Where is the strength you speak of?*

I could trap you in a crystal.

I could tear out your brother's soul.

Her stomach clenched, but she forced her thoughts to calm. *You won't. You need* him, *and he needs you.*

Peter shifted beneath her palm. His hand felt feather-light and too still. "What have you done?" he rasped, his gaze dropping to where their hands joined.

"My gift," she whispered, forcing a smile that didn't reach her eyes. "I've discovered new things about myself." She brushed his temple with her thumb. "Take the wolf, Peter."

She closed her eyes again and willed the spirit to leave her. *You'll never touch my soul.* She warned the wolf. *Save my brother or face my mate's flames.*

A hand slammed down over hers.

Gwen flinched, knowing immediately who it was.

"I see you have reunited with your brother," Cedric murmured, the whisper like poison-laced silk.

Her body locked up, every nerve lighting to protest. His grip was tight, fingers digging into the soft bend between thumb and wrist. Her stomach turned.

She didn't answer. She didn't need to.

A shadow moved near the doorway—one of Cedric's men. Another set of boots scuffed the floor.

"Get her a crystal," Cedric ordered. "My girl has discovered a new talent and brought us a new prize."

His hand rested on her shoulder, his fingers tightening just enough to bruise. Gwen didn't look at him. Couldn't.

Peter's eyes searched hers.

She forced her lips into motion. "Call on your magic. The wolf will come to you."

A soft breath stirred beside her. Patch had moved closer, his eyes bloodshot, jaw clenched. A smear of dried blood flaked from his cheekbone. "He can't. He's a half-shifter whelp with no spirit of his own."

Cedric snorted. "So useless, even with a bloodline." He turned his attention back to Gwen. "What a waste of power."

Her hands curled into fists. "Peter and I don't share a father," she snapped. "But his shifter heritage is there. The wolf will merge with him."

Lines furrowed and deepened on Peter's face. "I never knew him, so I don't even know what bloodline I have. It might not be a wolf at all."

"Weak and useless." Cedric spat.

Patch looked at her. Something strange glimmered behind his eyes. Sympathy, maybe. "Or . . . his blood isn't strong enough to call the spirit."

"My brother and I have no secrets from each other," Gwen said.

What must I do to get you to leave me and help my brother?

He is of no importance to me. You, great hehewuti, *mother of spirits, can aid me in my search. It's time. Our kind must meld again.*

Cedric stepped aside, one hand lifting in silent command.

Gwen followed the movement with the corner of her eye, her pulse stuttering. A man entered. His shoulders heaving, sweat slicking his temples, iron cuffs clamped tight around his wrists.

A strangled gasp broke from her throat.

Taran.

His dragon burned behind his eyes like wildfire straining against steel bars. Furious.

"I found your shifter," Cedric said with a smirk.

Gwen's gaze snapped between Cedric's triumphant grin and Taran's controlled, unreadable face. Her heart lunged in her chest.

"Won't you introduce us?" Cedric asked, all mockery and malice.

"I . . ." She tried to speak, but her voice caught, stuck in the knot of panic twisting her insides.

What are you doing? She cried silently, her thoughts reaching for him.

This is why you pair best with me, the wolf whispered, curling in her bones like smoke.

A memory surfaced. Taran's arms around her, his dragon humming through their connection, warm as firelight. The wolf broke apart the memory, replaced by a surge of tingling magic that made her limbs tremble.

Her stomach flipped. Something was wrong. *Do you sense other wolves?*

No.

Then why was Taran— Her thoughts trailed off as dread crept in.

Beside her, Peter stirred weakly, his hand pressing faintly against her chest.

"Where is the crystal?" Cedric's voice exploded like a cannon blast, and Gwen flinched hard.

Patch stepped forward without hesitation, holding up a soul crystal between thumb and forefinger.

Inside her, the wolf snarled, possessive. Her eyes burned as she blinked. Suddenly, the room sharpened, edged in spirit-light. Cedric glowed faintly. Taran's aura crackled with red-gold. And the crystal, white as bone,gleamed in Patch's hand like a trap.

"Take it," Cedric barked. "Expel the wolf inside you." He motioned to Patch. "Grab another crystal. She can take this one while she's at it." Cedric hitched his thumb in Taran's direction, like he was offering nothing more than spare meat.

Not Taran. She screamed the warning in her mind. *If they detect his dragon—*

He can't. He *can't* let it show.

She turned to him, eyes pleading, but his expression didn't waver. Stone. Steel. But she could still feel the fire in him.

"Hey," Peter whispered. "It's okay."

Her heart stilled.

His fingers loosened, sliding from her. "I'm the one who failed."

"No." Her breath hitched. "Peter, no." She clutched his hand tighter.

Go to him, she begged the wolf. *Please. Save him.*

Peter's body grew heavier against hers. Taran stepped closer, and the air shifted. Gwen's entire body responded—drawn to him without thought, without choice. Heat bloomed through her, slow and steady like water warming on a hot stove.

It comforted her. And terrified her.

The presence of his dragon pushed back the wolf from her soul.

Where is Aluk? she asked. *Why hasn't he come?*

But the wolf stood in the way of her reaching Taran, her thoughts trapped by the wolf in her mind.

It matters not. The wolf murmured. *It matters not. Let go,* hehewu-ti. *We are stronger together. The time has come.*

No, her rejection burned like wildfire.

Inside the room, a guard stood beside Taran, with two more behind him. Taran's gaze locked on hers. He didn't speak, but she didn't need words. She saw it in his eyes.

We'll get out of this.

You will get out of this.

But that's not what Gwen wanted.

Her gaze dropped to Peter. His life was slipping away. The wolf inside her surged, pressing closer, until her skin burned and her skull ached with pressure. Patch shoved the soul crystal towards her. When she didn't take it, he tossed it carelessly between her and Peter. It landed with a sharp *clink* on the floor.

Another hunter stepped forward, half-carrying a man who sagged between them. His skin was ashen, gray like Peter's. "The shifter took Butcher's wolf."

"We can replace it with this one's grizzly," one man beside Taran said.

Cedric shook his head as he approached, his expression curious. Calculating. "His spirit isn't a grizzly."

"Let him go, Father. *Please!*" Gwen cried.

Taran stood tall, shoulders squared, matching Cedric's height and intensity without flinching. Neither yielded an inch. They were both towering figures, but only one held her heart.

"What is he?" Patch moved to Cedric's side.

Cedric's eyes darkened, pulsing red as he drew power from the bear. He looked Taran over, dissecting him like prey. Gwen's breath hitched. She knew that look. Knew what it meant.

She moved, placing herself between Taran and Peter, half-turning to shield them both.

Peter's hand slipped off the cot.

"No—" She caught it, gripped it. Held on.

"Here is your chance," Cedric said to Gwen. "You know this shifter. *Well*. I can smell you on him."

Her skin crawled.

"Tell Father what he is," he continued, "and I might forgive you."

Tell him. Gorak will smell your lies.

Don't you tell him.

You want your brother to die?

What are you saying, Wolf?

Tell them, the wolf said, *and I'll help your brother survive.*

You'll go to him? She asked.

For now.

No harm will come to Taran?

"Gwen . . ." Peter rasped.

She'd run out of time.

Gwen swallowed hard, her voice trembling. "He's—"

Taran met her gaze and gave her a slight nod.

She turned her attention back to Cedric. "He's the man who helped me come down the mountain after they dropped me there."

Okay. Her thoughts echoed. *Okay. Save my brother.*

Her head bowed. Her temples pulsed with the swell of her magic.

Tell him more.

She lifted her chin and met Cedric's hard glare. "I-I love him."

She hadn't meant to say it. Not here. Not like this.

But it was true. And in this room full of enemies, with her brother dying and her mate shackled like a criminal—truth was the only power she had left.

Cedric laughed. "You've been gone three days. Is it because he touched you?"

He stepped closer.

Taran growled, low and lethal. His muscles bunched, arms straining against the iron cuffs. Gwen's stomach twisted. Peter let out a breath, his chest caving.

"No!" she gasped and threw herself over him.

Pain lanced through her abdomen. Her veins pulsed with something dark and ancient. Emptied. Her stomach clenched, cramping hard. She gagged, heaving forward.

The spirit inside her rose like bile. Darkness surged from within, clawing its way up her throat. She exhaled it, choking, unable to breathe, the air leaving but not returning.

Behind her, Taran struggled with the guards. Something slammed against the roof above, and distant howls shattered the night.

Hope flared and died as the cold press of a gun barrel settled against her neck.

"Move," Cedric hissed, "and she's dead."

Peter convulsed. His back arched as the shadow wolf poured into him.

Gwen gasped, forcing herself to exhale what remained. Peter inhaled the darkness with a shuddering breath, his body swallowing what she could no longer contain.

Tears streamed down her cheeks.

She kept breathing, little by little, forcing it out, mouth wide, air whooshing from her chest like a broken bellow. Her vision blurred as

Peter's eyes shifted. The dull green of his irises lit with red. Wine-colored veins laced through them, flooding outward.

His pallor went from ghost-gray to golden bronze. Dark markings, thick and jagged, carved their way down his neck, disappearing under his shirt. They glowed faintly, like smoke-charred runes burned into his skin.

"*Wôli ehta ne wôhtamakugo wôbanaki*." Peter sat up, voice deeper, older. *It is good to see you, my friend.*

His teeth elongated into canines. His eyes bled into a richer, more terrifying red.

Gwen's head spun. Dots danced in her vision, and for a moment, the blackness took her.

The air returned.

She gasped, lungs greedy, and crumpled to her knees on the cold tire floor.

"Breathe." Patch reached for her.

She flinched away, but his fingers brushed her sleeve. Even through the fabric, the crystal on his wrist pulsed. Its spirit essence trickled into her veins like a mild current, enough to shock her awake.

She groaned.

Patch eased her onto her back, trying to open her lungs. She blinked past the blur, past the spinning room.

Taran.

He was still restrained, guns aimed at his chest, red swirling in his eyes. Anguish and fury mingled. He bared his teeth, and the rumble of his beast vibrated between them.

Gwen looked up, finding Taran restrained with guns pointed in his direction and his gaze swirling amber with anguish.

"I'd ask you what he is again, daughter, but soon he'll reveal himself."

She wanted to believe Cedric wouldn't shoot her. He needed her. Her body trembled with exhaustion, her lungs raw, her stomach aching from the wolf's departure.

Peter rose slowly. His boots hit the floor with an eerie, grounded finality.

"Peter?"

His gaze snapped to her. Red bled back into green.

"*Ohunko,*" she whispered.

He knelt beside her. His hand closed around hers. She braced for the pain, but it didn't come.

My essence still lingers within you. The wolf said in her mind.

Where is Peter? she demanded. *You promised to keep him alive.*

Shocked, she heard Taran's voice in her head. *Gwen?*

Her heart jolted. Taran.

He was in her mind.

The *ohunko,* inhabiting her brother's body, hauled her to her feet.

"Get your hands off her," Taran growled, the rumble of his dragon bleeding into his voice.

"Easy," Peter said, but it wasn't Peter. It was the wolf who'd merged with her brother's soul. "She has yet to reveal your secret."

"Neither will you." Taran warned, more of his dragon pushing forward, heating his gaze to molten gold.

"I am bound to this world until the balance is restored," *ohunko* said.

"What balance?" Cedric asked.

Stop.

Gwen pushed the thought toward Taran, focusing all her will on him.

Think of your people.

She coughed again, lungs still raw, the ache stretching through her ribs. Both Taran and the *ohunko* stiffened. They heard her. She knew it.

"Can you do this to others?" Cedric asked, his gaze on her, ignoring Taran's rising fury.

"Do what?" She inched away from the *ohunko*. Peter's grip tightened.

"Bestow a spirit inside non-shifter-bloods without a soul crystal," Cedric said, dangerously intrigued.

"No," Taran said.

Guns raised. The hunters tightened their aim at him.

A loud thud landed on the roof above, shaking the ceiling. Cedric waved his gun toward the door. "Go. Find out what that is."

Patch and another hunter sprinted from the room. Only Butcher remained, still unconscious on the floor.

Cedric turned back to Gwen, positioning himself so he could watch both her and Taran. "Now, where were we?"

He stepped closer.

"Can you do this to others, Daughter?" he repeated.

Gwen looked at Taran. He gave a single, slow shake of his head.

"No." She didn't break eye contact with him.

"What should we do about him?" Patch hovered near the doorway, pointing toward Butcher.

"You have the crystal," Cedric said, eyes narrowing at Gwen. "Take the shifter's spirit and restore my hunter. Show me this new power."

He reached for her.

Gwen backed into Peter—no, the *ohunko*. Taran growled, the sound low and rumbling.

His eyes were wild, feral, and focused on her.

"I told you, I can't," she said.

Cedric's nostrils flared. He stepped closer to her, rage tightening every muscle in his face. "Do not play with me, Daughter. You will do as I say."

"What she means . . ." Peter said, his voice his own. "Is that she can't do it *here*."

She turned, surprised. Green now swirled with the red in his gaze.

"Yes," she added quickly. "Not here. I can't do it here."

Cedric's eyes narrowed. "Then where?"

Shouts rang out down the hallway. The scrape of claws against tile echoed closer.

Wolves.

The pack had come.

Panic surged. She forced herself to stay still.

Taran?

They will not take you. Taran yanked against the cuffs, gritting his teeth.

They're infused with dark fae magic. Gwen warned. *They're designed to suppress a shifter's spirit.*

My dragon is far superior to the average shifter.

With a roar, Taran pulled hard until the chain between the cuffs snapped. Metal clattered at his feet.

He went for the hunter left with them. The gun fired. The bullet flew wide, and Taran slammed into him, dropping him like dead weight.

The room exploded with sound.

Gwen screamed. Cedric lunged and caught her. His arm locked around her neck, claws unfurling, pressing against her skin. She froze. Raising her chin, she avoided making eye contact with Cedric.

She looked at Taran.

He stood over the unconscious hunter, chest heaving, golden eyes burning. He let the body drop with a *thud*.

"Call off your pack." Cedric's claws pressed lightly into her throat. A massive black wolf stood in the doorway, watching.

"Surrender your spirit," Cedric warned, "or I put my claws in her throat."

Twenty-Six

A DEEP GROWL RUMBLED from Taran's chest, echoing with the fury of the dragon caged within him. It wasn't just anger. He was hers. The terror frozen on Gwen's face, the way her shoulders trembled, her pulse visible at the hollow of her throat. His dragon thrashed against the barrier of flesh and bone to protect her.

Cedric's gaze glinted. Feverish. He glanced at the wolves now blocking the clinic's only exit. Rourke, cloaked in black fur, and Trace in storm-gray, both stood broad and tall, like ancient sentinels. Their teeth bared.

Patch had crouched near the body of the spiritless hunter. Rourke lunged.

Peter grabbed Cedric's arm, wrenching it from Gwen. "Run!"

Gwen stumbled. Taran caught her, dragging her behind him. Her breath hitched against his neck.

Peter tackled Cedric to the floor. Patch yanked a pistol from the hunter's limp hand, but Rourke's teeth sank into his arm with a wet crack, and the weapon clattered across the linoleum.

Taran exhaled relief, but it was fleeting. The dragon snarled inside him. Not enough, not safe.

"Go!" Peter's voice rang out, strained but still human. "Get her out of here. I'll handle him."

Cedric let a roar. Not human. Bear.

Taran's throat vibrated with a growl of his own. The air around them thickened, pulsing with magic.

Claws. Snarls. Flesh. The fight exploded into chaos. Peter's eyes flashed red. They met Cedric's, gleaming with unfamiliar intensity.

"They're *ohunko*!" Taran shouted.

Rourke paused, black fur bristling. Patch backed away, cradling his arm, eyes wide with animal panic. The black wolf stalked forward, low and deliberate. Taran followed. His jaw clenched.

"Find Conleth," Taran urged Gwen, his dragon on the verge of emerging. "I can sense him. He's close."

"What about you?" Her voice cracked. "Peter? The wolves?"

Taran brushed a strand of hair from her cheek. His fingers itched with the desire to pull her into his arms, to drag her away from all this blood and bone and spirit fury. "I can't shift. I can't protect you like this."

Her spine stiffened. "I'm not leaving."

"We're bonded now." His eyes burned, the dragon snarling behind them. "If something happens to you . . ." He didn't finish. He didn't need to.

Her lips parted, but she didn't speak. Instead, she stepped back.

In the corner, Peter's body contorted—his eyes flickering green, then red again. He swayed, caught in the flux between man and beast. Cedric struck him, a savage punch to the jaw.

"Gwen, please. Go." With a final, lingering touch, Taran pulled his hand away.

Peter let out a soft whine, stuck between wolf and man. Cedric rained blow after blow upon Peter. Rourke growled. Both the black wolf and Taran launched forward. Cedric slammed against the far wall, cracking the plaster.

Taran gripped the man's shirt, twisted, and forced both arms behind his back.

Peter scrambled upright, but the spirit shimmered behind his gaze. Red, like molten rubies.

"Keys!" Taran called, struggling to restrain Cedric. "Cuff him. We can't let the *ohunko* possess him."

Rourke shifted in a shimmer of bones and fur, blood slick down his arm, but his wolf had already knitted the skin. He reached for the nearest hunter and tore the soul crystal from around the medic's neck. A ghostly snarled echoed as the wolf spirit inside was freed.

Gwen rushed forward before Taran could stop her. She reached into Cedric's coat, finding the keys with shaking fingers.

"Fast," Taran growled. His muscles screamed under the strain.

Cedric stopped resisting. "Go ahead," he said, smirking. "Turn me in."

Gwen hesitated.

"Not him." Taran jerked his chin toward Peter. "Your brother."

Her eyes widened. "He hasn't—he didn't—"

A rush of relief sent pinpricks up his arms at the removal of the enchanted metal. Once the cuffs fell from his wrists, he placed his hand on her arm.

"If you don't, I will." Taran didn't want to frighten her, but his dragon coiled tight beneath his skin. "It's the only way to keep him, and us, safe."

Rourke took the cuffs from her. The moment they clicked shut around Peter's wrists, the red bled from his eyes like ink in water. He turned to Cedric and pried the crystal from his neck. Cedric groaned, hunched over as if part of him had been ripped away.

"Don't." Taran held up his hand. "Don't break it. We can't risk releasing the *ohunko*."

Rourke frowned at the pulsing red light in his palm. "Why would the Great Hunter free them now?" He looked at Peter. "*Ohunko*."

Peter lifted his shackled hands, eyes burning red. "It doesn't like the cuffs."

Taran didn't trust the grin behind his teeth.

Trace returned naked and unbothered, handing another pair of cuffs to Taran. "Found these on one of the hunters. Figured we could use them."

"Shift back," Taran muttered, eyeing Gwen flanked by two unclothed men. "Let's get these two out of here."

Outside, a pack of wolves waited. Aluk and Conleth stood like statues in front of the clinic's door.

Taran led Cedric out, Gwen trailing Peter.

"I hate this," she whispered.

"You did what you had to do," Peter said.

"There are three back in the room. Rourke will send his men in to take care of them," Taran said, approaching his brothers.

Cedric lowered his head, acknowledging Aluk. "Alpha."

"Kelly." Aluk's jaw twitched.

"You two know each other?" Taran asked.

"Kelly is the government agent for this region," Aluk informed them. "We have spoken many times but not met in person before now."

"He's behind the spirit thefts and the deaths of our people," Taran said.

"You have to turn me over," Cedric cut in. "Or the government will strip you of your land and your rights per the treaty." He spat out.

"He's right," Aluk said, jaw tight.

Conleth walked over to Peter, giving the man a more thorough look. "Nor can we allow him to go free."

"Then don't give him to them," Peter said, a glint in his eye.

"What do you suggest?" Conleth asked, still studying Peter.

"The Great Hunter's Forest."

Murmurs ripple through the pack.

"Impossible," Aluk muttered. "No one has access to the spirit realm. Not even the dead."

Rourke padded up in his wolf form. He dropped the red crystal on Aluk's bare feet. Each of his brothers stood in green scrubs, no doubt scavenged from the clinic, and no shoes. Aluk reached down and picked up the red crystal. "*Ohunko.*"

"Someone trapped one of the ancient guards?" Conleth held out his hand, but Aluk shook his head. Taran kept Gwen at his side. He noticed her quietness. She and Peter exchanged looks. "Is the wolf bothering you?" he asked, lowering his voice.

Cedric snorted. "You can't kill me. You can't put me in prison, and it takes a special magic to open the portal to the *Great Forest,* as you call it."

"Shut it," Aluk growled. "I'd like nothing more than to crush you as I would this crystal to release the spirits you have stolen from my people and the lives you have cost us. I could kill you and turn your body to ash to be carried away by the wind in hundreds of flecks, but I would not want to litter my mountain with your remains."

Peter grinned, tilted his head toward Gwen. "She can."

Gwen shook her head. "I-I don't know how to open the gate."

"It's in your blood." Peter, eyes regaining their green hue, stated. "She births and banishes spirits."

Taran placed a hand on her shoulder, glad when she didn't flinch. His mark warmed and his dragon spirit slid out to comfort her. *You're angry with me.*

Not you. This situation. She relaxed against him.

"Tell me where this is," Aluk questioned Peter.

"You're asking him? He's human," Cedric scuffed.

"She knows." Peter lowered his chin. "I have lingered there in wait for a long while."

"I do." Gwen's gasp was sharp, jagged. Her gaze flew to Taran. She reached for him, not with her hands, but with her mind. She sent a vivid flash of memory. His dragon wrenching free from his chest, the woods ink black around her, the icy crawl of the wolf spirit as it slipped beneath her skin.

Taran flinched at the sensation, his gaze going to his brothers. Aluk gave a single nod, his expression carved from stone. *It solves dealing with the government if she can do it.*

Conleth raised a skeptical brow. *I'd like to see this.*

Even Cedric's arrogance faltered. His mouth hung open, no words following.

In one swift movement, Taran caught Cedric from behind and locked him in a sleeper hold. The man thrashed, boots kicking against snow, until his limbs went limp and he collapsed like a dropped sack.

"How far is it from here?" Aluk asked.

"Not far if we fly." Taran left no room for argument. But the moment the words left him, a tidal wave of fear crashed through him. Not his. Gwen's.

"There's no other way. The place is too far to reach on foot. We have to fly."

Her face drained of color, breath snagging in her throat. "We can take a snowmobile. You all can go ahead."

Peter laughed, the sound coming out hollow. "You're the one we need to open the gate."

"You can ride on my back this time," Taran said, keeping his tone even though his chest tightened.

"I can't wait to see this," Conleth muttered with a smirk. He stripped off the hospital gown and shifted in a flash of shimmering scales. Massive wings unfolded, and he tossed a startled Peter on his back like luggage.

Peter's yelp echoed through the trees as Conleth launched into the sky, his wings slicing through the frigid evening air.

Aluk hauled Cedric over his shoulder. Taran cupped Gwen's cheek and kissed her forehead. She didn't flinch. No pain. Relief flooded him. "On my back, or in my arms? Either way, I'm not letting anything happen to you."

"Then hold me," she whispered.

Taran shifted, the dragon clawing to the surface. Skin became scale. muscle rippled. The bond between them vibrated, and he caught her, careful and close. Her fear-filled scream pierced the air. He flooded the bond with warmth and the memory of their last kiss. Slow and consuming. Toe curling.

The flight blurred around them. Mountains below. Stars above. But the pull in his chest sharpened. The pull in his chest, tethered to his mate, guided him like a compass.

They descended first into the blackened woods nestled between Sentinel Peak and the village below Avalanche Ridge. Gwen dropped from his hold the moment his feet touched the snow, stumbling into the nearest tree. Her fingers gripped the bark, and she kept her eyes anywhere but on him.

"I'm human again, *solanu*," he teased, after shifting back and stepping toward her. "Whole and ready for your inspection."

She glanced, startled. A flush crept up her neck, and he chuckled, her embarrassment warming something tight in his chest.

The others landed moments later. Aluk and Conleth disappeared into a cabin nearby. Abandoned, by the look of it. They returned dressed. Conleth tossed sweats and a shirt in Taran's direction.

Peter brushed snow from his arms.

Aluk dropped Cedric near the trees and let him stand. "He woke mid-flight." Aluk grumbled. "You need to work on your sleeper hold."

"Could be the *ohunko*," Conleth said, eyes narrowed. "Still clinging to him."

"Where from here, mate?" Taran asked.

She hesitated. "I don't know. Not exactly."

"Feel it. You've always been able to. Open up to your gift," Peter said.

Taran gave Conleth a look. His brother fell into step beside Gwen as she started forward, her boots crunching softly in the snow.

The air changed. Thickened. Like walking into breath held too long.

Taran's dragon stirred. His tattoo burning.

The trees pressed closer. Snow muted the sound of their passage. Shadows gathered under the branches like waiting things. He kept Gwen in sight.

Behind him, Cedric stared at her. Then at him.

"What are you?" the man asked, voice brittle.

Taran felt Gwen tense even before she stopped walking. No visible breath puffed from her lips anymore. The air here was wrong.

She looked at Peter. His chin dipped, red flickering in his eyes.

"He's—"

"Is this it?" Aluk cut in.

Above them, the trees knitted together, blackening the sky. No stars. No wind. The air had warmed, but it wasn't welcoming. It pressed in too thick, too still. Ahead, two rows of trees formed a perfect corridor, eerie in their symmetry.

"I feel it," Gwen whispered. "Like . . . like I belong here. And I don't. It's like home and nightmare stitched together."

"It's the fae in your blood," Peter growled. His silhouette wavered, his glowing eyes nearly the only thing visible. "It's what taints you."

The scent of rotting wood and wet fur hit Taran. His dragon recoiled.

"Open the gate, *hehewuti*," Peter said. His voice was deeper. Rougher. The wolf guardian taking possession once more.

"Yes, open it," Cedric echoed, eyes alight with something too eager.

Twenty-Seven

"How?" Gwen looked to Taran. Icy dread pooled in her stomach like water collecting in a grave. Her gaze darted between Peter, his eyes changing in a constant battle with the wolf spirit, and Taran, whose amber gaze was darkening. His dragon spirit brushed against her. *Not alone. I've got you.*

But she didn't feel strong. Her ribs tightened, as if her body would betray her if she dared try.

"What if . . . What if I can't? What if I mess up and something terrible happens?"

Taran stepped forward, gently taking her hands. The expected flare of pain never came. Just warmth.

"You won't mess up, Gwen." His eyes anchored her. "We're in this together. But tell us, what do you need?"

"You have the power within you. Use the gift your mother's people bestowed on you and call upon the hunter who awaits the mother spirit to free us. You are the key," Peter said.

Her pulse stuttered. *I am the key.*

She stepped forward toward the trees. Wind curled around her ankles like recognition.

"You don't have to do this, mate." Taran's steps followed hers. "We can lock him in a place where no one shall find him."

"You might as well bury me in the mountain," Cedric drawled, "if you think no one will know or come to free me."

"No!" The vision of a woman—mother of spirits—flashed through Gwen's mind, and something sparked beneath her ribs. A heartbeat. Ancient and wild. Her veins lit with it like kindling.

"Burying him will cause more problems." Her fingers curled at her sides. "It'll upset the mountain more."

Cedric scoffed. "Upset the mountain? Please. Spare me the theatrics."

Taran's gaze turned flinty. "Keep your mouth shut, or we might bury you."

Gwen turned slowly, searching. The air thickened—charged with something that didn't belong. Her vision sharpened. Colors deepened. A vibration threaded through the night, low and constant, like a hidden heartbeat.

Drawn forward, she walked toward the sound. The darkness ahead shifted, deepened, became something more than shadow. She pressed her palm against it—cold, solid, humming with power.

"Gwen," Taran said from behind.

Energy prickled under her palm. She flinched.

"Taran." Her fingers pressed against the surface.

"I'm here."

She bent forward, resting both hands against the icy wall. Taran stood behind her, presence warm, dragon coiled and ready within him.

"Don't touch me." Color bled from her fingers—red, then golden. Light streaked across the surface, forming glowing patterns like veins remembering how to live.

Peter's eyes turned black. *"Nimitqwa ktelo."*

Those words echoed through the clearing. Light surged over the surface. Gwen stepped back, hitting Taran's chest. His arms wrapped around her. His dragon's presence wrapped tighter.

Her hands still glowed, tingling with power she couldn't hold back anymore.

"*Nimitqwa ktelo*," she whispered.

Relief flooded her limbs, warm and sweet. The electricity under her skin intensified, but this time, she welcomed it. The light churned and morphed—then melted into a veil of water. It shimmered, then stilled, revealing a dark forest on the other side.

A mirror of where they stood—but older, sparse.

"The Great Forest is supposed to be a place of rest, but this—this feels alive."

Peter moved beside her, his eyes locked on the portal. He didn't blink. Didn't speak.

"Peter?" Panic rose in her throat.

Peter surged forward, his steps gaining speed as he rushed the portal—but Taran intercepted him, shoving him hard away from the shimmering veil.

Peter snarled, his eyes blazing red. "Get out of my way, *Bodaway Achak*."

"You brought us here to open the portal for you?" Aluk's voice cut through the night like a blade. "Go, *ohunko*, back to your forest if you wish."

"No." Gwen's blood roared in her ears, dizzying. Her knees nearly buckled. "My brother—you can't leave him to die."

"Oh, I'm not leaving him." The voice wasn't Peter's. "Your brother may walk with me in the Great Forest."

Her heart seized. "No."

The portal shimmered, beautiful and terrible. Gwen pressed her hand against its surface, desperate to seal it.

Behind her, Cedric's laugh cracked like ice breaking, setting her nerves on edge.

Peter lunged.

Taran tackled him mid-stride, both men crashing into the snow.

Gwen gasped, but her hand refused to move. It stayed fused to the shimmering veil. The surface rippled like disturbed water beneath her touch.

Taran and Peter tumbled, kicking up powder. Taran grunted, finally flipping Peter and pinning him, driving his face into the snow.

"Don't hurt him!" Gwen screamed. She tried to rush toward them, but her body jerked to a stop. Her hand was still stuck to the mirrored surface. She strained harder, feeling the burn in every muscle. It didn't budge.

She stilled. Something moved on the other side of the veil.

A silent scream built in her throat.

A chilling silhouette emerged from the shadows of the trees. Her heart hammered. Before she could focus on it, dizziness struck. Her vision swam.

"Shut it down," Aluk commanded, his alpha authority like a physical blow.

She tried. "What is that?"

Taran dragged Peter upright. Snow clung to his clothes and hair. He spat to the side, blinking hard.

Cedric cackled, his shoulders shaking with either cold or madness.

"The Great Hunter has come to see who enters his forest," the wolf *ohunko* murmured.

Gwen's heart cracked open. "I don't want to enter."

"Step aside," the wolf *ohunko* urged, "and allow another to take your place."

"What are you talking about?" Taran tightened his grip on Peter's arms.

"Once you enter the Great Hunter's Forest, there is only one way to leave." The wolf *ohunko* said. "Pull away."

"I won't sacrifice my brother."

Gwen yanked, but her hand slipped further into the portal. The pull became a grip. Unseen fingers curled around her arm, drawing her in inch by inch.

Each jerk brought fresh pain, screaming up her nerves. Her muscles fought. Losing.

The portal pulsed. Its edges twisted, greedy and alive, brushing her skin like tendrils.

Taran reached for her. "Gwen!"

Aluk raised his arm to block him. "You might get pulled in too."

"I won't stand and watch it take my mate!"

Aluk's lip curled, and a growl rumbled deep in his chest.

"No! Stay back!" Gwen threw all her weight into yanking her hand free.

Aluk moved. In one fluid motion, he shoved Cedric toward the portal.

Cedric stumbled forward.

Taran pushed Peter aside as Aluk grabbed Gwen.

Cedric hit the ground shy of the swirling portal, grunted at the impact.

"You're all doomed," Cedric rasped. "Since I know the source of your spirits, I'll take them and return them to those more worthy."

"More *wealthy*, you mean?" Taran snapped, catching Cedric by the arm and yanking him to his feet.

Peter bolted toward Gwen.

Aluk intercepted him, tackling him mid-stride.

"Taran?" Gwen clung to this side of the portal, her feet slipping. Beyond the veil of the portal's mirror, the shadowed figure approached, the hunter making the very darkness bend in his wake. Light glimmered behind him.

Taran glanced at Cedric, and his eyes shifted, deepening into molten amber.

"What are you?"

"Dragon." Taran shoved Cedric, wide-eyed and suddenly silent, into the portal.

Taran grabbed Gwen as he wrenched Cedric through the portal. The mirror rippled, releasing Gwen. She collapsed into Taran's arms with a sob of relief.

Behind her, the portal dimmed. The golden light faded like dying embers. Peter's eyes lost their red hue, the green returning slowly.

Aluk still held him tight.

From his coat, Aluk drew out the red, pulsing soul crystal of the bear *ohunko*, Gorak. He tossed it through the portal as it sealed.

Taran took Gwen's face in his hands. His forehead dropped to hers. "Does this hurt?"

She shook her head. "No." She went up on her toes and kissed him. Soft. Uncertain. His lips answered, warm and sure. The kiss reignited the flames protecting her soul, spreading and chasing away the cold of her veins. She sagged against him, relief threatening to undo her.

A cough behind him. Aluk.

Gwen pulled back, resting her head against Taran's shoulder. Her breath came in ragged puffs. She turned her gaze to her brother. "Peter."

But the look he gave her wasn't Peter's.

The red glow returned.

"Not Peter," he said flatly.

"Nituwe he?" Aluk asked. *Who are you?*

"Asigwani." Peter bowed slightly, a solemn grace in his posture.

Aluk didn't move, but something in his expression shifted, tightening around the mouth, a glimmer in his eyes that Gwen almost missed. His dragon stirred behind his stillness, its aura rising like the heat of sunbaked stone.

"Peter?" Gwen tensed. "Give me back my brother, wolf."

"Are you ready to trade?" Asigwani tilted his head.

"No trade." Taran said, stepping between them.

"Are you sure?" Asigwani's eyes glinted.

"Stay inside, my brother wolf, or greet your Great Hunter. The choice is yours," she nearly growled.

Taran drew her closer, his arm wrapping around her. Across from them, Aluk stood firm, his grip tightening on Peter's body. The wolf spirit bared its teeth.

Aluk's dragon surged forward, shimmering around him.

Taran turned Gwen's face away just as Aluk seized her brother.

Aluk launched into the air, a blur of pure black in the sky. Aluk and Peter broke through the treetops, vanishing into the dark.

"Peter!" Gwen screamed. Her cry echoed with fury and heartbreak. She twisted in Taran's arms. "Let me go! I have to get him back!"

She bolted, snow crunching underfoot as she ran after them, her breath hitching. Midway to the cabin, a frustrated cry ripped from her throat.

Taran followed in silence, his footsteps crunching in the snow behind her.

She spun around to face him. "Where is your brother taking him?"

He didn't answer.

Instead, his dragon spirit reached out, brushing against her like the warm wind of a summer storm. When had her blood stopped recoiling at his nearness?

"Taran?"

"We must leave this place." He stepped back, letting his dragon rise. Before she could argue, claws closed around her, gentle but firm. He lifted her off the ground, wings unfurling.

She heard the hiss of air, the pop of shifting heat.

Then they soared.

Darkness vanished beneath them.

Twenty-Eight

THEY LANDED AT THE top of a cliff. The icy wind howled a banshee's wail that tore at Gwen's sanity more than the wind rushing against her face.

Where was Peter? What had they done to him? What were they going to do to her?

Panic twisted in her gut, a cold serpent coiling tighter with every passing second.

She spun around, searching the swirling white chaos. Sounds of Taran's bones popping and transforming brought a distant comfort above the roar of the wind and the frantic drumbeat of her own heart.

Relief flooded her momentarily until a hulking figure emerged from the blizzard—Taran shifted back into his human form. He strode across the cliff top and bent to pull up a metal hatch.

"We're going down there," Taran shouted. "Go ahead. Get out of this wind."

As her eyes fell on the winding stairs, she cringed.

"What is this place?" she asked, peering over her shoulder.

Taran huffed and waved for her to go. "Aluk and the others are waiting."

On legs like jelly, Gwen descended downstairs, each step uncertain like her fate.

Taran followed close behind.

They took the large stone steps carved from the mountain down to a narrow hall. At the bottom, a man stood dressed in dark pants and combat boots—a prison guard. The thought hit Gwen like a physical blow. He brought her to the shifters' prison.

"Where's Peter?"

"You'll see him soon," Taran said.

A surge of bittersweet acceptance filled her. He'd done everything he could, protected her, but in the end, Taran had to obey his alpha.

Light flickered from flames burning down the sides of the wall in small troughs, much like inside Taran's dragon lair.

The man stepped forward. Gwen stepped back into Taran's chest. His hands came up to grab her arms. She jerked away, and Taran let go. "Did I hurt you?"

Guilt plagued her at the worry in his voice. She'd done this, not him. "No."

"Welcome to Crag's Cliff." The man smiled, his wolf showing through his eyes.

Gwen forced her chin up.

Taran held out his hand from around her to the man, who reached for his belt.

Gwen squared her posture. She should have expected this. Raising her arms, Taran grasped her nearest hand. "We won't be needing those, Finn. A pair of pants and a set of boots. My mate isn't into public displays."

Finn lowered his hand and tilted his head down the hall. "First room to your left."

Taran gave her a nudge to walk past the man. Finn's gaze burned into the center of her back. His wolf spirit caused the hair at her neck to prickle. Could he have known about the other wolf shifter at the resort? Did they tell him of the ones freed from the hunters?

"Nothing will happen to you." Taran kept her moving forward.

"You don't know that." Gwen swallowed hard. Taran opened the first door for her.

Inside, Conleth's head jerked up. He paused from lacing a pair of boots.

Gwen reached out, brushing her fingertips against Taran's arm.

"Thought you might have got lost." Conleth straightened from tying his boot. "Aluk sent word for the council to come here. They may not arrive until morning. Until then, they're arranging a cell."

Gwen's blood ran cold. Her hand tightened around Taran's, and he looked down at her grip. He took her wrist and slid his hand away from her crushing hold. "Easy, *solanu*."

"I can take her until you grab some pants. Unless you want some alone time first?" Conleth wiggled his brows.

Gwen's stomach sank.

Taran pulled Gwen into his arms. "That works."

"Of course." Conleth grinned at Gwen on his way out.

Taran gave her another squeeze, then released her. He sorted through pants lined on shelves on the far wall. The entire room reminded her of a giant walk-in closet. It held boots, pants, shirts, socks, and jackets.

"I never meant to put you in this position."

Taran slid on black cargo pants, much like the ones the guard wore. "You can put me in any position you want." He winked at her.

Gwen's face flamed, and she pushed back her hood. "Can you be serious? I understand you didn't have a choice in bringing me here."

Taran reached for a dark, long-sleeved shirt and pulled it over his head. Her insides clenched, missing the broad lines of his abs and the glow of his dragon tattoo.

"I will stand beside you no matter what." Taran cupped her face in his hands. Those amber eyes darkened, making it even harder to imagine saying goodbye to him.

Taran's fingers warmed against her chilled flesh, his dragon peering through his gaze.

"What's going to happen now?" Exhaustion tugged at every muscle in her body.

"Let's find out before you draw any more conclusions in that mind of yours." Taran kissed the top of her head. He took her from the room and down several flights of stairs.

They walked the narrow halls, just wide enough for two people to pass. Warmth radiated from the stone ceilings, walls, and floors. They came to another set of stairs, winding down. The air cooled. Moisture froze against the rough stone as they descended deeper into the heart of the mountain.

Alcoves appeared ahead, each barred, each humming with quiet power. Gwen slowed. Her chest tightened.

She reached out, brushing the wall with her fingertips. The shone pulsed faintly beneath her skin.

"I can feel them," she whispered.

Taran gave a single nod. "This level holds spirits that have gone feral or criminals. Most are dormant. They can't shift, so you have nothing to worry about from them."

What did she have to worry about with a dragon for a mate?

But a shiver still found its way up her spine. "Who built this place?"

Taran was silent for a long beat.

"The dragons before the war with the fae. It was carved into the mountain with fire and sealed by the spirits of our thunder. This was once the home of the dragons."

"And now?" Gwen asked.

"It contains what can't be destroyed. It protects those outside from the ones within."

Dread sank into her bones. "I've heard no one who ever went in has come out."

Taran didn't confirm or deny it.

A rhythmic clinking echoed from deeper inside the corridor.

A shadow shifted in the last cell on the left. Gwen stepped toward it, her breath catching. The spirits pressed closer. Come curious, some furious. The pulse of magic thickened in every step.

"Peter," she breathed, heart lurching.

Gwen raced to his cell, skidding to a stop in front of the silver bars. Dark magic pulsed from them—a hum of power too close to her own blood infused magic.

Peter sat on a cot and looked up. His eyes returned to their usual green. He rose and approached the bars. His skin had mostly regained its color, and he moved with surprising confidence.

"Why do you have him locked up? I'm the one who broke your laws!" Gwen's heart hammered in her chest. She reached for the bars, and an electric shock jolted her fingers. She hissed and yanked her hand back, rubbing it.

"It's okay." Peter lifted a hand, stopping just short of the bars. "It's this, or I die—and the shadow wolf goes free to possess someone else."

"Why would it go free? It's part of you now?"

"The wolf spirit inside him is an *ohunko*." Taran said, sounding grim. "One of the four ancient guardians. They can't bond with anyone outside their bloodline. When the fae cast them into the shadows, they became lost. The wolf is desperate to return—either by finding a true heir or taking someone with enough shared blood to survive the binding. Most believed the guardian bloodlines were wiped out when the fae cursed us. The guardians protected us. Now they are just as much a threat as the fae."

"You can control it," Gwen told Peter.

Peter glanced past her to Taran and then back to her. "It doesn't work that way. This place keeps the animal at bay. The cuffs prevent the wolf spirit from escaping. But I'm not sure how long. Eventually, the wolf will take over."

He held up his wrists for her to see. "If I shift, the wolf takes control, in either form."

"And if you can't shift?" she asked.

"I've already shifted, Gwen."

Gwen's hand flew to her mouth as she stumbled back. Taran steadied her, keeping her upright.

"Once it merged with your soul and shifted," Taran said roughly, "I would have lost you."

"But Peter . . ."

"Is at the mercy of the guardian who now possesses him," Taran finished.

"No. We'll find another one. There are more spirit animals out there. We just have to find one that matches his bloodline."

"It's too late, and even if it weren't, there are none." Conleth joined them outside the cell.

"My shifter blood isn't strong enough," Peter said with a grimace. "Besides, I'd end up here eventually for all the other lives lost because of my foolishness. At least this way, I can try to make it right."

"If the wolf guardian leaves him, he'll die," Taran said.

"Might be best," Conleth murmured.

"No." Gwen's throat tightened.

"Gwen." Peter drew a deep breath. A fleck of red bled into the green of his irises. "The spirit within me will not leave. It can't escape this place. The magic infused in the walls keeps the animal from breaking free.”

“Peter . . .”

He raised a hand, cutting her off. “If it leaves me, Gwen, it comes for you again. You felt it, didn’t you? That seething hunger for revenge. As long as I am alive, it can’t hurt anyone. This is where I need to be.”

“Peter, you don’t have to do this. You don’t have to keep protecting me.” Gwen clenched her jaw against the dizzying flood of spirit energy pressing in from every side. Her tainted blood responded, burning beneath her skin, aching to draw those lost essences closer. She pressed her palm to her temple.

“You need to get her out of here,” Peter said. “There are too many shifters down here.”

“Come, *solanu*. You need to go where it’s safe.”

“Safe for who?” she whispered. “Didn’t you bring me here for your brother to lock me away, too?” She spun toward Taran, fury in her eyes.

He lifted both hands in surrender. “I brought you here to say goodbye to your brother.”

“Goodbye?” Her heart splintered. Blood pounded in her veins. Gwen closed her eyes, fighting the rising pressure and pain.

Taran scooped her into his arms.

“Wait,” she protested, trying to wiggle free.

“He’s gone,” Conleth said quietly.

Gwen looked back. Peter’s eyes had turned fully red. A wolfish grin curved his lips. “*Nimitqwa ktelo*, spirit woman.”

Gwen’s breath caught.

Taran growled, striding up the stairs with her in his arms. Gwen sagged into his embrace.

What had she done?

Twenty–Nine

ALUK SENT WORD WITH one of the guards to grant Taran's request that Gwen not be summoned until morning. Now, with the commotion behind them, he led her through a secluded corridor. Relief eased the tension in her chest.

Taran paused before a heavy wooden door carved with swirling animal motifs. He opened it and gently guided her inside. The room, though sparsely furnished, radiated warmth. A fire crackled in the stone hearth, casting flickering shadows over worn tapestries. A king-size bed dominated the opposite wall, its black fur comforter inviting her to rest. Familiar scents of wood smoke and pine wrapped around her like a blanket.

Taran sat beside her, their shoulders touching. Silence settled between them, comfortable and still.

Gwen slid her hand over his, the tattoo on her wrist flaring faintly as his dragon's spirit soothed the turbulent energy in her blood.

"Rest," Taran murmured. "Tomorrow will come sooner than expected."

She nodded, the last of her adrenaline fading. As her eyelids drifted lower, Taran leaned in. Their lips met in a gentle kiss filled with unspoken promises. Gwen gripped his arms, holding onto the moment. His dragon pushed forward in the kiss, desire rising. Finally, he pulled back. "If we keep this up, I won't want to stop."

"Don't," she whispered, brushing her lips against his again.

"The wolf is no longer in you. My touch—" He cupped her cheek, and Gwen shivered.

A soft smile graced his lips. He kissed her once more. "Rest. I'm not going anywhere."

She curled up on the bed, sleep finally overtaking her, comforted by Taran and his dragon. His spirit sent her pleasant images, softening the edges of her exhaustion.

But morning came too quickly.

A knock roused them. A guard stepped inside. "The alphas await you."

Together, they walked through the prison fortress. Gwen's nerves churned, but curiosity helped anchor her. She took in the towering stone halls and winding tunnels of interlocking pathways curved deep into the mountain. How could a place built into stone have towers?

When they reached Aluk's office, a guard swung the heavy oak door shut behind her with a bang. Gwen flinched. The mahogany walls of Aluk's office seemed to close in on her. Two guards with wolf spirits stepped in front of the doors, blocking her exit.

Taran remained at her side until they entered fully, then peeled away, leaving her alone on the ornate carpet facing Aluk and the two men beside him.

The air held the scent of scorched cedar and something older—like ancient stone warmed by dragon fire. Shadows flickered over the blade mounted behind Aluk's chair.

Three wolf alphas stood before her. Rourke. Sia. And another she'd never met, but the bear spirit within him pressed against her with dominance.

So many alphas in one room. Their power was suffocating. Gwen staggered, her body trembling under the pressure.

Taran stepped forward. "There are too many powerful spirits in here. You're hurting her."

"She deserves a little pain," Sia snapped. The scar on his brow marked him clearly. She remembered him from Conleth's clinic, standing beside Rourke that night.

"That's enough, Sia," said Rourke, the man with a stare like winter storm winds. His black wolf spirit radiated from him with strength like the iron bars that awaited her.

Silence stretched thick. Gwen steeled herself for their judgment. She swallowed, a lump rising in her throat. *I love you, Taran.*

A flicker crossed his expression, and his voice met her mind.

I love you. Nothing will change that.

Tears pricked her eyelashes.

"Are the bear and mountain lion alphas coming?" Taran asked.

She glanced around. Conleth wasn't here.

He returned to the resort last night, Taran answered silently.

"This is a wolf matter," Rourke said firmly. "There is no need to involve them."

"Any matter of spirit hunters is a matter for the council." Aluk rose from his seat behind an expansive desk. "I have discussed the matter with both of them." He glared at Sia, who shifted his weight, avoiding Aluk's gaze.

A frantic pounding echoed on the door, followed by a desperate voice. "Wait! Please!"

Gwen's arms folded over her stomach before she could stop them, trying to hold the panic in. The pounding of the door echoed like a second heartbeat in her ears. She found Taran's eyes. The storm she saw there mirrored her own. Her breath hitched. If she looked away, she might unravel.

"Let them in," Aluk said, gesturing to the guards behind her.

The door opened. Ben and Kaya strode into the room.

Kaya approached Aluk, carrying a large leather satchel. She stopped between Gwen and the dragon alpha. "You can't lock her away. She didn't know she was hurting anyone."

"Taking someone's spirit animal isn't hurting them?" Sia exclaimed.

Taran growled, slipping his arm around her. "She knows the truth now. Give her a chance. Lye still lives."

Gwen had never dreamed so many people would stand up for her. For most of her life, it had only been Peter. Then Taran, her mate. Her eyes watered, exhaustion catching up with her. The mix of overwhelming emotions and the intensity of the spirits around her stirred her blood magic again. Now Kaya.

"I deserve it," Gwen said. "I knew there were consequences of getting caught. I never wanted to hurt him. I wanted to save my brother. And in the end Peter still lost his life." A tear trickled down her face. "I've never had a friend outside of him." She looked at Kaya, a small, aching smile forming. "You were too kind to even let me in your kitchen. I can't explain how much that meant to me. I appreciate you thinking enough of me to come here to speak on my behalf."

Kaya's expression softened, the spark in her eyes burning brighter. "Tell them, Father. Tell them they can't lock her away. She can stay at the resort and serve her time there."

The man closest to Aluk, tall, with a calm presence with streaks of silver in his beard, stiffened. His eyes, so much like Kaya's, glanced between her and Aluk. "I'm sorry, Kaya. I have no say in this. It's a wolf pack matter."

But something passed through his gaze, tightening around his eyes. Gwen didn't know him, but she sensed it, the way the room seemed to quiet around him for a breath. The air shifted. A subtle vibration beneath her skin made her blood magic prickle in warning, like the mountain itself had leaned in to listen.

"We can't put her around others whom she could harm," Sia scoffed.

"Ben?" Kaya turned to her husband, voice rising.

Ben shook his head. "I have no say in this matter, my love. I warned you before we came, but you insisted." He shrugged and looked at Aluk as if asking what he should have done.

Aluk leaned back, gaze fixed on a point in the distance. He pursed his lips. "She can't go to the resort."

The room erupted in a cacophony of shouts. Kaya's voice rose above the rest. "There must be another way! We can monitor her, have her wear a tracking device—"

"A tracking device?" Sia scoffed. "She's mated to a dragon. He can fly her off to who knows where and hide her from us."

Kaya's jaw tightened, but Ben placed a calming hand on her shoulder before she could retort. "I admit I've had mixed feelings about her since she arrived. I believe she's part of the solution to the curse, but she puts us all at risk. More hunters could come, not for us, but for her and what she can do." He turned to Aluk, a hint of guilt in Ben's voice.

"Gwen risked her life to save her brother, and he sits in your prison for the rest of his life to protect us from one of the *ohunko*. Not one, but two *ohunko* have been eliminated from the shadow forest." Kaya must have spoken to Conleth to have known. Gwen remained quiet, not sure what to say.

"She's a danger," Sia insisted. "She holds the gifts of the dark fae in her blood. Even if she no longer hunts us, her heritage alone should be enough to forbid her on this mountain."

"Or a warning we should not be quick to ignore," Ben said.

"Leave it to the historian to educate us," Sia said with a grunt.

"What does that mean?" Kaya's father asked, his brows drawn.

A hush settled over the room.

Gwen tightened her arms around her middle. A pressure curled in her gut, a low hum in her blood, as though her magic had pricked up its ears to listen. Even the air in the room felt . . . off. Like it was waiting.

Aluk leaned forward slightly, fingers steepled. "Ben's right. She's not the only fae blood we've encountered over the last few days. First her. Then Kelly. There will be more now."

Kaya gasped softly. "Here? Why would the fae risk crossing onto the mountain after all this time?"

"Because they feel it too," Ben said, his tone a growl wrapped in dread. "The *ohunko* are no longer drifting in the shadows."

"The mountain isn't sleeping anymore," Rourke added. "Something—or someone—must have awakened it." He looked at Gwen.

A chill spidered down her spine.

"There hasn't been fae blood on the mountain in centuries," Kaya's father said, stroking his beard. "Perhaps this is what we needed all along. She's unlocked something."

Gwen's heart skipped.

"Perhaps we take her back up to the peak and spill her blood," Sia said, too casually.

"Only if you want to die," Taran said.

"Or reseal the curse," Aluk murmured as he rose. His eyes flashed between red and darkness. He clenched his hands into fists, then slowly opened them again. "The fae don't act without reason. If they're returning to the mountain—"

Ben's voice cut through the silence. "The fae don't just come. They're summoned or drawn."

Everyone stilled.

Kaya's father furrowed his brow. "By the queen?"

"Or something older," Aluk said softly, the words hanging like smoke in the air. "Something that remembers the mountain before it was ever cursed."

Gwen's stomach tightened. The dampeners hadn't even touched her yet, but already it felt like something inside her was bracing against them. Not out of fear—but recognition.

"She's awake," Ben murmured. "Or she's waking."

Taran's hand brushed Gwen's. *We'll be ready.*

She nodded, but a shiver ran through her despite the warmth of his touch.

Aluk met her gaze, his amber eyes glowing with the power of his dragon spirit. "I believe Conleth sent something along with you to give me?"

Ben glanced at Kaya, who stepped forward and carefully pulled a wooden box from the bag slung over her shoulder. She set it on Aluk's desk.

Gwen's gaze fixed on the ornately carved box. Her skin prickled as Rourke lifted the lid.

Inside, two silver and gold arm cuffs pulsed with a low, unsettling hum. Gwen's blood went cold.

"These," Rourke explained, his voice grave, "are dampeners. They'll suppress your powers while you remain on the mountain. Enough to keep you from calling upon another shifter's spirit or opening anything that should remain sealed."

Sealed. Not broken . . . not yet.

They'll keep the spirits from causing you pain.

Gwen's breath hitched.

Taran moved closer, his presence shielding her from the storm of alpha spirits that scratched beneath her skin. She tilted her head toward him. *You know about this?*

A slow smile spread across his face. *I want to be with you, Gwen.*

Sia scoffed. "Dampeners? Are you mad? Who knows what kind of side effects those things have?"

"Would you rather I lock Gwen away in a cell away from her mate?" Aluk asked without looking at him.

"She could take them off," Sia argued.

Rourke shook his head. "She can't. Only the one who places them on her can take them off."

All eyes turned to Gwen.

She looked at Taran. Was this freedom or a leash? Then she thought of Peter, of the spirits, of the lives she nearly destroyed, and she already knew the answer.

I want to be with you, too. I love you, Taran.

She nodded to Rourke.

"Then it's settled," Aluk said. "Gwen will wear the dampeners and remain on the mountain under the supervision of her mate."

Sia opened his mouth but caught Rourke's glare and muttered, "Yes, Alpha."

Gwen slipped her arms from her sleeves, grateful for the thin-strapped undershirt beneath. Rourke slid the cuffs into place. Cold metal kissed her skin, and power surged like icy water through her veins. The hum of magic quieted, and with it, the pain.

She exhaled. "Thank you."

Rourke gave her a nod and stepped back. "We're done here."

Gwen had just slipped her arm back into her sleeve when Kaya wrapped her in a sudden hug. Gwen froze, startled, then melted into it.

"You're the best friend I've ever had," Kaya whispered fiercely.

Gwen smiled. "Tell me that again after a few hours in the kitchen."

"And she'll need the help," Ben added, rubbing his neck. "We're expecting again."

Kaya touched her stomach, her eyes gleaming.

Ben turned to Taran and Aluk. "I've been overprotective lately."

"A bit?" Taran raised a brow.

As Aluk, Rourke, and Sia filed out, the remaining wolf guards followed. The heavy door shut behind them. Gwen leaned into Taran, her breath finally steady.

"What is it?" he asked, wrapping his arm around her.

She blinked, swallowing the unexpected emotion. "I just . . . I think I'm okay."

A silence settled between them, one that hummed with something deeper than peace—*possibility*.

We can have babies.

Taran chuckled, lifting a brow. Babies, *as in more than one?*

Ben and Kaya will have more than one, she teased.

That's a whole lot of touching, Solanu.

Her body flushed with warmth, anticipation curling low in her belly.

Ben groaned. "Alright. Whatever the two of you are discussing—get a room."

Kaya swatted him on the arm. "See you back at the resort."

Thirty

A CROW CAWED HARSHLY, its silhouette slicing across the bruised-purple twilight that bled over the resort. Gwen's breath hitched as she paused mid-step, skis slung over her shoulder. The call echoed like a warning, sharp and insistent. A prickle tiptoed down her spine. It wasn't the mountain chill—this was something else. The air had a texture now, thick and almost humming, like static before a storm.

She unclipped her skis with deliberate care, letting the familiar motion anchor her. Muscles ached from the run, but it was a good ache. Real. Tangible. It reminded her she was still here. Still herself.

A blur of red snow pants broke through the gloom, barreling toward her. "Gwen!" Levi's voice rang out, high and thrilled. He slammed into her with a force that almost toppled her, and she laughed despite herself.

She caught him easily now—there was no jolt of pain, no explosion of another's spirit against her skin. The cuffs worked. Relief bloomed in her chest, fierce and unexpected. She hugged him back tighter.

"Levi, slow down!" came the amused voice behind him.

Taran's golden eyes met hers as he strode across the snow. The sun had almost slipped away, but the glint of dragon fire still lingered in his gaze. When his arms came around her, the last of that strange chill melted.

"You took your time," he murmured, his breath warm against her hair.

"What are you talking about?" Levi asked, glancing up at him. "Did you see how she flew off the mountain?" His eyes sparkled with admiration.

Gwen tousled his hair. "He's just jealous. He's seen my moves."

The boy beamed, his mountain lion spirit thrumming faintly under his skin. She could feel it now, just a whisper—but it didn't hurt anymore.

Wind snapped through the flags outside the gear shop. Gwen stiffened. Her hair lifted, tugged by a sudden gust that seemed to crawl over her skin like invisible fingers. She glanced up.

The sky churned with heavy clouds, unnaturally fast. Too fast.

Taran's gaze fixed on the churning sky as he took her hand. "Looks like we might have some interesting weather on the horizon."

Another caw rang out. The crow circled overhead. Gwen's heart gave a stuttered thump.

"It's a test," she whispered.

"I don't like tests," Levi groaned. "I always end up with a bad grade."

"You should study more," she murmured, though her voice lacked its usual humor. Her gaze remained locked on the darkening sky.

"What is it?" Levi stepped away, nose twitching. "The air's weird."

"It's more than the air." Conleth's voice came from behind them. He approached with Lissette, Levi's mother, beside him.

"Come, Levi," Lissette said gently. "Kaya made snacks."

The boy pouted but obeyed, skipping off without question.

As soon as he was out of earshot, Gwen turned to Conleth. "What's going on?"

"Sentinel Peak is thawing."

She blinked. "That's . . . good, right? People can return to their homes?"

"Not if the snow melts too fast," he said. "The mountain can't hold that much water all at once. We could be looking at floods."

"Floods?" Her stomach clenched. "And the lower towns—?"

"Mudslides," Taran cut in grimly. "Fast ones."

"Avalanches weren't enough?" Gwen's throat tightened. "What else is coming?"

Conleth clapped Taran's shoulder with forced levity. "Duty calls, Ranger."

Taran's face tightened, the lines around his eyes deepening. He didn't laugh.

Gwen tried to lighten the mood. "Does this mean the ranger station's finally getting a makeover?"

But neither man smiled. Their expressions darkened—dragons speaking in silence. That look. That shared gaze. That quiet between them spoke of things ancient and dangerous.

Men and their dragon conversations. She shook her head at them.

Her tattoo pulsed gently, warmed by Taran's spirit. A reassurance. *You're not alone.*

Still, her magic—dampened though it was—felt uneasy. Like something inside her was curling inward, bracing.

"Our brother was right. They'll be sending others soon," Conleth said.

Others.

"Taran?" Gwen's fingers tightened on Taran's arm.

They faced so much together in the past month—defeating the hunters, trapping Cedric, and restoring a semblance of peace. But she'd stirred something within the mountain. Its looming shadow gathered from within the trees and the rocks.

"Is it the shadow spirits?" Her thoughts spun wildly. Peter was imprisoned with the *ohunko* wolf spirit. The crystal that held the bear spirit. Cedric. The portal. Everything she'd touched was twisted now, steeped in the mountain's ancient magic.

Steam hissed from Taran's nostrils. "It's the curse. The mountain's growing impatient. And you . . ." He trailed off, sharing another look with Conleth.

Her pulse drummed in her ears. "I triggered it."

"I think Ben was right," Conleth said. "Your fae blood might have been enough to wake her, but now that you've mated with a shifter, it's changed the temperature around here. I think you might have enraged her."

Gwen closed her eyes. "*Nimitqwa ktelo,*" she whispered. "The shadow spirits. There are more, aren't there?"

Conleth's jaw clenched. "There is at least one we haven't encountered yet."

"I unleashed them, didn't I?" Gwen tugged on Taran's arm.

Conleth's expression darkened. "You may have woken them, but you didn't unleash them."

Silence stretched between them. A determined expression formed on Taran's face. Those amber eyes she loved darkened with his dragon spirit.

"Are you going to hunt them?" Gwen hoped the wolf enforcers from Rourke's pack confiscated a few soul crystals from the hunters they imprisoned. If they intended to go shadow hunting, they would need them to contain the dark spirits of the ancient guardians.

Taran cupped his hand against her cheek. "We must rebuild and prepare for the spring. If there is any hunting to be done, it'll be the rangers who protect the forest and the wolves who enforce the laws of the mountain."

"Kaya's been teaching me to cook, but don't expect me to help feed a pack of hungry wolves on the hunt." She ignored the twisting in her gut at the mention of wolves. Rourke and Sia still made her tremble. Not that she would admit it to Taran.

"You'll feed them with stories," Conleth teased. "And maybe a few burn marks."

Gwen flushed. "Hey—some of those cookies turned out fine."

"Speaking of packs . . ." Conleth gave Taran a knowing look. "Looks like yours is getting started."

"It won't be long." Taran looked at Conleth, a glint in his eye. "You're next."

Her heart swelled. Shadows stirred beyond the trees as they walked together toward the lodge. Snow crunched beneath their boots. The wind whispered through the evergreens. Darkness gathered on the mountaintop. But for now, she and Taran had found their peace. Even if the curse was only catching its breath.

Thank you

Dear Reader,

Thank you for taking a chance on my book! I know this was a risk on your part, never having read anything written by me yet. You always remember your firsts! Anyway... I hope you found it worth your time in Sentinel Peak and enjoyed the story as much as I loved writing it. If you did, I would be eternally grateful if you took a moment to hit the stars to rate this read or drop a review.

Every single review and rating makes a difference in helping others discover my stories and support my dream as an author.

Your thoughts and kind words are an inspiration that navigate me to keep writing more stories like this one. You never know when you might see those words shared in my marketing or in posts because they're important to me. Without you, I wouldn't have made it this far.

THANK YOU.

Suzy

P.S. *Marked by an Oath* is my next book! You won't want to miss Conleth and Trinity in their adventure to solving another piece of the curse.

Glossary

Solanu – Mate

Bitatelo - mountain lion

Hehewuti - warrior mother spirit. - One who could hold and bestow a spirit to anyone.

Bodaway Achak - fire making spirit

Unahu - mate

Nimitqwa Ktelo - as you once were and will be again.

Ohunko - guardians whose dark hearts stain their spirits

Wakinyan - thunder/ thunder spirit

Nituwe he - who are you?

Mal'drathir - Shadow snatcher

About the author

S.E. Lower writes urban fantasy, paranormal romance, and epic fantasy, bringing readers into worlds filled with magic, hidden realms, and supernatural intrigue. Whether it's dragon shifters, fae, or the forces of darkness and destiny, her stories are packed with immersive adventure. When I'm not writing, she loves thrifting for hidden gems, walking through the woods, and spending time with her kiddos and husband traveling open roads and looking for her next adventure.